IN AN EVIL PLACE

One side of the passage opened into a pit, and Kyle recoiled mentally at once. *OhmyGod* ran through his mind, and he gulped hard as his stomach flopped.

Bodies. Rotten ones.

A shiver shook him from toes to head. The top layer was two recently dead adult males. One had had his throat cut, the other had been shot through the head. Below them were older bodies reduced to mostly gristle and bone, and below that was a pit of bones, hacked and broken and still wearing moldered rags of fabric and leather. The bones were old and blackened. Even in night vision, the cut ends were dry and withered. They'd been dumped here decades, even centuries earlier.

"Keep alert," Kyle warned. "There can't be anything honest in this place. Assume enemies and shoot if needed. But only if needed."

"Roger that," Wade said. "Just wish I'd brought silver bullets."

"Yeah, me too."

Books by Michael Z. Williamson

TARGETS OF OPPORTUNITY
THE SCOPE OF JUSTICE

TARGETS OF OPPORTUNITY

MICHAEL Z. WILLIAMSON

AVON BOOKS
An Imprint of HarperCollins*Publishers*

This is a work of fiction. Names, characters, places, and incidents are products of the author's imagination or are used fictitiously and are not to be construed as real. Any resemblance to actual events, locales, organizations, or persons, living or dead, is entirely coincidental.

AVON BOOKS
An Imprint of HarperCollins*Publishers*
10 East 53rd Street
New York, New York 10022-5299

Copyright © 2005 by Bill Fawcett & Associates
ISBN: 0-06-056525-X
www.avonbooks.com

First Avon Books paperback printing: March 2005

Avon Trademark Reg. U.S. Pat. Off. and in Other Countries, Marca Registrada, Hecho en U.S.A.
HarperCollins® is a registered trademark of HarperCollins Publishers Inc.

Printed in the U.S.A.

10 9 8 7 6 5 4 3 2 1

To PFC Gail Sanders,
enlisted at age 35.

A target of opportunity I'm glad I hit.

TARGETS OF OPPORTUNITY

SERGEANT FIRST CLASS KYLE MONROE WAS doing the one thing everyone in the U.S. Army had to do: paperwork. Napoleon had said that an army moved on its stomach, but the twenty-first–century U.S. Army moved on piles of paper and computer files, liberally lubricated with red tape.

Kyle was an instructor at the U.S. Army Sniper School. At the moment, no class was in session. That didn't stop the paperwork. Nothing stopped the paperwork. It was an enemy more pervasive, insidious, and overwhelming than the Nazis, the Communists, Muslim terrorists, and the IRS combined. At least, that was Kyle's opinion.

His phone rang, and he was glad for the distraction. "U.S. Army Sniper School, Sergeant First Class Monroe, this is not a secure line, how may I help you, sir or ma'am?" The official phrase rolled off his tongue without conscious thought. Because to think about a line that long just to say hello was ridiculous.

"Sergeant Monroe, I'm wondering if we might discuss another assignment?" said the gravelly, powerful voice at the other end. Kyle recognized it at once. General Robash

"I suppose we might, sir," he said, stalling for a moment to think. The last "assignment" had been a temporary one, a month of sheer hell in the highlands of Pakistan. The end result, however, had been a dead al Qaeda leader, a Bronze Star with Combat V, a Purple Heart, and a sharp reduction in terrorist activity in Europe.

And, Kyle recalled, a very pretty young local woman who'd hired on as their translator, gruesomely killed by a burst of machine-gun fire. That, added to the death of his spotter in Bosnia before that, was a heavy burden on his soul.

The general interrupted his musing with, "Good, let me give you the basics. We can talk more if you say yes."

"Go ahead, sir," he prompted.

"Romania. We've got someone staging through there with explosives for Europe, and it's causing sheer hell for the NATO forces in Yugoslavia, er, Bosnia-Herzegovina, or Macedonia . . . all over that Government of the Month Club, whatever the hell they're calling it now." Robash was joking slightly, Kyle could tell from his tone. The general was very familiar with that area and its geography and politics. He had a Ph.D. in international relations, after all.

"What's the game plan, sir?" he asked.

"Similar to last time. You and Wade"—that would be Staff Sergeant Wade Curtis, his spotter for the last mission—"with whatever gear you deem necessary. We'll insert you quietly, the CIA will furnish you with intel as to these assholes' whereabouts, and you eliminate the problem with a well-placed bullet or two. Or fifty. Whatever it takes, as long as civilian casualties are minimized."

Kyle thought for a moment. Romania was far better than the wastelands of the Afghan/Pakistan border, he thought. Europe had plenty of water, food he would be partially familiar with, phones, and—language trouble aside—the alphabets would have to be easier to work with than translating Pashto.

Still . . . "I'd like to consider it, sir. Can I let you know tomorrow?"

"Sure. I'll have an outline emailed to you. Will be coming through secure in about thirty minutes."

"Yes, sir. I'll be back with you ASAP."

"Rangers Lead the Way, Kyle." It was a friendly greeting and farewell from one Ranger to another.

"Roger that, sir," he said, and hung up.

Kyle finished his day's paperwork and drove home automatically. He didn't even notice the trip until he found himself opening his apartment door. Another assignment performing as what amounted to a role as an assassin. He had no

moral qualms about shooting terrorists, but he
didn't want to encourage the idea that he was a
hired gun. Hollywood glamour aside, there were
too many agencies with too many agendas for
that to be a safe job. Sooner or later the odds
would catch up with him.

He unlaced his boots and grabbed a Sprite
from the fridge without taking off his shirt. At
one time he'd been a light drinker. Then he'd lost
his spotter and become a heavy drinker. Then
he'd been a very light drinker after returning
from Pakistan. Gradually, he'd stopped alto-
gether. Heavy drinking made him morose and
depressed, light drinking didn't do much of anything. There was no point in wasting money for
the flavor of cheap beer, and expensive beer was
not something he'd ever learned to appreciate. So
he stuck to soft drinks.

He sprawled back in his recliner. It and a
good used loveseat that didn't match were the
only casual furniture in the room. He had a
small desk and computer against the wall, with
an office chair. If he ever invited more than
three people over, he'd need to get some cheap
plastic seats.

The TV was in front of him, but he left it off.
Right now he needed to think, and TV and
thinking didn't go together.

He stared at a place on the wall above it. On a
cherrywood rack he'd built in the post hobby
shop hung a World War I British Lee-Enfield rifle.

It was uglier than hell, but had meaning for him.

The rifle had floated around for seventy years God knew where, then had been bought and refurbished by the U.S. government for the Afghan mujahideen during the early 1980s, with a shortened forestock and hard parkerized finish. After that, it had found its way into Pakistan, where Kyle had bought it in a hole-in-the-wall shop for local use. It was less blatant and bulky than the massive M107 .50-caliber rifle he had taken, and better suited to the environment. At Kyle's direction, a local smith had lengthened the butt and built it up for precision shooting. The wood didn't match, the finish was spotty, but it was an amazingly accurate rifle for something so old and abused.

Battleworn, ugly, and deadly. It matched Kyle's soul. Perhaps it was time to take it shooting again. Feel the kick, hear the roar, watch the bemused and bothered expressions at the old piece of crap the sergeant was shooting.

Or maybe it was time to shoot something new.

He sank back into his thoughts again.

A few minutes later, there was a knock at the door. He rose automatically, quite sure who it was, and opened it.

He'd been correct. It was Staff Sergeant Wade Curtis, a former Sniper School instructor and his spotter during the last mission. They were friends, despite being posted separately, and the fact that Wade was at Benning rather than his current posting of Meade meant that there'd already been some planning for this mission. Wade was grinning broadly, his mouth a yard of gleaming white teeth against his coffee skin. He carried a small cooler.

Kyle smiled, reached out a hand and pulled Wade into the apartment, into a manly hug and grip on his shoulder. "My man," he said in greeting.

"Back in action! Their most hair-raising mission yet! Can our heroes top their previous brilliant exploits?"

"Get stuffed!" Kyle laughed. Wade had a knack for humor that took the edge off.

"How ya been, Kyle?"

"Getting better, I suppose. Have a seat," he said, gesturing.

"Thanks." Wade dropped down into the couch, the cushions whuffing out air from the impact of his 180 pounds. Both men were tall, lean, and in formidable shape for their early thirty-something ages. They were "old" by Army standards, but still at the far end of the curve as far as physical fitness.

"So what do you think? Romania. Europe, at least. Theoretically Western and modern," Kyle offered to get things started. "We need weapons we can carry on the street that aren't obvious. Stuff that blends in."

"I'm waiting for them to figure out I don't blend in some places," Wade said.

Kyle laughed aloud, because he'd been thinking the same thing during their last mission. Blacks did not blend in in Central Asia, and likely not in Eastern Europe, either.

"Yeah, you laugh," Wade said. "Someday, we'll go to Zaire and I'll be the one amused."

"It might be one of those tribes who wear beaded skirts. You won't laugh then."

"Right," Wade said. "So assuming we're doing this, what are we going to use that's discreet?" he asked, bringing the subject back to the mission. "Unless and until they change the rules of engagement on us?"

"I was thinking of a Ruger Ten Twenty-Two. Have you seen the takedown kits for backpackers?"

"No," Wade said. "What about them?"

"Carbon fiber barrel, stainless liner. Slots in and snaps in with the fore end. Stock folds. Whole thing fits in a briefcase. Add a good scope, bipod and a silencer. We can use it near witnesses and no one will ever know."

"Such nifty toys the free market system comes up with. God Bless American Capitalist Greed," Wade said and they both laughed. "But how do we get close?"

"If it's city, we'll get a room or roof nearby and drop him. Cities are much the same tactically, whether it's Bucharest or Hong Kong. And I did some in Bosnia." That brought up more memories, though they were just ghosts now. "If he's hiding in the mountains, then we either use a real rifle—the M Four will do fine—or we do a

Ranger sneak and get close enough to bag him with the twenty-two or pistols."

"Given the choice, I prefer distance," Wade said. "It's neater."

"Sure," Kyle agreed. "I don't want another knife fight if we can avoid it."

"I'm not sure about the M Four, though," Wade said. "It's blatantly American and new. And I hope we won't need any forty millimeter this time. We can get a Romanian SKS or AKM or even an AK Seventy-four that will blend in much better."

"Hmm . . ." Kyle considered. "Don't they suck rocks, accuracy wise?"

"Yes," Wade agreed. "But from what I understand, that's mostly an ammo issue. If we work one over well and load some good ammo, it's discreet. We can fit it with a suppressor, and have something good for four-hundred-meter shots."

"I like it," Kyle said. "Good idea. But let's stick to seven point six two, not the five point four five." The older AKs and SKSs came in 7.62 × 39 caliber. The newer AK74 was in 5.45 × 39. That was a good battlefield infantry round, but fast and with a tendency to oscillate. The 7.62 was a bit more stable, and being older, more common and nondescript. Properly loaded, it would be better for long-range shooting. It lacked the power of 7.62 × 51 NATO, the .308 Winchester round; or .338 Lapua or 7mm Remington Magnum, the monsters of the precision-shooting world, but one had to use what was least obvious. The only good large-caliber round in the area would be 7.62 × 54 Rimmed, the old Russian round that fit the Dragunov sniper's rifle. But that was a large piece of hardware, and hard to hide.

"So, an old AK or SKS, and sixteen inches of barrel?" Wade asked.

Kyle nodded. "That should be accurate enough, if what you say is true."

"Good. The bottom folding stock is an inch longer than the fixed wooden, which will let us pack it down in luggage or under a coat, and we can get a cheekpiece that snaps on for better long range."

"You seem to know the weapon better than I do. You take charge of it, you carry it. I'll have the Ruger."

"Good division of force," Wade said. "I'll want some civvy ten-round magazines that are less bulky than the thirties, say two, with match ammo. Hell, it may as well all be match ammo. But we can load up with local seven point six two for suppression. Better sculpt the grips and stock, float the barrel, use a match barrel, the usual state-of-the-art precision modifications for which we, the world's best observers and shooters, are justly infamous for."

"You should switch to public affairs and write press releases," Kyle quipped, chuckling and rubbing his eyes. "Okay, so the gunsmith is going to be busy with your weapon, the contractors are going to be busy with mine, and Robash is going to be busy having his people write checks."

"You know, I think that's a *very* good division of labor," Wade said. "Meanwhile, we shall study the maps and drink beer. That way, when they change the rules on us yet again, it might make sense."

"Pistols," Kyle reminded him.

"Pistols, of course. I need a suppressor for the Beretta. Damn, this is starting to feel very James Bondish. Think I should carry a Walther PPK?"

"Thirty-two caliber?" Kyle asked, eyebrows raised.

"Right. Better stick to the nine. You going to leave that cannon of yours behind?"

"No way," Kyle said firmly, shaking his head once. Kyle had a highly customized Ed Brown 1911, smooth and easy to draw, accurate and reliable, with all the internal mods necessary to shoot any junk ammo that came along. Typically, though, he shot high-quality ball, or jacketed hollowpoints when allowed. "I can get a silencer for a forty-five. Brown will have to make a threaded barrel to fit. And Uncle Sam is paying for it. They'd have to, anyway. And this way their name isn't on the weapons."

"What about your three-eighty?" Wade asked. Kyle had a Colt Mustang stainless in .380 caliber he carried for backup.

"If it gets that bad, noise is the least of our problems. I'll take it as is."

"It could really suck to be us."

"Oh, Romanian jails can't be fun," Kyle said, frowning. They would want to check on that. They might be really unpleasant, and there was a strong if sporadic government presence to work around. "But the cops will have to deal with the government. But we don't want to be caught in the first place."

"We didn't want to get caught last time, remember?" Wade said.

"Yeah. Nasima." It was still a sore spot for Kyle, and would be for a long time. Especially the occasional half-snide comments he overheard about his "girlfriend." She'd been a remarkable lady. It had been a strictly professional relationship, though he'd certainly wondered what it would have been like romantically. He wasn't sure if the strict professionalism made it easier or tougher. All he knew was she was dead, and it was a waste of a good person. Then there'd been Jeremy, killed by that Bosnian countersniper. And why was that coming to mind now? Likely because they were going to the same part of the world again. What had Robash's joke been? "The Government of the Month Club."

Sadly, that was a fairly accurate statement.

His reverie was interrupted by Wade saying, "Sorry. Didn't mean to bring up a sore spot."

"It's okay. I'm not riddled with guilt. Just sad." He really was okay. But it still hit him now and then. In which case, it was good he wasn't a drinker.

"At least the alphabet is familiar," he said, to

get back on track and not dwell on life. "And Romanian's not far from Spanish."

"Really?" Wade said. "I guess that makes sense, given the name. I would have figured it for some Slavic thing if you hadn't said anything."

"Yeah. I had four years of Spanish in high school. A few days listening to a Spanish radio or TV station should get me brushed off and cleaned up. We should be able to manage. We'll still need to talk to Mister Gober, though."

"Right." Bill Gober was a civilian contractor who seemed to know every language on Earth. He'd drilled them in Dari and Pashto before the trip to Pakistan, and they were assuming they'd meet him for this trip. "What else? This is essentially clandestine and more cloak-and-daggerish than front-line military."

"Yeah," Kyle agreed. They'd still need a lot of military hardware, but they'd have to trim the excess. "I suppose we can look like backpackers. Enough of them in Europe. We could pass you off as Algerian or Moroccan."

"Kyle, you don't know much about African history, do you?" Wade was chuckling and shaking his head.

"No," he admitted. "Why?"

"Because we all look alike to you," he said. His tone was friendly, though. "My ancestry is west and southern African. North African blacks have a lot of Berber, Arabic, and Mediterranean influence. I don't look like them. I look like an American."

"Oh," was all Kyle could say. He was too embarrassed to continue.

"No sweat," Wade said, breaking the pause. "We can be reporters. We can use a good telephoto for initial spotting, and get some intel with the cameras while we're at it. That will explain us having backpacks to travel with, and money . . . we are getting money, right?"

"I assume so," Kyle said. Last time, they'd been handed $50,000 in cash in three currencies for expenses.

"Check on it. We need the money for our tuxes and to impress the fine ladies of Eastern Europe. Assuming we can find a couple with less facial hair than you."

"Funny. I'd rather have it for renting cars, bribing petty thugs, and eating, thank you."

"Well, there's that, too," Wade agreed. "But I think we can pull off being reporters. We'll take a laptop, audio recorders, and all that crap. I wonder if we can get a good pair of walkie-talkies and justify it?"

"They all look the same. I think Motorola or someone has the military contract. It wouldn't be surprising for reporters to have them. And we'll have a satellite cell phone again, I'm sure."

"Good," Wade said. "Let's make lists and cross check. Mind if I use your computer for a few minutes?" He rose as he spoke.

"It'll be an hour, as slow as that dial-up relic is, but sure."

"No hurry. And at least this time, we're doing the chasing."

"We agree we're doing it, then?" Kyle asked, though he didn't think either of them had doubted it. All they'd had to do was get in the right state of mind.

"Sure. We're soldiers. It has an immediate, positive payoff. And it's what we signed up to do."

"Yes, that it is. Kill enemies. And these scum are everyone's enemies. I just don't want to lose any more friends."

"That's always what we want . . . but Kyle, even Nasima was a volunteer. It's painful, but better than kids in day-care centers or on buses." He stared levelly at Kyle.

"Yeah, I know," Kyle said. It was true. It still hurt like hell. "Yeah, let's do it."

Wade reached down and drew a bottle of Heineken from his cooler, went to the kitchen nook, popped the cap and poured a bare taste in a glass for Kyle. He kept the bottle. "Toast?" he suggested.

It was barely a mouthful of beer. Kyle decided that was acceptable. He raised it and said, "Sure. Absent companions."

"Absent companions," Wade replied.

"And death to terrorist assholes."

"Amen, brother."

2

THE TWO MEN MET WITH GENERAL ROBASH
two days later, Thursday. As before, they all
gathered at the Sniper School's classroom. It was
remote, quiet, and unobtrusive, and thus a perfect place for the purpose. The twittering birds
and sunlight on red Georgia clay had always
seemed to Kyle to be in ironic contrast to the
controlled death discussed within.

"Sergeant Monroe, Sergeant Curtis." Robash
greeted the men as he walked in.

They stood to attention. "Sir," they replied together.

"Please be seated. I'm informal, and we're
here to talk business."

He fiddled with his unlit cigar for a few seconds while they relaxed their lanky forms out in
chairs. Once everyone was comfortable, he said,
"We've got a bit more lead time than last time,

and better data to start with, as I said. We'll go through what we can here, and more in theater. Also, Romania is more Western, urban, and modern, so it's going to be a different operation."

"What we've got, gentlemen, is a terrorist cell linked to al Qaeda who's moving explosives from the east, across the Black Sea, through Romania, into Europe and parts of the Middle East, and killing people. We've linked them to bombs in Iraq, Bosnia, Germany, Israel, and Egypt. Likely the same group who supplied material for Spain last year and France this year. You're going to help stop them the old-fashioned way."

"Well-placed shots," Kyle said.

"I knew you'd approve." Robash grinned, eyes twinkling, and chewed on his cigar.

"The main pipeline is across the Black Sea through former Soviet Georgia and Azerbaijan. They were going through Turkey, but the Turks don't take too kindly to it and shoot them readily. So they come from Pakistan's fundamentalist areas and Iran, across the Caspian and Black Seas, into Romania and up into the rest of Europe."

"Why not stop them on the sea?"

"We're doing some of that, our SEALs and the Turkish Su Alti Taarruz, but there's a lot of ships and it only takes a few pounds of explosives here and there. That slows them down. To stop them, we have to nail the command and control, which is based out of the Carpathians. We have names, we have the general area. What we can't find is a base of operations. We're trying to get a live one for that information, or bag a few at meetings."

"How's the Romanian government on this?"

"It sucks, to be frank," Robash said, tapping his lip with his cigar stub. "We've made some inquiries, and they were favorable in response. But there's so many holes over there that we can't risk setting it up. Unlike Pakistan, there's no dictator we can talk to as sole source. We'd have to talk it over with the cabinet and defense ministry. That would mean leaks. All I can promise you is that I'll back you to the hilt if you get in trouble with the locals. But that does mean the mission is likely to be compromised."

"Mission, yes, but will the U.S. be in trouble?" Wade asked. Kyle understood what he was asking. Were they deniable and expendable?

"We've got a good cover story. Not that you wandered over the border, but something that will cause the whole incident to be forgotten in a couple of days. We won't leave your asses hanging out."

"Good. It's the only ass I've got," Kyle said.

"Beat me to it," came from Wade. He continued, "We'll be as discreet as we can until it hits the fan. I don't think we can promise after that, sir. Once we nail a bad guy, the rest seem to respond unfavorably."

"So we noticed last time," Robash said. He slipped the stogie back in his mouth. "If it's quiet, walk out. If not, we'll come get you. But you won't have to wait long for pickup, we hope. Air Force Pararescue will be ready in Turkey, about two hours away, to do a low-key extraction. If it gets really messy, just go to ground and we'll have some Rangers ready, too. We'll drop them in. Of course, that means we'll need permission from the Romanians."

"What if they don't want to give that permission?" Kyle asked.

"Then it's going to be ugly, so try to throw yourselves on any local official. We'll have the embassy and CIA take it from there."

It didn't sound very reassuring. Hope the locals played along and didn't shoot them, or weren't in cahoots with the terrorists, who likely spent much money locally for cover, or that it was quiet enough to allow them to sneak out or be roped by a chopper, or that some bureaucrat gave permission for a drop. Kyle said so.

"Yeah, it's your turn in the barrel," Robash said. "But we have set up a war game in that general time frame, forty to seventy days from now. If you can make this happen in that window, we can have an 'accident,' where a drop goes bad, and run you out in spare uniforms."

Kyle nodded. It wouldn't be quite that easy. Governments generally wanted passports and ID from any foreign soldiers coming in to play games—and again on the way out, just in case they were spies trying to infiltrate. Still, it had obviously been thought about in some detail. "This is getting a bit spooky," he said, referring to spycraft, not ghosts.

"Yes, it is," Robash agreed. "But you're the men we've got. It worked last time, even after everything turned to crap. It should work now."

"Yeah, it should. I agree. Wade?"

"Hell, it's why we're here. Kick ass and take names, chew bubble gum and drink coffee. Or some junk."

"We're on," Kyle confirmed with a nod, as team leader.

"Outstanding, gentlemen," Robash said. "Our intel people will find what they can, you get in close and observe, pull out all the details and photos possible, and make the shots. Done right, we'll severely cramp their planning and execution, which will make it easier for the locals to find them. We'll feed you, you shoot. Rangers Lead the Way."

"Roger that, sir," they both replied.

"Stop shaving now and grow some hair. Scruffy is good. Moustaches are good."

They nodded. That was expected under the circumstances, and thirty days was enough to get a bit shaggy.

Robash continued, "Now, as to transport, you'll fly in on the Rotator as far as Aviano, Italy, catch a hop to Rome, fly commercial to Bucharest. After you get your gear and meet with the embassy intel people, they'll brief you up to date and help arrange local accommodations as needed."

"You can't use SATO to book transport, obviously." SATO was the military's travel agency. It would be rather clear who they were. "You'll have to call a civilian company and get them to book any trains, taxis, and hotels. Your contact is Mister Mick Cafferty at the embassy, and he'll provide you with local links for more stuff."

"You'll rent a car, because you may have to travel some distance, and follow targets from the sea up to the mountains."

"Communications?" Kyle asked. "Anything special?"

"Will be available there," was the reply with a nod. "We're giving you both new encrypted satellite cells plus Motorola civilian jobs with headset radios to keep in touch with. They look like cell phones, because they're that, too." That was something Kyle and Wade had discussed, so it was one less thing for them to chase down.

"Good," Kyle said. "What about other gear?"

"Laptop, PDAs, anything you can think of for cover," Robash agreed.

"Cameras," Wade said. "And other stuff to make us look like reporters. We might even get some footage you can leak or even sell."

"Yes to the gear, maybe to the pictures, no to selling anything for cash due to conflict of interest, and no to the Army publicly admitting we did this."

"I suppose that's fair," Wade agreed.

"Two stars says it's fair, sergeant," Robash grinned while tapping his collar insignia. It was friendly. "But if you get a chance to get good pictures without risking the mission, by all means do. It's PR, it's also evidence and intelligence."

"Yes, sir," Wade said. He looked happy.

Kyle was fairly happy, too. It was definitely going to be a better mission than the last one. The Army did learn from mistakes on occasion.

"What about disposable assets?" Kyle asked, humor in his voice. Though the question was real and serious.

"Your mission cash is going to be U.S. dollars, euros, and lei," Robash stated.

"Lei? Like the Hawaiian wreath?"

"Same spelling, different language. We'll make sure you get leid," he joked.

"About time the Army took care of important needs like that," Wade returned.

"So we do have on-site intel this time?" Kyle asked.

"Yes. CIA has information from the Romanians, their own digging and whatever they get from our intel-sharing program. Of course, the Saudis and the Pakistanis only tell us as much as they think won't send the Wahhabis into a bombing frenzy, and there's so many holes in their intel that we have to double-check all of it. But you'll have in-nation backup. That was the big problem last time; we assumed the starting intel was accurate."

"Yeah," Kyle said. After a moment he added, "Sir." He didn't want to think about that last mission, or the one before it. Whenever there was a screwup, someone died, and there was always a screwup. All you could hope for was that it was someone else who took the bullet, and that the mission got accomplished anyway.

"Also, we've got a month to prepare. Gather what you need and train up. I've got you a language briefing, a political briefing, and some tourist books to read so you're familiar with the area."

"Good," Kyle said. Robash was a good man, and tried his damnedest to take care of his troops. He also accepted responsibility for mistakes and tried to prevent recurrences. In this cover-your-ass-and-pass-the-blame era, that was something to inspire confidence.

"Have you given any thought to weapons yet?" Robash asked.

"Yes, sir," Kyle said. "I've got a list."

"Good. Finalize it, find NSN numbers on everything you can, and push it through Colonel Wiesinger. You remember him?"

"Yes, sir," Kyle said. Wiesinger was the nominal intermediary between them and Robash, through 3rd Infantry Division, whom they had been temporarily assigned to for the last mission. Kyle remembered him as an overbearing ass more concerned with administrative details, most of which he got wrong, and throwing around his weight, which Kyle had heard was considerable and above Army standards, than with getting a job done.

Still, there was nothing in Army regs that said you had to like people you served with, or that they had to be competent. You just did what you had to and tried to keep a safe distance from idiots. Wiesinger was in Washington, only at the end of a phone line. That seemed a safe distance to Kyle.

After emailing his list in, he wasn't so sure.

He spent all morning the next day looking at National Stock Numbers, with their thirteen digits, all seeming to start with 8 and with a 00 or 01 in the fifth and sixth places. Everything in the military, from buttons and paperclips to tanks, had an NSN. At least Kyle could look them up on computer. He'd heard horror stories of the days when they'd been in huge binders.

The radios and other communication gear, the cell phones and PDAs, already were listed and numbered. The weapons were a bit trickier. Wade had read up and decided to go with an AK104, a later, better variant. A few did exist in the U.S. military for training purposes and clandestine missions, but were not readily available. The suppressors, on the other hand, were custom, and the takedown Ruger had never been issued.

It took some time to find a soldier at the post armory who could tell him which form to use to request custom-made weapons. Then he had to provide justification, in the form of a mission order. Naturally, being non-standard, those were questioned. If he'd ordered a bomber and a nuke, likely they would have flown in within the day, no questions asked; they had numbers. But try doing something different . . .

He knew there was a problem when the phone rang. He could feel it. Someone had seen the request, called in on the orders, asked for a decision from higher up, and now shit was rolling downhill. He also knew who the problem was before he picked it up.

He'd barely identified himself when the ranting started.

"Sergeant Monroe, why are there civilian weapons on this list? And mods for your personal sidearm?" It was Wiesinger, of course.

"Easiest and best way to handle the job, sir," Kyle said. He supposed it did look a bit funny, but he'd included a detailed write-up of what and why.

"You're wanting a militia survival-nut twenty-two with space-age gadgets, and a silencer for a very expensive personal pistol, plus extensive custom work to a cheap-ass former Commie rifle. Any idea how that looks to Uncle Sam, Sergeant?"

"Sir, I included an explanation for the request," he said. "It's—"

"Yeah, I read it. Nice try. But I'm not going for it. You can use standard Army issue rifles and carbines, or buy something locally with the cash you'll be issued. A local weapon which you will not attempt to bring back CONUS this time, you understand." CONtinental U.S. The man was too much an official prig to say "Stateside."

"Sir," Kyle started, then took a second for a very deep breath to get his anger under control.

This pencil-pushing REMF was going to be a pain in his ass. "Sir, we need to be discreet, and we need accurate weapons for intermediate range. The two circumstances are contradictory in nature, and therefore—"

Wiesinger cut him off, which was a shame, as he thought he'd sounded properly bureaucratic.

"You're not going to be discreet with a God-knows-how-expensive pistol with a silencer on the end. You're a goddamned soldier, not James Fucking Bond!"

There was just no way this jerk was going to grasp what they were doing. He could try to explain that no one should see the pistol until too late to worry about it, that few people including soldiers would be familiar enough with the hot-rod gun market to identify it, and that it was backup only for close range in an urban environment, but it would be a waste of breath. "As you say, sir," he said.

"Just do your damned job and don't try to think too much, Monroe," Wiesinger said.

"No problem, sir. I'll leave it to you." He gritted his teeth and scowled. Ten more seconds. He just needed to hold on ten more seconds.

"You do that. Resubmit your list and I'll approve everything reasonable." His voice had a sneering tone that almost pushed Kyle over the edge.

"Yes, sir," he agreed, and waited for the click.

He placed the phone carefully down, dropped his fists to his desk, and clenched and shook. He hated what was going to happen next, but he was damned if some desk-warming bean counter was going to screw Kyle's mission over an amateur opinion of how it should be done.

Deep breath, he told himself. Deep breath. He let the shakes and the flush subside.

That done, he leaned back and smiled faintly. He punched another number into the phone and leaned back in his chair.

"General Robash? I seem to have run into a problem . . ."

When Kyle finished the call, he turned to see the school commander standing in the doorway, smiling faintly.

The current commander of the Sniper School and Kyle's immediate commander was Captain Schorlin. He was not yet thirty, but deadly competent and with a very sharp mind. "TDY again, Kyle?"

"Er, yes, I meant to tell you, sir. But we've been busy."

"It's okay," Schorlin smiled. "The general did brace me first. He's not stealing you from under me."

"That's good," Kyle said. He realized he hadn't thought about his chain of command and how his leaving would affect the training schedule. All of a sudden, he was back, his mind working on exercise problems and thinking about the weather and curricula. He shook his head to come back to the matter at hand. "We're not clearing post for about a month, but I'll be TDY at once, briefing and prepping. I'll be using my office here, if that's okay."

"Sure. If it helps you, and lets me claim the materials on our budget."

"Thanks, sir. As to mission, I'm not sure. I'd say at least thirty days. Maybe longer." He frowned slightly. This was rather open-ended.

"Just do come back, Kyle. We need you here."

"Planning on it, sir. I'm not looking for fame, just to do a job. Can you do me a favor and watch out for Lucas? He's overeager with the students, and . . ."

Schorlin cut him off with a faint smile. "We'll manage, Sergeant. Go kill terrorists."

Kyle smiled despite himself. "Yes, sir."

The weapons were delivered despite Wiesinger's complaints. No doubt he was shitting a brick somewhere in the bowels of the Pentagon, Kyle thought, smiling thinly to himself. Not that he gave a rat's ass.

Actually, he did. Anything that inconvenienced a bureaucrat was a good thing. It wasn't that most of them were bad, though most were, but that almost all of them got out of the habit of thinking. Choose an option A through G. Refer to manual 35-10. Fill out form NMS-2112 in triplicate. Why think, when one could refer the decision elsewhere? And when enough decisions got referred, nothing got done.

Although, Kyle thought, where the government generally was concerned, that might not be a bad thing.

He called Wade and they got together at his apartment. Technically, the weapon shouldn't be there. But it was a private place to meet and the weapon was perfectly civilian legal if a bit unusual in the configuration in question. Kyle made the decision, and there was no one to know he'd violated the reg. Except Wade.

The little Ruger and kit was as Kyle had said. It had been purchased new from Butler Creek, under the category of "training weapons," which wasn't entirely false; they *were* going to train with it. The receiver and its custom folding stock were one assembly, with the barrel separate. It assembled as a break action shotgun would, the fore end snapping in place, thanks to Ruger's clever wedge attachment for the barrel/receiver mate. The case also held a fine Leupold scope, two factory ten-round rotary magazines, and two twenty-five-round curved box magazines. The barrel was short, barely legal for civilian use, barely long enough for good velocity. It couldn't be shortened further, being a wrapped carbon-fiber sleeve around a stainless steel liner, with a screw adjustment for tension. "That's going to make a silencer hard," Wade commented. There was no way to thread the carbon.

"No," Kyle said. "G-Tech in Indiana is building one that slips over the front sight, from aluminum, that will muffle it down to nothing. Light weight, thirty-eight decibel reduction."

"Damn!" Wade said. "That's as close to silent as you get. Subsonic ammo?" With the muzzle blast dissipated and no supersonic crack, the weapon would be untraceable even in the dark.

"Yes, but also some hypervelocity," Kyle said. "I'll see if CCI can special-load us some even hotter than their Stinger loads. Damned near twenty-two-magnum energy. We won't always want close and quiet, after all, and pistols aren't the best for sniping."

" 'Aren't the best,' " Wade replied, snickering. "Aren't you funny?"

"Anyway," Kyle said. "It fits in a standard briefcase with room to spare for ammo, we can carry extra in our pockets if need be, I'll fit it with a picatinny rail for the scope and whatever else, and I think with practice we can get down to thirty seconds to uncase, assemble, and shoot."

"That sounds like fun," Wade said. "The practice, I mean. Not that gapping terrorists is less fun."

"Remember to be professional," Kyle replied with a grin.

"Always," Wade said. "But there's nothing wrong with enjoying my work."

"Right."

"Going to use that scope?" Wade asked.

"We'll take it along. I'll also bring an AN/PVS Ten scope, in case we need to shoot at night. Actually, I'd prefer to shoot at night."

"Suppressed twenty-two in thick, cold, humid air in the dark would be ideal," Wade agreed. "So naturally, we'll have to do it in daylight."

"Yeah, Murphy's already packed his bags, I'm sure. Anyway, we're waiting on the suppressors at my end, and CCI's hottest ammo. How's yours?"

"Got the AK," Wade acknowledged. "The armorer is flogging it. It actually doesn't need much, because the barrel's the right length and it's already got fiberglass furniture. He's removing the bayonet lug and cleaning rod—I won't need those—and threading it. So we're waiting on a suppressor and some custom ammo. I ordered a thousand rounds from a civilian loader who insists that it won't possibly work properly. I told him it was for a custom hunting pistol. He seemed to buy that."

"Fair enough. Where'd you get the ballistics figures for the round?"

"I asked a ballistician at Natick Research Center, who checked with a physicist and with Olin. They offered to load some rounds up, but it would take four months and they have a two-hundred-thousand round minimum order."

"Uh . . . yeah," Kyle said. "So we'll need to test this ammo, then." It wasn't a question. Sniping was as much science as art, and everything was checked and measured before being tried in the field.

"I figure to use half the ammo for practice," Wade said. "Maybe more. I'm hoping not to shoot more than a magazine of the special stuff for keeps. Standard Eastern Bloc fodder can fill in the rest, and I'm taking some civilian stuff that I know is reliable, too. But I have a question."

"Yes?" Kyle asked.

"How the hell do we get the weapons there?"

"I'm told State Department will ship them to the embassy, and that it's done all the time."

"Oh. Reassuring. I think." They shipped special weapons into embassies all the time? How many operations like this were being run by the CIA, NSA, FBI, and God only knew how many other agencies?

"Yeah, that was my reaction."

3

IT WOULD BE SEVERAL DAYS BEFORE THE REST of the accessories and gear were ready. In the meantime, there were more briefings. Kyle didn't mind. He was a natural tourist, loved seeing other cultures, and was learning to appreciate Wade's fascination with the details and differences. The briefers seemed to know what they were talking about, and they didn't waste time. Facts and key items only.

Neither of them knew a lot about modern camera gear. They were brought up to speed in a hurry. Their instructor was a slim, dark-haired man with a faint Russian accent who was very engaging and informative.

"You've goht the three still cameras," he said. "Point and shoot. They've had the circuits disabled so they won't beep when you shoot. Fifty photos on each memohry stick, and you can carry extra ones."

"Roger." Wade was handling this, but Kyle took notes, too, so he could double up.

"Yohr best bet is the camcorder. With memohry sticks it can take passable stills. It can use digital tapes for up to two hours, and it has an IR illuminator good for about ten meters or so. Telephoto lens, and you've goht a two-hundred-millimeter lens adapted to fit it. Eastern European power supply and spare batteries. Make sure you carry the spares."

"Yeah, definitely," they both agreed. Batteries were the ammo of the modern army. Bullets could sometimes be done without. But batteries were essential.

"Now, the betacam is noht going to be used much, but it has to look like it is. I'll show you how to operate it, and how to look professional."

The man knew nothing of their mission, but he really knew cameras and photography. Wade was delighted to take a minor hobby and improve upon it with good lessons.

They spent a morning looking at the economics and social fabric of Romania, which hadn't fared well under the madman Ceauşescu and the Soviet Communists before that, and was still only slowly entering twenty-first century Europe.

Their briefer was a college professor. All he'd been told was that they were going over to act as liaison with the Romanian military for a training exercise and needed to know about the culture and people. As a result, there were important questions they couldn't ask him and would have to catch up with later.

"The economy is still in a recovery phase and social systems are in a state of flux," he told them. He was full of information, but much of that was hidden in heavy babble. He gave figures about GNP, GDP and relative worth, told them of the excesses of the former regime, and even described several amusing and informative misunderstandings he'd encountered on his own trip to the Universitatea din Bucuresti. They made notes.

When they broke, Kyle expressed an opinion. "You know, it's always some kind of goat rope. We've got all this support, so it seems, but they don't want to make it obvious to foreign intelligence that we're doing anything. So we can't ask State Department to brief us here, we can't take enough backup, and we can't even ask some questions, and have to hope they have someone on site who can help us. It's really, really . . . aggravating."

Wade agreed, "Ours not to reason why," he said. "Which is a damned good thing, because we'd go crazy trying to figure this out."

After a lunch of Taco Bell, cold but better than chow-hall takeout, they were ready for their language briefing.

"Greetings, gentlemen," Bill Gober said as he walked in. As always before, his arms were full of CDs, books, and notes. A bag slung over his shoulder was stuffed like Santa's pouch with more documents. He was portly and balding, roundfaced and smiling, dressed in a casual sport shirt and jeans. He wasn't a stuffy type, and had done an excellent job of prepping them on the basics of languages they'd never even heard of for the last mission.

"Mister Gober," they both replied.

"Let's talk about Romanian, which is, of course, a Romance language."

"I wondered about that," Kyle said. "They're in the middle of all those Slavic countries."

"Yes, and it's corrupted their language," he agreed as he sat down. "There's Slavic endings and vowels stuffed into the degenerate Latin. But there's good news."

"Yes?"

"You speak Spanish, I'm told. Spanish has better than seventy percent commonality, so you should be able to be understood. Of course, dialects can vary, and if they speak quickly, you'll be hard-pressed to extract more than a few words."

"Understood. I haven't used it much in some time."

"I've got CDs of Romanian and Spanish you can listen to that should make comprehension much easier. Anyone who wants to understand you should grasp the gist of what you say." He tapped the stack he'd arranged on the table.

"Yeah, that's the key," Kyle nodded. Of course, if someone who clearly understood most of what he was saying tried to pretend they didn't, he'd find ways to make them understand. "What about other languages?"

Gober took a sip of his water before replying. "The Gypsies speak Romani in various dialects. But they almost all speak Romanian. There's a smattering of Hungarian, Turkish, Bulgarian, and of course Arabic might crop up."

"Right. And the local alphabet is based on the Latin one," Wade put in, looking over one of the guide books.

"Yes. They switched from Cyrillic when the Soviet Union collapsed. Or rather, the Soviets imposed Cyrillic on them, but it's a Romance language, so it used a Latin base originally."

"So I read up, use Spanish as needed, and you, Wade?" he looked a question at his partner.

"Oh, I can pick the written parts up at least," Wade said. "Looking at this page, I see 'natura,' 'interiorara,' 'primul,' and 'arhitectura gotica.' Much of it looks easy to extract."

"Yes, much easier than last time," Gober said. "We've got more than three weeks before you depart, I'm told, so there's time to practice."

"Any chance of practicing with you, Mister Gober?" Kyle asked.

"I wouldn't be of much help. I'm not a linguist, I'm an ethnologist. I study the development and relationships of languages. I can handle basic grammar and vocabulary, and advise on pronunciation, but I'm not fluent in a great many."

"Okay," Kyle said. That cleared up a great many things. It would have been amazing had

Gober actually spoken all the languages they discussed. This made more sense. Though he did wish the Army could dig up a linguist to work with them.

On the other hand, that would mean either flying to Monterrey, where the linguists were, or bringing one here, or trying to get a clearance for a civilian instructor of unknown loyalty. Any of which would make it obvious something was going on, and wouldn't be of substantially more help in a few days. Gober was likely more useful to them in that regard.

And Gober was cleared. He knew approximately what they were doing, and could give them military terminology and specialized language that most non-military experts wouldn't know, and would immediately get suspicious of. They worked with him three afternoons a week, the three days they weren't practicing shooting and spotting, just to keep the basics fresh.

Then there was all the research they did themselves. As with most military installations, Fort Benning had a decent amount of material in the post library, and both men knew how to use computers. They swapped links, dug through sites, made and compiled notes, and then sat down to compare. The problem with online information was deciding which was accurate, which was amusing fabrication, and which was ignorant hearsay.

Wade came over every couple of nights and they discussed their findings. One of the first things he'd looked at was the religious background.

"It's not far from what used to be Constantinople, and is heavily Christian. But not like America," he said. "Here's a chart." He laid out a printed page for clarity, and brought up a file on an Army laptop he'd acquired.

"Okay," Kyle said, digesting the figures. "So ninety percent Orthodox, five percent Catholic, and the rest a mix, with only point oh oh three percent Muslim? Why is that such a problem? They can't all be troublemakers."

"Indigenous Muslims aren't a problem. These are Muslims from Bosnia and the Middle East. You'll recall that the Romanians arrested an al Qaeda member a while back who was using his cover name in the Iraqi embassy."

"I don't, actually," Kyle said. He hadn't known that, and he really needed to get up to speed. The government claimed WMDs and conspiracies and terrorists. Its detractors denied everything. The truth was likely somewhere in the middle, as usual. "They're coming from elsewhere?"

"Yes, it looks as if much of their explosive is former Eastern Bloc and sometimes former Yugoslav military munitions. They load up in the quiet parts of Romania then go elsewhere. And it's easily within range of the MidEast."

"Ain't it amazing how these scum are so devious? If they spent half this much effort on real work, there wouldn't be any trouble in the world."

"'A policeman's lot is not a happy one,'"

Wade said. "Someone has to be babysitter and playground attendant."

"And trash collector."

"Yeah, it all sucks," Wade said with a nod. "So let's pull on the gloves."

Changing the subject, Kyle asked, "How are you doing on supplies?"

"Adequately," Wade replied. "Still waiting on the suppressor and ammo."

"Damn. We've only got a week left."

"Yeah, I keep a calendar." Wade winced. "Better than last time, but your pessimism is rubbing off on me."

"Pessimism?" Kyle asked. "I think positive. I'm positive the Army is going to screw up again."

"And on that note, I need a beer." He'd brought his own in a cooler again.

There was no friction between them over drinking. Kyle didn't think of himself as an alcoholic, just as someone who increasingly thought drinking was a bad idea for himself. Wade didn't drink to excess; this was the same twelve-pack he'd been working on for three weeks. He drank, Kyle didn't, and that was all there was to it. But Wade didn't seem to feel it was sociable to drink alone, so he always grabbed a soda for Kyle.

They dove back in to a history of Romania from the time of the Turkish occupation through Ceauşescu's butchery. "That was one seriously insane dude," Wade said.

"Yeah. Forced breeding program to outpopulate the West? And what were they going to eat in that little country?" Romania had less than 23 million inhabitants, and was no larger than a couple of Midwestern states. How he'd planned to increase to where the nation would even be noticed by most Westerners was a mystery.

"I think it was an attempt at individuality for him, seeing as how Moscow was threatening to march on him, and an ego trip against the modern world. If it's not that, I have no idea why he was such a twitch."

They kicked it and assorted maps and photos around until 11 P.M., when Wade said, "Time for me to get back to billeting. When and where tomorrow?"

"Call me at oh eight hundred," Kyle said. "I'll know then."

"Maintain a rigid state of flexibility?" Wade asked.

"You got it. Later." He showed Wade to the door.

The next morning at the school, a package was waiting on Kyle's desk. It was from post logistics, and contained multiple layers of cardboard and padding. He sliced the top with his Benchmade, and took enough of a glance to determine it contained round, black phosphated shapes: suppressors, magazines, and some assorted other parts. He left everything packed for privacy and to protect it.

Now what they needed was a place to practice. The choice was obvious but problematic. He grabbed the phone and speed-dialed Captain Schorlin, who was out on the range, prepping for the next class.

"Captain, I need to see about reserving some range time."

"Shouldn't be a problem. When?"

"Sir, we need to do some shooting inside to . . . well, we need to shoot inside." He needed to know it was going to be quiet enough before he tried it in the field.

"I assume these are weapons you really don't want seen in a civilian range?"

"Yes, sir," he said. They were somewhat distinctive. It was unlikely the word would leak out from here, but taking military automatic weapons with suppressors onto a civilian range was guaranteed to draw attention from someone, even if it could be legally arranged. "Rumors. This has to be on base somewhere."

"Kyle, there's some things I can't beat, and political correctness is one of them. You're going to need to call General Robash for that."

"Understood, sir," he said. "I just wanted to make sure I checked with you first."

"I appreciate it. If he'll help, I'll cover for you. But I'm only a captain. I can't buck the system that much by myself."

"Yeah, I don't blame you, sir. But thanks, and I'll make that call."

* * *

General Robash hesitated, too. "Son, I know what you need, and I know why you're doing that, but damn," he said. "There is absolutely no legal way."

"I was afraid you'd say that, sir," Kyle replied. "I'm just trying to figure out a discreet alternative."

"No, hold on a moment," the general said. "Just hold the line."

Kyle said, "Yes, sir," but the phone was already clicking. He waited, receiver to ear for fifteen minutes, fumbling with papers and his computer, until he wondered if he dare hang up on a general officer and await a return call.

Just as he was thinking that, Robash came back. "All right, Wade, call Sergeant Major Jack Parsons at this extension," he said and rattled off the digits. "He's expecting you to call now."

"Thank you, sir."

"For what? I didn't do anything. I don't know anything. I don't even know why I'm talking into this phone, since there's no one there." He hung up, but not before Kyle heard a snicker.

Kyle reset and dialed the number. It was answered on the first ring by a deep, gravelly voice. "Sergeant Major Parsons."

"Sergeant Major, I'm Sergeant Monroe."

"Right. General Robash told me you need some indoor time?"

"Yes I do, Sergeant Major. Quietly and without spectators."

"Right. Tomorrow at zero nine hundred suit

you?" Parsons clearly wasn't one to waste time.

"That works for me," Kyle said. Parsons gave him a building number and a road. "We'll be there," Kyle agreed.

The next morning, he and Wade took their weapons from the Sniper School armory and loaded them into his truck. Military weapons were never supposed to be in private vehicles, but these weren't crated like military weapons, they didn't want anyone to think weapons were going into the building in question, and he figured the captain and the general could run interference if need be. Not that anyone should notice. The Ruger was in its metal case, and the AK was in a sleeve in a duffel bag.

"I didn't even know there was an indoor range here," Wade said.

"Neither did I. That was a certain amount of luck."

"Right," Wade said. "I'm still amazed you could pull this off."

"Actually, Robash called a sergeant major."

"Ah, sergeant majors," Wade said. "Is there anything they can't do? When God needs backup, he calls his sergeant major."

"About the truth," Kyle agreed.

The building was like many at Benning: brick, aged, and well maintained. But this one had a long forgotten secret: an indoor twenty-five-yard pistol range in the basement. Kyle was hoping the confines and closeness would give him a good idea of how the weapons would handle inside a city, with witnesses nearby, possibly even in adjoining rooms.

Simple enough on the face of it. But the reason the range was forgotten was because it had been closed before Kyle was born.

A very large, very black man in painted-on BDUs met them at the door. "Sergeants Monroe and Curtis? Good to meet you."

"Yes, we are, Sergeant Major Parsons. Thanks for meeting us." He winced slightly at a hand-shake that could crush pipe, and quickly passed the hand to Wade.

"I'm told it's for a worthy cause. If General Robash says so, I'm willing to bend the system. Once," Parsons cautioned. He motioned them in and turned to lead the way. He filled the doorway as he did, shoulders almost brushing the frame.

"So this was a common-use area once?" Kyle asked.

"Yeah, most posts and every National Guard armory used to have a twenty-five yard range in the basement. Lead complaints shut them all down," Parsons said as he led them through the building, now used for storage of desks, chairs, and crates, then down dim, dusty, echoing stairs. It was cool and musty, the air smelling of mildew.

"I can see that. Lead oxide," Wade said. As bullets were shot and impacted the backstop, they'd throw lead vapor into the air. It was toxic to breathe. Modern indoor ranges had filters and fans to handle it. Retrofitting old ranges was cost prohibitive.

"Yes. And that's why we aren't supposed to be here," Parsons said. "So do what you've got to, be done by lunch, and no one knows a thing."

"We'll be brief," Kyle promised. "And we won't shoot that much, anyway."

"Good. The lead risk is real. There's just times that's an acceptable risk militarily. But the EPA *doesn't* know that, so I've told the MPs to keep the area clear, and that some construction with nail guns is going on. Or rather, I told their first sergeant that, and he told them."

"That should do fine," Kyle said. If anyone could hear these weapons outside a concrete basement and on the street, they needed a new strategy anyway.

Parsons unlocked a thick, heavy door that had padding on the inside and a dirty, fogged window about four inches square set into it. The hinges protested slightly, but it swung easily enough. "Here you go," he said. "Call my cell phone when you're done and I'll come secure the building." He handed over his card.

"Thank you very much, Sergeant Major," Kyle said, and Wade chorused in.

"No problem, gentlemen. Whatever you're hunting, good luck." He smiled and left, boots thumping and echoing back up the stairs.

Wade closed the door. "Man, if I didn't know he was coming back, I'd hate being down here. It's like a forgotten dungeon." The building was so old it was lit by incandescent bulbs in metal cages. Floodlights illuminated the target area and backstop. Everything was old, covered in peeling white paint, and there were four lanes, each about three feet wide with motorized cables to run targets downrange. The area they stood in was perhaps five feet deep. The ceiling was seven feet high.

"Tell me about it," Kyle said. He felt creeped out, too. The echoes of his voice were tinny. "Anyway," he continued, "let's see what we have now."

He'd practiced with the .22, and had it assembled in short order as Wade watched. As claimed, G-Tech's suppressor slipped over the muzzle and pinned in place behind the sight. It was a can type, slender and about six inches long. He added the Harris bipod to the rail that had been fitted under the fore end.

That done, Wade screwed a larger suppressor onto the AK's muzzle brake. "We'll still get a crack, obviously," he said. "But the muzzle blast and flash should be minimal."

"Right," Kyle agreed. Nothing could be made silent. But if it didn't sound like a weapon to a witness, and if the flash and bang were reduced, the odds of being identified were greatly reduced. "And here's where the forty-five rules," he grinned. He'd never liked the 9mm.

"Yeah, the round is already subsonic, no crack," Wade said.

Kyle said nothing, he simply screwed another suppressor onto the specially prepared barrel Ed Brown had cut for him. It protruded a half inch beyond the slide and was threaded. He was glad to see it fit well. He'd assumed so; Brown was a very reputable maker. But they also had a hell of a waiting list at times, and had squeezed the job in among their other clients. All they'd been told was "urgent military contract," and they'd done it. It was nice to know patriotic support still existed among civilians.

There was nothing wrong with the workmanship. The barrel worked flawlessly; Kyle had already shot it in. The threads had been done perfectly, which was no big task, but accidents happened on some contracts. He was glad again to have insisted on first-rate work up front. The lowest bidder was often more expensive in the long run. And G-Tech's suppressors were functionally pretty, no-nonsense and sturdy.

"Oh, to reassure you on the lead," Wade said, "I bought us a box each of Winchester's fully jacketed stuff for the pistols. No exposed lead at the base." He indicated two boxes among the dozen he'd brought. They planned to try several rounds to find the best combination of weapon and cartridge.

"Good man," Kyle said. "I always wondered why they aren't more available."

"Production cost. They can't just pour the lead in."

"Oh." He felt stupid. That was a rather obvious problem.

"That still leaves lead twenty-two, and exposed lead on the AK."

"Gee, thanks."

"You know," Wade said conversationally, "the Romanians have the solution to that problem. Seven six two with wooden bullets."

"Wooden bullets?" Kyle asked.

"Yup. Specifically for indoor range practice. No lead, no ricochets, just holes in the paper."

"Wooden bullets. Romania . . ." Kyle muttered.

"Vampires and wooden stakes?"

"That's a hell of a coincidence," Kyle said. Weird irony.

"Yeah. Should we get some, just in case?"

"I really don't want to explain that to Wiesinger," he said with a frown.

"Yeah, better not. Still, it's funny."

With the suppressors on, no hearing protection was required. A faint *pop!* accompanied each shot of the Ruger, followed by the metallic *tink* of the empty brass hitting the side of the lane or the floor. The sound echoed on the block walls.

"Okay, we need a brass catcher. Twenty-five bucks and two screws to install," Kyle said as he finished a string.

"Sure. Meantime, this is one accurate little son of a bitch!" Wade marveled. He raised the weapon smoothly and quickly as he shuffled into stance, and commenced firing.

In ten seconds, he'd shot all ten rounds. He laid the weapon down, automatically extracted the magazine and observed the empty chamber through the locked bolt, and pressed the button to return the target.

As it swayed back toward them, rocking in the breeze created by its motion, one thing was clear: All ten rounds had hit in a circle no larger than a quarter inch, dead center on the forehead of the silhouette target.

"Nice," Kyle commented. "My turn."

The factory ten-round helical magazines functioned flawlessly. The twenty-five-round aftermarket ones were quite reliable. But the thirties Kyle had picked up . . .

"These are just crap," Wade said in disgust the fourth time one misfed and jammed a round against the breech face.

"Yeah, we'll scrap those. I don't expect to shoot more than five shots at a target, anyway," Kyle said. "The larger ones are just backup."

"Okay, well I'm happy with that. Let's look at the support."

The modified AK104 was an ugly little gun. The barrel was barely twelve and a half inches, and the stock folded sideways.

"The bottom folder was longer, but caught on the magazine when deploying," Wade said. "This is from the AKSU Seventy-four and works much better. The muzzle brake," he pointed under the suppressor, "reduces felt recoil and flash, and maintains pressure for the gas piston, and the expansion chamber stops it from getting louder." That was a positive thing. It was common for a good brake to actually *increase* perceived sound. "It's threaded, and the suppressor fits right over it."

"Nice," Kyle commented. He'd shot AK-series weapons, but wasn't an aficionado of them. He could strip and clean and employ. That was all he needed to know.

"Bad news is that with this short barrel, accuracy with standard ball will suck. Suck bad. Way bad. So bad that . . . well, it won't be much good over one hundred meters with standard Eastern ammo. With the stuff I had loaded, it's accurate for about three hundred, but it's about like a pistol for power at that range. So any kill will have to be precision, not trauma."

"That fits our plans," Kyle said. He grasped what Wade was saying. Below certain critical velocities, wounding effect was greatly reduced. There would be a hole, but not a catastrophic energy dump into the target. Still, they intended to shoot accurately.

"I figured," Wade continued. "The rail attaches here and here, with pins. So it looks mostly standard issue like this, but can take the rail, scope, and suppressor in a few seconds. I actually thought about using Russian night vision and scopes, but while the quality is good, we aren't familiar with them, and it's not going to make that much difference if we're found."

"Right. We'll work with what we're used to as far as possible. And who'd question it, anyway? Either they know who we are, or we're mercs of some kind."

"Glad you approve," Wade said.

"Hell, Wade, either of us could run this, you know that. I'm nominally in charge due to rank and because someone has to be the place where the buck stops."

"Thanks," Wade said, seeming to mean it. He obviously felt complimented.

"No problem. Show me how to shoot it."

"It's going to be zeroed fifteen inches high, because it's got a twenty-seven-inch drop at three hundred and a flight time of point five zero seconds exactly. Ballistics tables are in my PDA, soon to be in the laptop, and we can study them as we go. I've found a couple of support points that give it a very stable position," Wade began. "First is in front of the magazine, fingers wrapped . . ."

Unfortunately, the rounds still had a supersonic crack. Both men reached for earmuffs in a hurry.

The .45 was fun, rocking lightly, its kick reduced to a slow shove, and the additional nose weight keeping it stable. The Ed Brown platform was one of the world's best, and Kyle proceeded to blow the middle from a target with dull thumps akin to a phone book being dropped on a concrete floor.

"I think we're in good shape," he said. "The twenty-two is near silent, the forty-five sounds nothing like a firearm, the AK is loud but much reduced and the nine millimeter has a crack when you're using standard loads, but is still not immediately recognizable. Let's try two rounds each of our combat loads and I'll stand upstairs to get a listen."

"Will do," Wade agreed, and started loading. Kyle shoved the heavy door open and jogged up into the clutter upstairs, leaving the door wide behind him. He'd been so busy shooting, he'd forgotten the aloneness the building exuded, and was used to it now.

Shortly, there came clicks, thumps, and clatters. Then Wade shouted, "Cease fire! That's it!"

"Roger!" he replied and headed back down. "Didn't sound like anything threatening to me. We're cool."

"Good. Call the sar-major and let's go get lunch."

With all preparations made, all gear—from rifles and GPS to pocketknives and a handful of paperbacks—packed and ready to either travel as luggage or meet them there, they started their final outprocessing. They checked their government credit cards to ensure they were active, compiled lists of phone numbers and email addresses, and gathered maps and flight schedules. Kyle called ahead to speak to the Regional Affairs officer at the embassy in Bucharest, Mr. Mick Cafferty.

"You realize it's . . . eight hours ahead here?" he asked. His voice was gravelly and tired.

"Damn. I'm sorry," Kyle said. It was damned near midnight there, and he'd woken the man they'd be working with.

"It's okay. Let's talk," Cafferty said. Behind him, a female voice was protesting. She didn't sound happy.

"Okay," Kyle said, "I need to know what we do when we arrive."

"There'll be a taxi waiting for you at the airport. It'll take you to the Marriott. You'll call me and I'll arrange for you to stop by the office."

"Understood." He was writing it down to add to his file.

Cafferty continued. "We have to be careful not to let people conclude you're more than glorified tourists. It's fine for you to stop by and 'ask questions,' but if you stay any length of time, the locals may become curious, and there are leaks."

"Yes, sir," he agreed. "Do we have visas?"

"Yes. They should arrive there in the next day or so. You're photographers for hire. Some group wants to do a book and video about Dracula again, and they sent you to get footage. You're spending their money and snickering at their foolishness—it adds to the cover story. I had to find some way to explain your presence."

"I guess that makes sense," Kyle said. He didn't want to contradict or complain, as it wasn't his arena. It did call for some acting, and he wished they'd had more notice. "Is there any question over us being such unknown videographers?"

Cafferty chuckled, a rasping, scary sound. "No. Thousands of nuts and researchers from hundreds of agencies with dozens of nations come through here all the time to see the Dracula sites. As long as their embassy or a producer vouches for them, no one bothers to check up. It's just not worth the work."

"Understood," Kyle said. "You'll have more intel for us when we get there?"

"Yes, we're still building a report. You're going to be here early in the operation."

"Better than being late. Anything else I need right now?"

"You won't come to the embassy. Some things the ambassador doesn't need to know, so he doesn't have to deny them, and so he can't refuse to assist. But that's my problem. It's only your problem if things go to hell,"—Kyle thought, when *things go to hell*—"and then you've got DoD and State to bat for you as well as me. You'll stay locally, I'll deliver your gear and intel. I'll email you if anything else crops up. How often do you check messages?"

"At least three times a day at the school," Kyle said. "Let me give you my home addy, too." He read it off phonetically.

"Got it."

"Good. I'll let you sleep. You have our cell numbers?"

"I do. Good night."

"Good night."

"Okay, not thrilling but better than last time," Kyle said to Wade. "We have someone in country who speaks our language and can run interference."

"Good. Hey, even the Army learns from its mistakes. Eventually."

"Right. Let's check off the list and call logistics. I'll make sure they load it all."

"Okay," Wade said and pulled out his PDA. "First item, AK-one oh four with AN/PVS dash ten scope and suppressor, two ten-round magazines and four thirty-round magazines, hardshell case and four hundred and eighty rounds of match ammunition."

"Check."

Their gear made quite a pile, Kyle thought, as it was taken to be shipped. Weapons, rucks, local and military clothes, body armor for out in the field, commo gear and computers, cameras and recording gear for "reporting," maps, charts, suitcases, a few personal items, and credit cards and cash. Some would fly as luggage, some would be flown to the embassy and meet them there, and some went with them as carry-ons. Wade was staying at billeting, he at his apartment, and they didn't need to wake up at ohmygodthirty this time. Which was good.

Kyle had never learned to sleep the night before a mission started.

4

THEIR LAST MISSION HAD ENTAILED LONG hours trapped in commercial aircraft, pretending to be harmless civilians and getting shuffled around at airports.

This deployment was much the same, except the aircraft were military, or sort of.

"Sort of" meant after a civilian flight from Atlanta, the overseas Rotator flight from Baltimore to Rhein-Main Air Base, Germany, then to Aviano Air Base, Italy, where they'd debark before it continued on to Saudi Arabia. It was an old Lockheed Tristar, contracted to the Air Force from ATA, and all the passengers were military. Most were deploying unit elements on their way to Iraq, Kuwait, or Qatar, who'd transfer to military transport aircraft at some point. Kyle and Wade sat near the front, separated from others by a seat or so each way, and tried to get back into the tactical discussion.

"Pity it's not Pan Am like last time, with the free beer and that nice chicken," Kyle said. Though he recalled the chicken being Airline Standard Tasteless. And he didn't drink, even if there had been beer on this flight. But it was standard to complain. The military ran on complaints.

"True. But there's one really good thing about flying charter," Wade replied.

"Yeah," Kyle agreed. "We can talk about killing, and terrorists, and weapons, and not be dragged off by TSA." He met the eye of the passing flight attendant, who smiled thinly back at him. Clearly, she wasn't happy with the subject, but recognized it as something military and legitimate. It was a plus, but at the same time, they'd have to avoid slipping details that would place their mission to Romania. The other troops would tell tales, and those could become leaks. ComSec, it was called. Communications Security. Never say anything in the presence of those who didn't need to know.

Still, they could study background from books. Wade had a history of Romania he'd picked up online. He'd often expressed the theory that one could never have too much intelligence, and his schooling had been in sociology. He was engrossed in it when not dragged out to deal with mundane issues.

"Hey, Kyle, listen to this about Prince Vlad Dracula," he said, eyes wide as he leaned back and read aloud:

" 'Some Italian ambassadors were sent to him. When they came to him they bowed and removed their hats and they kept on the berets beneath them. Then he asked them why they did not take their caps off, too. They said it was their custom, and they did not even remove them for the emperor. Dracula said, "I wish to reinforce this for you." He immediately had their caps nailed firmly on their heads so that their caps would not fall off and their custom would remain.' "

"Damn," Kyle said, "And I thought the drills in boot camp were harsh about hats under cover."

"And this one: 'He [the Sultan] marched on for about five kilometers, when he saw his men pale; the Sultan's army came across a field with stakes, about three kilometers long and one kilometer wide. And there were large stakes on which they could see the impaled bodies of men, women, and children, about twenty thousand of them, as they said. Quite a spectacle for the Turks and the Sultan himself! The Sultan, in wonder, kept saying that he could not conquer the country of a man who could do such terrible and unnatural things and put his power and his subjects to such use. He also used to say that this man who did such things would be worthy of more. And the other Turks, seeing so many people impaled, were scared out of their wits. There were babies clinging to their mothers on stakes, and birds had made nests in their breasts.' "

"He impaled his *own* people to scare off invaders?" Kyle asked, guts churning. Dear God.

"Sounds like. No wonder he got the reputation he did. But he's a folk hero to some of the locals, because he kept the Turks out."

"Yeah. Who'd want to invade? Damn."

"And we think the scum we're fighting are obscene. They've got nothing on this."

"I think we can be happy they haven't read history," Kyle said.

"They haven't learned from it, either," Wade said. "Which is why we're here. God bless job security and precision shooting."

"I think I'd rather be unemployed," Kyle said, somewhat darkly.

"Me, too. But in the meantime . . ."

"Nothing wrong with enjoying our work," Kyle finished for him.

"Bingo."

Both men napped for a while. It wasn't restful. It seemed all the troops heading for Iraq were nervous—understandably so—and wanted to party as hard as was possible without booze. They were loud and boisterous. The crew seemed used to it, and neither sniper was going to complain about fellow soldiers de-stressing, but it did leave them a bit wired by the time they landed at Rhein-Main, Germany. There was a three-hour layover, just long enough for the troops to find an open German bar in the airport and get soused.

On second thought, Kyle wasn't sure bars in Germany ever closed.

The leg to Italy was much quieter once they replaned, but the lavatories were somewhat worse for wear, with one hundred troops times six to eight beers. Still, there were worse things, Kyle thought. Getting shot at. Getting shot. Getting friends shot.

He fell asleep over Poland, and still didn't get any rest.

From Aviano, Italy, they took a plane to Rome, then boarded one for Bucharest. The constant changing of planes did mean a chance to stretch and unkink. But it also meant no sleep. They switched to civilian passports in Rome, and took a few minutes to wash and clean up. The sodas aboard had been useful as time wasters, and slightly refreshing, but Kyle wanted a bottle of water. He needed replenishment, and his military training insisted on water, not sugary snacks. Wade downed another ginger ale, and Kyle wondered how he did it. They'd both had four sodas before reaching Aviano, and that was Kyle's limit for the day and then some.

It was 8 P.M. local before they arrived in Bucharest, and they'd been awake more than twenty-four hours with all the movement. A few minutes of naps here and there hadn't done much for their metabolisms.

Otopeni airport was as modern as they'd been told, at least at first glance. It was also small. It wasn't what Kyle thought of as a hub. He'd seen regional airports Stateside that were bigger. Yet this was the main international center for the entire nation. The fixtures were older desks in metal; there were guards with submachine guns and, then there was the drab, rundown effect that followed the former Eastern Bloc like a bad smell and took years to fade.

Going through customs was straightforward; they showed passports and visas, and declared their cameras and gear. The agent they dealt with was a woman who might be attractive except for a severe uniform of white shirt and blue pants, hair tightly pulled back and square-rimmed glasses that made her face look humorless. She spoke good if accented English.

"What is the purpose of your visit?"

"We're doing a historical background segment for a documentary. Poenari, Bran, and then across into Turkey."

"Ah, the history of the Walachia?"

"Yes, at least this segment is."

"You'll be seeing at Tirgovişte?"

"I don't think so. All we have is a list of places, and our specialty is getting good photos. The actual analysis is left to the experts on Dracula." He grinned.

"Ah, I see. Well, if you have time, do enjoy yourselves also," she said as she stamped their passports.

"We'll try to," Wade said. "Lots of travel, not much free time."

"Yes. Let me see in your camera bags, please?"

They opened the bags, which contained only a small betacam, a professional digital video recorder, two digital still cameras and a digital audio recorder.

She gave them only a cursory glance. "Very good, gentlemen. Enjoy your visit."

"Thank you."

They headed for the restroom, which was modern but in need of cleaning, and took turns in a stall. A quick drain was called for, but the main reason was to dig deep into their personal checked luggage and get out necessary accessories—folding knives, flashlights, and Kyle's SOG Powerplier pocket tool. These were the very useful items one carried everywhere, in Kyle's opinion, but couldn't carry aboard planes anymore. They went in one at a time, Wade slipping in after Kyle was done. Kyle watched the bags while Wade gathered his Kershaw Boa knife and Gerber tool. They'd rather have firearms, but that was not yet an option. But with the basics in pocket and on belt, they were ready to face the world again.

Outside the doors, they sought a Romanian *taxia*.

"There's supposed to be one meeting us here," Kyle said, looking along the ranks of dull vehicles. They ranged from slightly worn to decrepit, as did their drivers. One nearby car started toward them. " 'Otel?" he called firmly.

"Yes, hotel. Which one?" He wanted to make this man identify himself.

"Marriohtt," was the reply.

"Yup, that's it," he nodded to Wade. He motioned with his head and they started walking.

It was a worn but serviceable old Fiat, technically a four-seater but tiny by American standards. The driver tossed their bags casually into the trunk and they piled into the back, knees against seatback and heads brushing the liner. They clutched at the doorhandles—there were no seatbelts—as he took off and wove into traffic. There was no radio—the hole in the dash where it would go held a hastily mounted two-way for operations instead.

"You have cameras? Sightseeing?" the driver asked. He was about thirty, dark and swarthy with hollow cheeks, and not heavily built.

"Cameras, news," Wade said.

"Ah, very good," the driver grinned, nodding much. Perhaps he hoped for a quick image to make him famous. "Very good," he said.

He zipped through traffic quickly and agilely, shaking fists and shouting an occasional colorful curse at other drivers. The radio chattered, and he picked up a microphone and chattered back. He turned right and took them onto a long, straight street. They were quite some way from downtown, and it seemed there might be time for a nap.

Kyle leaned back and closed his eyes, trying to ignore the buzzing, rattling exhaust and occasional swerves. The radio chattered again and the driver replied.

It took a moment, but then Kyle opened his eyes. He tried not to move too fast, and eased forward again.

"Wade, I think I overhear something bad," he said.

"Yes?" Wade prompted, conversational and smiling.

"This stuff is almost like the other speech I speak, and I hear something about 'setup' and 'bring the cars' and 'they've got cameras, could be something . . . er . . . worthwhile.'"

Wade laughed as cover. "Oh, that's good. Got another one?"

"Yeah," Kyle said, grinning back. "An interception. They fumble, we recover. Pity it can't be at the forty-five yard line. Or the nine in your case," he said, hoping it would be cryptic for the driver. He might know some English, after all, and while it was technically a West Germanic language, there were enough words borrowed from Latin that the driver might recognize one word in five. Kyle chose his vocabulary carefully to avoid *language, valuable,* and any other word that would have a Romance language analog. *Never thought I'd want to thank Mrs. Howarth for those weeks of etymology in eighth grade*, he said to himself.

"Sure," Wade agreed. "That was a great game. Who's the referee?"

"I am. Unless you see the ball first."

"Got it," Wade said, nodding and grinning a

broad mouthful of teeth. Kyle grinned also, though he didn't feel cheerful. Fights were never fun, and if it were to be a knife fight, he'd prefer his Ed Brown, which was tucked safely away, he hoped, in the embassy, awaiting their arrival.

But starting a firefight on the streets of Bucharest would be bad anyway. Ideally, they'd talk their way out of trouble, or intimidate or punch. Gunfire would not be discreet. And it wasn't an option, yet.

They were definitely not getting closer to downtown, and the traffic was getting lighter. "I think we were told about this in passing," Wade said.

"Seems to be. Oh, well."

Shortly, another car pulled in front of them. Then they turned onto a smaller, darker side street. It was rough and gravelly in spots. *Here comes the pitch*, Kyle thought. He kept a bored look on his face.

Then two more cars pulled in behind. Still he stayed reticent, and so did Wade, even though alarm bells were jangling in his mind.

The three cars were pulling in close. Kyle nodded, but played along so as not to lose the advantage of surprise the enemy thought they had. "What's happening, driver?" he asked. "They're too close!"

The driver said something noncommittal with a shrug attached, and slowed. It was a bit too rehearsed for Kyle's taste; they'd obviously done this before.

But not to two Army Rangers ready for it, you sons of bitches, he thought with a grin he kept concealed. It was time for a lesson in manners.

He and Wade locked eyes for just a moment and nodded readiness. They turned back to their individual sectors of fire, Kyle to the left, Wade to the right.

Then all the cars stopped and men were piling out. They were quiet, which wasn't a good sign. Quiet meant professional. Professional thugs rather than soldiers, granted, but not amateurs. They moved quickly, they and their shadows darting around the car, clothes and hands brushing against the glass and metal, making whispering sounds that would add to the fear a victim would feel.

Kyle and Wade weren't victims.

A hand clutched at the door next to him, and Kyle followed it back with his eyes. The man attached to it was skeletal, swarthy and had a broad moustache and long hair around deep eyes. His garb was drab, a jacket and pants with a dark shirt underneath. He held what looked like a tire iron in his other hand.

As the door started to open, Kyle kicked it as hard as he could with his left foot, then stuck both legs down to the ground as he twisted and braced the door with his shoulder. He didn't crave having it slammed against his shins. His antagonist staggered back as the door hinges crunched from being pushed beyond their limits. It was a light door, and he'd kicked hard. Next to him, he heard Wade grunt with exertion as he did something. There was no time to look, and Wade didn't sound too bothered, so Kyle kept his attention forward where it belonged. One can't do the other guy's job in combat. One has to assume the other guy will do his job properly, even if he's an idiot.

But Wade was no idiot, and Kyle was perfectly comfortable with him flanking, or backing up, or even leading. They'd meshed quickly as a team during the first mission, and that was carrying over.

Kyle was out the door and standing tall. Crouching would give him better cover, but he was several inches taller than these punks, and meant to use that imposing height as a psychological weapon. See the big American who doesn't back off? See the big American as he clutches your friend's tire iron and pulls him in close? See him punch your friend in the face?

It was a close, dirty brawl, and rules hadn't even been considered. That was fine with Kyle. He could play dirtier than these jerks. His hand hurt like hell, but his attacker, now his victim, went down with his face pulped and gushing dark blood from nostrils and lips. And Kyle had the tire iron.

He was in front of the door, and a younger man, teen really, from the rearguard car was closing from behind. So he kicked the door again, backward, to smack this new threat in the hip. The kid gasped, his eyes popping large above his scraggly beard as he stumbled.

He could hear sounds from the other side that indicated Wade was holding his own, and grinned. In a way, this was fun, a training exercise or warmup for a real fight. But another man was starting to swing the pipe in his hand, and Kyle found himself unable to move. The driver had leaned out the window and clutched him around the waist.

Snarling and trying to do two things at once, Kyle reached in two directions. He tried vainly to get hold of the driver's fingers and break one, but the man had clutched his hands together. No luck. And that club was raised and close. Ideally, Kyle should just shoot him with 230 grains of persuasion, but that was not an option. He realized he should have had his knife out and ready and gone to town earlier. Rules? What were rules? Except Kyle had been thinking traditionally. He needed to think like a coward and be vicious at once.

It was time for another kick. He raised his right leg and threw his weight behind it. It went straight, the incoming thug ran into it gut first, dropped his pipe, dropped to the ground, and spewed vomit onto the road. Kyle dropped a booted heel on the back of his head, then kicked sideways into his exposed face. That last one wasn't very effective, but it should leave scrapes and dings.

Meanwhile, he pulled at his left pocket until he got his Benchmade automatic clear, clicked it open and ran the razor sharp tanto blade along the driver's left arm, from knuckle to mid forearm. He used the sharp corner where the point met the blade edge, and it cut easily.

The driver howled and let go, flinging the black drops that beaded along the wound off to Kyle's left, the front of the car. That left one more man standing, considering his move.

Which was when Kyle threw the tire iron at him. It smacked into his head with a dull, ringing *thunk*, and down the guy went. A step to the side cleared Kyle from the driver's reach. The youth he'd caught with the door was trying to get into position for a rush, and Kyle rushed him instead.

Then the driver cursed and started to drive off.

Most of the thugs were scrambling backward, stumbling to their feet and beating a hasty retreat. Three other cars squealed away, but Kyle was only concerned about the one that held their luggage and very expensive cameras, which Wiesinger would try to make him pay for, no doubt. Also, that he and Wade would be in the ass end of Bucharest with nothing but cell phones and a long wait for backup, "long" being defined as "enough time to get killed."

He turned to see if Wade was okay, then ran to help when he saw what was happening.

Wade's legs stuck out from the passenger side of the taxi. He was obviously entangled with the driver and the steering wheel. The vehicle was rubbing against the broken curb. Then it was on the curb. Then it bumped a building front, scraping metal and bouncing to a stop.

Kyle vaulted onto the trunk, then the roof, feeling the metal give under him. He reached carefully into the open window with a sharp knife and said, in Spanish, *"Llévenos reservado al hotel o le mataré. Muerte. Comprende?" Take us quietly to the hotel or I will kill you. Dead. Do you understand?* He added the basic verb because he wasn't sure *mataré* would translate. But *muerte* should be universal.

There was no argument as the driver replied, *"Da, domnule!"* in a squeak.

"I'm remembering that as 'Yes, sir,'" Kyle said. "'Da' like Russian and dominant something. If not, we'll deal with him. Let's go."

In moments, they were back inside, Kyle behind the driver with the point of his knife against his neck. Wade let his show in the mirror.

Wade looked like hell. His face had taken a beating, and still had a crease where it had been pressed against the steering wheel. He had some blood on him, but a quick check didn't show a wound. It was the driver's. Kyle had bruised knuckles and a sore shin, but was otherwise okay. He didn't remember banging his shin. The driver's arm wasn't critical, just superficial and running blood. *"Véndelo y conduzca." Bandage it and drive.* The driver nodded agreement, grabbed a rag from the front passenger footwell, and stuffed it up his shirtsleeve. He gingerly took the wheel and started off again, carefully and as directed.

"Want to call our friend now?" Wade asked.

"No, let's get to the hotel first. I don't think our boy here is going to cause any more trouble." This was, after all, a military problem. Unless it became political, Kyle wanted them to handle it firsthand. Calling for help over minor issues would give the impression they couldn't handle the job. As long as they were in control, they'd stick to the existing plan.

"Fair enough," Wade agreed. "Are we giving him a tip?" He indicated the driver.

"Yeah. Don't fuck with the Rangers. That's a good tip for anyone."

The streets were getting better lit and better traveled. There were some gorgeous buildings, reminiscent of old Colonial architecture in America, and Turkish, and old Soviet. Bucharest was big, over two million people, and was old enough that the streets were a confusing maze. But the driver made no further attempts at subterfuge. He'd been totally cowed.

Thirty minutes later, they pulled up in front of the Marriott. It was new, white, stylish, and a very welcome sight. Kyle let out a breath he hadn't realized he'd been holding. Things could have gotten bad again.

The driver was sullen as they took their bags

from the trunk and piled them on the curb. A bellman in Marriott uniform came to meet them. "Checking in, gentlemen?" he asked in English.

"Yes, reservation, Monroe," Kyle said.

"Yes, sir," he agreed. "You came in this?" he indicated the *taxia* with a concerned and curious wave. Then he stared at Wade's abused face.

"Eventually," Kyle said. He slammed the trunk and said to the driver, "*Tenga buena noche*, OK?" *You have a nice evening, okay?*

The driver muttered something under his breath and spun tires as he left.

The bellman looked quizzically at them, but led the way inside.

Twenty minutes later, they were upstairs and unloaded, sprawled on the beds and taking turns in the shower.

TV had nothing of real interest; it was all in rapid-fire Romanian that Kyle almost understood. He settled for a mindless game on the laptop until Wade came out, then went in to let hot water beat him senseless and ease some of the bruises from the fight. His hand hurt like hell and was going to be stiff for days. And it was his trigger hand, too. He'd have to be careful.

Within the hour, they were each crashed out asleep atop a bed. Neither one bothered with covers.

5

AFTER EIGHT HOURS, KYLE SIMPLY WOKE UP. His body just couldn't see sleeping longer than that, after years of training. They hadn't closed the curtains the night before, and it was sunny out. That took a moment to adapt to. He ran through a mental checklist and got started.

First, he fumbled for his cell phone and called the number provided.

"Cafferty," was the answer.

"Monroe. We're at the hotel."

"Fine, you need to get a *taxia* and come to the location where we can talk. I'll email you directions and address. Two hours, if that works?"

"Sure," he replied.

"Right. Bye."

"Bye," he said to a dead connection. It had been a really terse conversation.

"Come on, Wade, time to wake up."

"Yeah, I'm awake," Wade said, and dug fin-

gers into his eyes, screwing up his face against
the coming day.

They dressed and cleaned up, wearing slacks
and shirts as a good compromise between business and tourist.

"I never realized how important wardrobe is,"
Kyle said. He had a full suitcase of clothes in different styles for this.

"Clothes make the man. Or make him something else," Wade said. "I could handle being a
beach bum. Surfboard, chicks, piña coladas . . ."

"Doesn't take much clothing for that. It takes
attitude."

"Damn."

"Let's get breakfast. Maybe our next mission
will be somewhere with sunny beaches."

"More likely sons of bitches," Wade com-
plained.

The nice thing about an expense account was
that international chain hotel food was adequate.
If you weren't paying for it, it was far easier and
less adventurous than going out on the street.
They had bacon, eggs, and some pastries,
washed it down with Turkish orange juice, and
were ready to tackle the day.

"We should be in the lobby waiting," Kyle said.

"Okay, let's go get the stuff," Wade said. In
ten minutes they were heading back downstairs.
He wasn't a bad photographer, so he carried a
camera. Kyle was halting with the audio, but
could do well enough to fake it.

* * *

A *taxia* pulled up outside and waited. The snipers rose from their seats and walked out casually, making sure not to hurry or look around. Kyle still felt as if they were obvious. He knew it was just nerves, and he'd dealt with them before, so he stuck it out, waiting for the feeling to pass.

The driver looked at a paper he carried and said, "Mon-ro?"

"Da," Kyle agreed. "Monroe."

They loaded luggage and climbed in. This vehicle, a VW van, had rates painted on the sides, a meter, and radio. The driver set the meter and off they went.

A fifteen-minute drive took them out of downtown, past a business district of older shops, into a residential area with small businesses to a *panzione*—a house with rented rooms. The driver pulled up in front and stopped, then helped them with their bags. He smiled and tipped his hat, accepted money from Kyle, then jumped in and sped off.

An elderly lady waited at the door. She was dark haired, slightly rounded, and short.

"Is this the place?" Kyle asked.

"Address matches, and she looks as if she expects us."

"Okay," Kyle sighed. At least she didn't look equipped to be a mugger.

At the door, she waved them into a cozy parlor and closed the door behind them. Two men were sitting waiting, both Westerners. Kyle and Wade both stiffened just slightly, in anticipation rather than because of a threat.

The closer man stood and approached. "Kyle and Wade? I'm Mick," he said.

Mick Cafferty was medium height, about fifty, slightly balding and barrel chested under his nondescript suit. Age was obviously catching up to him, but he wasn't giving in without a fight. They looked him over as he gave them a quick glance, then they shook hands all around. "And this is Sam," he said. Sam was barely shorter, pale and freckled and with reddish hair. He was dressed in common local clothes and his smile revealed slightly crooked teeth.

"Gentlemen." He nodded, then rose to shake hands. He sat back down again.

"You hear the news this morning?" Cafferty asked, giving them a deep gaze.

"No, what?" Kyle asked. Mission change?

"Bombs," Cafferty said. "Nine hundred pounds of TNT on a train in southern France, and four huge car bombs totaling another thousand in Bosnia. That's the stuff that's coming through here."

"Jesus," Kyle said. Wade was silent.

"Yeah, you got here just in time. Looks like close to twelve hundred dead or injured in a couple of hours. Statistically not that important, unless you're one of the statistics. But it's a tremendous issue politically and socially."

"I thought the French and Spanish were safe from attack, since they stayed out of the new round in Iraq?" Wade asked. The sarcasm was obvious.

"Yeah, that's what bin Laden is alleged to have said. Now we see what happens when you give a terrorist what he wants."

"More terror," Kyle said.

"Right. So we need something concrete fast—a kill, a bust of explosives, positive intel to avert something with lots of camera time. The good news is you've got more budget if you need it."

"Thanks," Kyle said. "Though I'm not sure what we need, besides a target and a place to shoot." Dammit, he wasn't a spy. He was a soldier. He watched the battlefield, broke things, and killed people. Tracking down political intel was for computer geeks or skulky sleuths.

"Well, let me know. I'm trying to get more of a free hand from State if I can," said Cafferty. "This working across agencies is a pain in the ass. Everyone has a form to stamp." He grabbed a mug of coffee, took a gulp, "I don't want to be seen too much, so you'll be talking to me by phone and dealing with Sam in the field when needed," he said as he put his cup down. "Let's show you around."

The house was owned and run by the CIA. It was small but modern enough, and they had a lockable room. The bathroom was shared, meals provided, and there was a phone line. "Dial-up modem only, to stay discreet. Make sure you use the local phone a few times to order *taxia* or food or whatever. Use the encrypted cells to talk to me."

"Understood," they both agreed. Kyle tapped the deep pocket where his phone was. It was a habit he had.

"You can stay here and at the hotel. Keep your special gear here," Cafferty said, which they understood to mean the weapons. He grabbed another mug of coffee from the kitchen as he led them through. The lady, the housekeeper, smiled at him and refilled the pot. He waved behind him as they walked back through the front, down the short hallway, and into the bedroom they'd use. "Only the government suspects this place that we know of, and they think it's strictly a waypoint for SEALs and such heading south and east. They shouldn't take much interest in you for a few days. Even after that, any investigation will take time."

"They'll make us eventually?" Wade asked, sitting on the bed. Kyle dropped down next to him. The mattress was a lot softer than he expected. Or maybe it hadn't been designed for two heavy soldiers to use as a chair.

"They make everyone eventually," Cafferty said. "As long as you get some shots or we have intel to share with the Romanians at the end, it'll be fine."

"That assumes we get either. For that we need you to get us in place," Kyle said, barely frowning. "We're just shooters. The spy bit is not something we know."

"No problem. We'll have you something soon.

We're just waiting for one of our observers to find one of them again. It's never longer than a week, and it's been three days since the last sighting."

"Good, then."

"So how was your trip in?" he asked.

"Ah . . . exciting," Kyle said.

"Exciting, how so?"

Kyle and Wade looked at each other, then gave him a complete brief with observations and the plate number. "It didn't seem targeted at us specifically," Kyle said to Cafferty's wrinkled brow. "Are we wrong?"

"No, it was random," he reassured them. "They were fishing. Hotel is what tourists expect, and the Marriott is a common choice. But that's a bad sign, and I'll hint about it after you leave. The driver lucked out. Or didn't, this time."

"You seem to mean it's common. I'm surprised," Kyle said.

"Common enough. All part of the background here. You need to call the *taxia* service and ask for 'command,' which puts them on government notice and makes them honest. You got the low end. The middle end speak English until you're inside, then they don't speak it until you're twenty miles away. Twenty-five euros or a million lei and two hours later, you're where you wanted to be in the first place."

"Charming." Still, Kyle thought, it was better than Central Asia, where they shot at you or sold you out to another tribe or used you to settle local scores under the guise of fighting a war.

"It's been like this since the Wall came down?" Wade asked.

"Pretty much. Gypsies," Cafferty said. "Lots of them homeless and without family, from Ceauşescu's reign."

"How?" Wade asked.

"You read about all the orphans left from his forced breeding program?" The two snipers nodded. "Well, they grew up. Almost none have social skills, most aren't very bright—they never got any input as infants. Some can't talk. Most are illiterate. Almost all are unemployable. They sleep in the sewers, steal and rob to eat, and snort paint to pass out so they don't feel the cold and hunger. A worse nightmare than any stupid Dracula movie."

"Damn," Kyle said. "What can we do for them?"

"Nothing," Cafferty said, grimacing and sipping at his coffee. "There's not enough millions anywhere to deal with it. Some were adopted, the rest are abandoned, and there's still another few years' worth in orphanages who are kicked out as they turn eighteen."

"Shit."

"Yeah, and something we can't help with. Close your eyes, grit your teeth, do your job, and pray for them. That's all there is."

"Roger that," the snipers agreed together. It was the standard response to a situation one had to deal with, no matter how disgusting it was.

"As for you gentlemen, the *taxia* isn't the only thing to watch out for."

"Crime's bad?" Wade asked.

"Yes and no. Lots of scams you need to watch out for. Don't trust the hotel housekeepers—use a safe or keep your stuff with you. If you leave before cleaning time, leave the Do Not Disturb sign. Locked cases are probably safe, but any cash left out or in clothes or open luggage might wind up as a tip. Assume all teenagers and large kids are pickpockets, and keep cash split among pockets, ID up front and high. Don't eat anything unless prices and an actual menu of food are posted. Same for services—always assume they're screwing you and offer them one quarter what they ask. Settle for one half. Don't drink. The drinks are watered, overpriced, bad liquor that can give you a hell of a hangover, and they'll bring them until you say to stop. As soon as it hits the table, bang! you're charged for it.

"Watch out for fake cops. Real cops wear suits and carry badges. So do frauds. They'll whip out a badge, demand to inspect your currency to ensure you complied with the exchange law, then peel off a couple of big bills for themselves. So will the real cops sometimes."

"Goddam," Kyle muttered.

"Oh, it's worse than that," Cafferty said. "Drunk driving can be settled on the spot for a million lei. That's twenty-five bucks. If you've had a drink, you're drunk. Either pay up or go to jail. You don't want to go to jail."

"How bad are the jails?" Wade asked.

"You'll need SERE training to survive them,"

Cafferty said, not smiling. Survival Evasion Resistance Escape was not a fun course. It involved bugs, snakes, and being tortured by the "enemy."

"What?" Kyle burst out, surprised.

"We take MREs to the poor American bastards who get nailed over here, so they'll at least survive the ordeal. And God help a woman in jail. Not as bad as Turkey. But not good." He scowled deeply. "We've got one now State is trying to beg out. Her family is trying to come up with a bribe. I rather hope it's not taken, because she'll need that money for therapy afterwards."

"Fuck me," Kyle said.

"As bad as that," Cafferty confirmed. "Most people here *are* honest. But assume otherwise, because there isn't 'always one in every crowd' here. There's always a dozen. And you better be *very* discreet with your firearms."

"That's the plan," Wade said. "We shoot when and only when we have a target. Otherwise, cased."

"Good," Cafferty nodded. "The police will bust you in a second, and even diplomatic means here might not get you out. Might take DoD and State to do it."

Or a platoon of Rangers, blown off-course in a parachute drop, Kyle thought. But that would *really* create an incident. Even with Robash's assurance, Kyle's blood was running cold. The worst he'd faced in life was being shot and killed. He was starting to realize there were worse things, and that even with his combat experience, he was very naïve and vulnerable to cultural issues.

Coming back to the core of the mission, Kyle asked, "So you don't think they're going to be hard to find?"

"Actually, no. We have good intel. The problem is the local government leaks. We can fix them to a couple of regular places, but once away from the coast and the capital, no dice. We need to get on them and stay on them. That's why you're here."

"How do you mean?"

"Anything my people do is known. We need people who can shoot, aren't known, and don't drag a lot of paperwork with them. That's you. We don't want the Romanians knowing, we don't want them wondering why I'm breaking my routine tasks, and we don't want to try getting too close. Shootings happen. Up-close brawls with foreign officials don't."

"I'd hoped to have all this before we arrived," Kyle hinted.

"So did we," Cafferty nodded. "But as I said, we're still building the database. That's the key here—we're trying to get them before they do anything."

"Are you sure these are the right guys, then?" Wade asked. "I'd hate to wait for a bomb to go off, but we do want to nail the right people."

"Oh, it's them," Cafferty nodded. "They were involved in Chechnya, and some attacks in Georgia. That was more the Russians' problem, and they gave us some intel that is solidly corroborated. But it got too hot there, so they moved to the Middle East. With the current screwup there, they're moving this way. Have moved this way now. Gutless freaks won't ever stand and fight."

"That sounds like the right people, then," Wade said.

"Yeah, fits the pattern, doesn't it? Anyway, here's the dossiers so far," Cafferty said as he handed over five folders. Wade opened them, Kyle read over his shoulder, and Cafferty narrated.

"They'll have probably twelve to twenty lower people with them, to do hauling, security, and buying supplies so they aren't seen. If you get a chance to bag them, they're gravy, but don't hit a pawn and miss the bishops and kings. Underlings are only a symptom."

"Right," Kyle agreed. Though killing enough underlings would still cramp operations, there were enough suicidal idiots that it was only a temporary fix.

"So, from the bottom is Vahtang Logadze. He's Georgian. Not directly al Qaeda but a fellow traveler. He blends in locally, and we suspect he's their expert on shipping, which local officials to bribe, et cetera.

"Enis Altan is Turkish. He's facing death if he goes back there. He was 'helping' the Kurds, but somehow they kept getting ambushed. We figure he was helping Iraqi intelligence. On the other hand, the Kurds aren't popular in Turkey. He may have been working for a private group. But both the Kurdish movement and the Turkish government want him dead. If you kill him, we get some good bargaining points.

"Number Three, Anton Florescu is Romanian. He's helping get the stuff out of here into the rest of Europe, likely through the woods and north into Hungary or Slovakia. He's also seen a lot in the Carpathian Mountains and near Sighişoara. We're looking for a base there, but haven't pinned it down yet. But it's there, we're sure. So he's only a target of opportunity, and hold off if you think he might lead us to more. Like whoever orchestrated Bosnia and France." The snipers looked up from the binders and nodded.

"Number Two. Behrouz Jalali is Iranian, and a very bad boy. He's definitely part of al Qaeda, orchestrated several attacks on British troops in Nasiriya, and has now moved up here, figuring he just might get a lungful of cannon fire from a chopper there, but can kill babies at random in Europe, where no one is armed. He's come in twice, but we don't know where he is now. Shipped back out, gone to ground, hiding in Europe, who knows? Keep an eye out, and we'll snatch him if there's a chance. If not, just kill him on sight. There's nothing we want from him bad enough to risk letting him get away.

"And that just leaves our prime target, who you've heard of if you're following the news."

"Dammar al Asfan," Kyle said.

"Synagogues, Shia mosques, buses . . ." Wade recited.

"And a standing reward of fifty thousand dollars to the family of anyone who kills Americans or Israelis," Cafferty said. "Again, we'd like him alive, but if there's any doubt at all, shoot him. Shoot him twice. Run over him. Drag him down a gravel road. Stake him through the heart. Whatever it takes. You can even walk up to him in front of the police station in Bucharest and shoot him dead on the steps and we'll cover for you. The headlines alone would get you out. But discreet is better."

"Roger that," they replied.

"We don't expect you'll get all five," Cafferty said, answering the question before they asked it. "Just get one. If you find one, there might be another nearby. Get him, too, and then as many minions as you can."

"Terrorist Poker," Wade joked.

"Pair, three of a kind, four of a kind, full house?" Kyle smiled back. He turned to Cafferty and said, "We'll see what we can do. We'd rather find them in the woods, or some quiet little burg where we can disappear in a hurry. An urban kill that's not in a dedicated war zone . . . you really need a police sniper for that."

"I know," Cafferty said with a twist of his lips. "But we don't have one. So it's up to you to make the call. Don't create an incident if you don't think it's worth it. Except for al Asfan."

"What about military support?" Kyle asked. "Near the sea we've got Air Force and Navy, you say, and a possible exercise to cover for us. What about inland? Is there someone with a chopper or a truck who can come get us?"

"Truck. Sam. Me, if it comes down to it," was the reply. "Anything more than that is going to get us seen. And we can't trust the government at any level—city, county, or national. Too many leaks, too many moneygrubbers. They're worse than dedicated idealists, because they don't stay bought."

"Right," Kyle nodded. Behind him, Wade started singing, "It sucks to be meeeeee." Kyle ignored him. Wade sometimes went too far when he was stressed. He understood it, he just wasn't going to feed it.

"There's no way to get the Romanians involved?" He really preferred the idea of local backup.

"To do what? Unless one of them commits a provable crime here, any kind of local activity only serves as a warning to the bad guys that we know they're up to something. And to be honest, the Romanians wouldn't be able to round them all up. The local police are used to petty crooks and thugs, not international rings with cutouts and multiple IDs. Their military arm might manage it, and I'm still trying to get a hint through to the right people, but it has to be the right people or all I have is more leaks."

"I just wanted to check."

"Yeah, your ass is in the sling. I understand," Cafferty shrugged. He took another drink of coffee. He'd gone through three cups already. He wouldn't have a stomach left at this rate.

"Do you have our luggage?" Kyle asked.

"Oh, yes," Cafferty nodded vigorously and smiled. "It was still sealed. And nobody said I shouldn't look, so I hope you don't mind that I peeked but didn't touch. You gentlemen have unique tastes."

"Just what we need to get the job done," Kyle said.

"Wait here, I'll get the bags," Cafferty said and turned.

Before he left, the two snipers were conferring.

"Definitely the twenty-two in urban settings," Wade said.

"Yes, and pistols. If we get close, we might set one with a rifle to cover, and one with a pistol as bait or beater, and do it that way."

"We might," Wade agreed with what was almost a frown. "Though that's not something we've trained in. I don't worry about one of us shooting the other. I do worry about getting in the way and spoiling a shot, or taking a piece of it, or being ID'd."

"True," Kyle nodded. "We were hired to do it from a distance."

Cafferty came back with Sam, dropped three cases on the bed, then went for another load of bags. "All sealed when it arrived," he said. "It was transported in a lead-lined box, which we do all the time. No one has questioned us, and things are usually undisturbed. So we're co-pasetic unless you get seen."

"The weapons are safe here?" Kyle asked to confirm. Wade reached for the AK104 and started checking it over.

"Yes. The lady, Mrs. Cneajna"—whose name Kyle knew he'd never be able to pronounce—"works for us. This door locks. No one else comes in here. If the weapons are seized, there's nothing to tie them directly to you. Which doesn't mean someone won't try to rope you in."

"Right."

"It's up to you if you keep them with you at the hotel, keep them here and have to drive over and get them, or carry them on your persons. Try to avoid the latter, but I don't want to tell you how to do your jobs."

"Thanks," Kyle said. He wasn't sure if *he* knew how to do this job. "Are we going to have a car at our disposal? We can't carry these things on the subway or buses."

"Right. Get a rental car tomorrow. Go for something a couple of years old, not flashy, and that can take a bit of abuse. An Audi four wheel drive, maybe. SUVs are too obvious, and most of them are useless in this terrain." Most SUVs were built for looks only, as everyone who drove real military vehicles had figured out years ago.

"That means we'll have to actually use it a bit."

"Yes. I can recommend some restaurants that are worthwhile, there's the museum, and anything locked in the trunk should generally be safe. We've got to get you up into the mountains soon, though, because that's your cover, and that's where we expect some of the action. Small villages. You can shoot there?"

"We can shoot anywhere," Kyle said. "Open terrain is easier, woods make for better concealment, and in any urban setting witnesses and hard cover are problems. But with that," he pointed at the Ruger, "the AK and pistols, we can nail targets from five meters to four hundred."

"Good," Cafferty said. He sounded confident and reassured. "I'll get you the targets and try to get you in range, and run interference over anyone who might see you. Meantime, you can go. There's nothing to do but wait."

"Great," Kyle said. He hated hurry-up-and-wait.

"It shouldn't be so bad," Cafferty smiled. "You can be real tourists on tax dollars for a couple of days. You'll earn it."

In theory, they could play tourist. They had cell phones and could be reached anywhere. But they needed the weapons close at hand, didn't want to confuse a pursuit by having to get unlost from where they were before getting lost following anyone, and they were antsy about more of the local color. It hadn't taken much to convince the two snipers to stay at the hotel, no matter how boring.

The kicker had been lunch. They'd called the same *taxia* they'd used earlier. The driver was an elderly man who gave them a quick tour on the way to the car rental, which was a familiar Western chain.

In short order, they had a recent Audi Quattro in a tan color that was nondescript and, once dusty over its shine, would be invisible in almost any terrain. It hadn't taken much asking for the tan. Apparently, most customers wanted a brighter color.

The car was right-hand drive, and driving was on the left, so it was a mirror image of what they were used to. But the pedal layout was the same as they were used to. "You want to drive?" Kyle asked.

"Sure, I'll give it a whack. It's not far, anyway."

They were only about five miles from the hotel and they could see its silhouette from several blocks away. Just down the street from the Marriott was a Mexican restaurant. It was a little hole in the wall, looked clean, and had a bright awning in green.

"Worth a try?" Wade asked. It wasn't one Cafferty had mentioned.

"Why not?"

The restaurant had prices posted, they nodded agreement that it was honest and took seats outside, it being a modestly warm noontime. The

menu was clear enough, and they ordered que-
sadillas and tacos. Ten minutes later, plates were
set in front of them. Wade nodded and said,
"Mulţumesc," and dug in.

His face told all. "Paprika?" he said, confused
and shocked. "And something like sage? In *Mexican* food?"

Kyle agreed with his assessment. The stuff was
greasy, overcooked, weirdly seasoned, and of
low-quality ingredients to start with. They
forced it down and headed back for the hotel.

"Christ, that's worse than stringy goat and
beans in Pakistan," Wade muttered on the way.

"Disgusting," Kyle agreed. "Let's stick to
American staples or real local food, not their attempts to internationalize."

"Yeah. We got anything in the room to get the
taste out with?"

"*I* have cookies and chips," Kyle said. "I can
share, this once."

"You're my hero."

After expensive sodas from the hotel and some
cookies, they felt better. "Damn, it burns me to
pay that much for a drink," Kyle said.

"Uncle Sam is paying for it," Wade reminded
him.

"Damn, it burns me to help people screw over
my dishonest uncle, who nevertheless gives me a
job and a roof and a chance to risk my ass over
stupid things."

"Yeah, well. When in Romania . . ."

They tried to watch TV, took turns surfing the

Web for games, news, trivia, maps, and anything of interest. It was a long, slow day, and they left early for dinner at the nearest restaurant Cafferty had recommended. It was walking distance.

"Local food, which hopefully they can manage to cook properly," Kyle said. He was still feeling a bit odd from lunch.

"You know, I see the international appeal of McDogfood's now."

"Yeah. You know exactly how bad it will be, and it's cheap."

They arrived at the restaurant and were shown in. They were seated shortly, in a smoky corner. Eastern European cigarettes, pipes, and cigars all clashed. There was a stale acridity to the green plastic curtains near them. The floor was linoleum and the tables were plastic and worn chrome. "Points for atmosphere," Kyle said.

"Hey, the food smells good," Wade replied.

It did. Aromas of real meat and potatoes, vegetables and fire combined to flush the queasiness from Kyle's stomach and make him hungry again.

The waitress was young, lacked curves and had the classic cheekbones and deep eyes of Slavic ancestry. Her English was very broken and accented, but the menu had some English and Kyle recalled his Spanish. She had a cute smile which she flashed when she understood him.

"*Salata de Creier*. Brains salad?" Wade read from the menu. He looked more than a bit bothered.

"No, thanks," Kyle replied. "Is that a vampire thing?"

"Veal brains," Wade said. "I'm not sure they've heard of Mad Cow. And it doesn't sound appetizing, anyway."

"Yeah, what else is there?"

"*Salata Primavara*. Lettuce, radishes, carrots, potatoes, green onions, sour cream."

"Okay. Anything weird in it?"

"A bit of sugar."

"I think I can deal with that," Kyle agreed. "And here's an entrée: *Biftec Rusesc*. That's Russian beefsteak. Sirloin with onions. That sounds good. Sprite or whatever to drink instead of alcohol, and *Prajitura cu Zmeura*, cake with raspberries."

"Just no brains."

"No. We should just not ask, let them serve us, and enjoy it." It was common advice for soldiers going to exotic locales.

"I'm not that brave anymore," Wade admitted.

The food started arriving at once, and they ate quickly, trying to enjoy the food for its cultural differences.

"Not bad," Kyle said. "Steak's a bit tough, but not bad."

"Needs more seasoning," Wade replied. "And the portions are a bit small."

"I think we're just pigs who eat too much."

"That could be it."

The crowd was building as evening grew later,

and it was boisterous and cheerful. Drinking and talking, talking and drinking. Entire families were out together. It seemed weird. There were what appeared to be couples on dates, dragging parents and younger siblings.

"They seem happy at the decline of communism," Kyle said.

"Yup. No matter how bad things are now, they were worse fifteen years ago."

"That's depressing." Kyle had known that intellectually, but to actually see it was shocking.

They polished off dessert, paid, and left a tip, which neither of them was sure was considered appropriate. But they wanted to be remembered as dumb but friendly tourists if anything. The waitress smiled gleefully and waved as they departed.

It was a cool spring evening. It had drizzled while they ate, but then cleared slightly. They tucked their collars up as they headed for the car.

Wade turned his head slightly and asked, "So what do we think?"

"I think it's riskier than last time politically," Kyle said slowly, "and safer as far as military threats go. For some reason, that doesn't reassure me." Kyle didn't like military threats, but he understood military threats. This was new territory. They reached the car and he waited while Wade unlocked it.

"Yeah. Watch it," Wade said in warning, nodding very slightly. "I'm sure Robash is on our side. I'm equally sure other people would just throw us to the wolves and claim it wasn't their problem."

"Yeah, that's what I'm thinking. And we keep volunteering. I ask myself why."

"Why did we volunteer to get our asses kicked, frozen, drowned, abraded, and burned in Ranger School?"

"Same reason," Kyle admitted. "Because we can, and others can't, and the job needs doing."

"Yup." Wade started the engine and screeched into traffic. He'd picked up the local style quickly. Or maybe that was just how he drove.

"I dunno. I think if I'm second-guessing myself it means I'm getting too old."

"Well, you can retire at thirty-eight."

"You know, that seems old now. But I know it won't then." Kyle mused.

Back at the hotel, they took turns playing computer games and reading intel. There was a great time waster that involved computer representations of little plastic toy soldiers, complete with breaking them in pieces and melting them in puddles from the effects of weapons. The only problem was, every stage had an "objective." That was too much like work. Kyle just wanted to kill things for a while, mindlessly. The usual backpack-of-weapons-and-hundreds-of-mindless-ghouls-to-kill game was less fun without a network of participants, and was too simplistic. After two hours, Kyle figured out he wasn't going to enjoy anything.

"Look, I've got to take a walk or I'm going to

go nuts. This is a Western hotel, it's like being down the street but with no TV. Once around the block should be safe. I can even hang out with the bellmen. But I need some more outdoor time."

"Let's both go," Wade said. "We'll keep it short." He grabbed a camera just to maintain appearances. Coats, knives only, though Kyle really wanted to carry his pistol, considering the trouble so far, and they took the elevator down. They were staying among crowds, and didn't want an incident, but Kyle still felt naked.

Downtown Bucharest was alive in a gritty, trashy way. There were surface trams and a subway, *taxia* vying for parking spaces and passengers, and lots of people. The people were dressed in every style from working-class pants and shirts with sturdy shoes to Euro-chic leather coats with Italian-made shoes and silk shirts. A few stood out even in that spectrum as unkempt bums.

"Like parts of Bosnia, only classier," Kyle said.

"They had less problems here. Which is still pretty frightening, when you think about it," Wade replied as they walked around the Central Market Square. "There's 'The Harp,'" he said. "Irish pub, owned by a real Irishman. Good place for food and intel, he said," referring to Cafferty.

"Right, we'll note it," Kyle agreed. "Food should be of at least British standards."

"Is that a good thing?" Wade asked.

"Compared to here? I . . . don't know. I'd say yes," Kyle said. He was joking, and tried very hard to keep a blasé expression.

"Smartass." Then they both chuckled and kept walking.

As they turned a corner, there were the signs of nightlife. Two or three late restaurants and a club or two lit the street. "I think we should avoid those," Kyle said.

"Yeah. If we get mugged in a taxi, I'd hate to see a bar brawl."

They let their eyes wander briefly. It didn't do to look like tourists, but they were obvious foreigners. They'd have to convey confidence, to hint that they weren't the kind to be messed with. If that failed, words or hands would have to get them out of trouble. Pistols were a last resort.

Kyle turned back around and almost bumped into a girl. She was almost as tall as his chin and was skinny. She also had worn jeans and an oversized shirt and lanky, unwashed hair. She was caressing his chest through his shirt and saying what could only be an offer of temporary romance for a few euros.

He wondered how she'd react to a counter offer of a shower, dinner, and a place to sleep? Or maybe that was part of the deal. He wasn't familiar with that aspect of the local customs and didn't want to be. But he knew what she was offering at her end, and said, "Nu," forcefully enough to make it clear he wasn't negotiating, hopefully not strongly enough to scare her.

She simply gave him a look of disgust and turned on her heel. She pulled up short to Wade's hand on her wrist. He twisted it and Kyle's ID folder appeared.

Kyle said, "*Buen intento, pequeñita.*" *Nice try, little girl.*

He saw what looked like a cop, decided he didn't need any kind of scene, and let her go.

She spat on his jacket and ran.

"Charming girl," Wade murmured.

"Yeah. I've had enough fresh air. Let's go be bored."

"Suits me."

A few minutes later, they crashed gratefully onto boring, hotel-standard beds. "You know, boredom means no excitement. No excitement means no danger. No danger means no compromise of the mission before we get a chance to screw it up the Army way. I think I can live with that," Kyle said. He breathed hard and sighed.

"I think I agree. We must be getting old. Or wise."

"Let's say it's wisdom," Kyle suggested.

"Wisdom it is."

6

DAMMAR AL ASFAN WAS TENSE. HE KNEW
there was no reason for it. His cover was
solid and he never handled shipments himself.
Nevertheless, a ton of explosives was a sizeable
amount, and there was a risk of discovery. Not
everyone at the port was dishonest, not even
most. All it would take would be for his pet in-
spector to be sick. He should call ahead if that
happened, of course, but the type of men who
needed and took bribes were the type of men one
didn't want to depend on.

Still, there were several cutouts, and things
should go well enough. The nervousness was predictable and familiar, so he concentrated on the
task at hand and tried to avoid the worry.

He studied his list on the screen again. From
here, the TNT had to be split for various destina-
tions. There were the soldiers in Germany, fight-

ing the American pollution. There was the new target of France, now that those filth had prohibited the proper wear of scarves among faithful women. The Balkans always needed some against NATO's intervention against the efforts to secure Muslim territory there. Then there was a need to ship some to Egypt for the African missions, and a sizeable amount for their brave Palestinian brothers, fighting the Zionist entity.

If it were up to him, some would also be sent to America to fight the Satan on its own soil. But he'd been ordered not to. The Americans were like a nest of hornets, angry when disturbed. That was true. But like hornets, they were a menace that had to be done away with, and one didn't deal with hornets by being nice. One dealt with them with fire and accepted a few stings. All the better to slaughter Americans now and bring on the jihad they so obviously craved. Let them attack the faithful. Every day they lost more soldiers in Iraq. If every Muslim nation was thus attacked, the Americans would be too weak to defend any of the whole, and would have to accept peace on terms imposed by those Righteous in God.

But for now, those were not his orders. The Zionist pigs had to be punished, Europe had to be reminded that angry Muslims, denied their place under God's Will, were more important than the filthy money of American corporate and tourist whores.

After blood had washed the corruption from Europe, then the end war could begin. And al Asfan was patient and obedient, even as he looked forward to that day.

Kyle and Wade were still bored the next morning, and getting fidgety. After breakfast, they headed back to the room.

"You know, this whole vampire thing confuses me," Wade said.

"Oh? What specifically?" Kyle found it all confusing and amusing.

"A wooden stake kills vampires," Wade started.

"Yes."

"So what about other wooden items? I mean, wood-pulp paper can cause paper cuts . . . could you torture a vampire with a death of a thousand paper cuts?"

"Ah . . . I don't know," Kyle replied. Wade was really weird at times. Maybe it was the boredom.

"And then I got to thinking . . ." Wade said as Kyle muttered, "Uh-oh." "Diamonds and coal are fossilized trees. So if a woman smacks a vampire with her engagement ring . . ."

"I don't think myths are supposed to be logically followed through," Kyle said.

"Obviously. Those wooden bullets got me wondering . . . There's graphite lube we could use on our bullets. Would that work?"

"Can't hurt. Though we could use blanks and pencils."

"And then there's maple syrup."

"What?" Kyle asked.

"It's refined from tree sap."

"Ah." That was true. Was there a point? "Would it have to be injected? Or would just eating it be harmful? They don't have sugar maples here, so I doubt it ever came up."

"Right. We should try an experiment. On a U.S. Government grant, of course."

"Uh, Wade," Kyle interrupted. It had just hit him, and it was so totally ridiculous he couldn't avoid sharing.

"What?"

"*Latex* is also a tree sap."

For a moment there was silence, then both men roared with laughter.

"So assuming it's a *female* vampire . . ."

"Always wear your condoms. The life you save may be your own . . ."

"This is gonna hurt you a lot more than it hurts me . . ."

They laughed hysterically.

"Snipers shoot holes in myth. Film at eleven," Wade said.

The time they spent wasn't totally boring. They reviewed maps of downtown, the city as a whole, the region and of the nation and its routes elsewhere. Romania was poor, largely cluttered and chaotic, and had a large city and plenty of wilderness. Once in Romania, travel to the rest of Europe was easy and relatively paperwork free. It was ideal for what the terrorists wanted.

"If we're shooting in town, I recommend being inside somewhere," Wade said. "The field of fire is better from a rooftop, but there are helicopters. Sticky tar, rain, sun, and visibility are problems that seem to counteract any advantage we get."

"Yeah. If we can find old warehouses, of which there seem to be some. Or vacant apartments we can get access to," Kyle mused. "I'll call Cafferty."

Cafferty assured them there were buildings they could use. "I'll email you some addresses, you'll have to look them up on the local maps and place them. Got a printer?"

"No, but we have time to sketch. What about apartments?"

"Enough, vacant even, but that's another problem. You'll have to break in, and quietly enough no one comes looking. Then there's the homeless and orphans using some . . ."

"I get the picture," Kyle said. It sucked. They'd have to sneak everywhere. "We'll do what we can. But we're really better in the field."

"I'm trying to work on that," Cafferty agreed. "But you're likely to see Logadze within a few blocks of that area I marked, if you see him at all. Bye." The signal dropped.

Kyle clicked off and said to Wade, "Man, he hangs up in a hurry."

"Likely a CIA thing. Afraid of being traced from back when regular phones were used? Or maybe he's got some other missions going."

"That's possible. We may not be the stars of the show, just the stagehands."

After a moment, Wade said, "I want to get some video of the area. It helps our cover story, gets us familiar with things, and we can review it for good positions."

"In turns, or together?"

"That's a good question," Wade pondered. "What do you think?"

Kyle thought for a moment. "I'd say in turns right now. I'll stay here with the car, and can call you if I need to pick you up. You show me what you saw, and I'll go out later to confirm."

"Okay. Just hand me my trench coat and fedora . . ." It was only a half joke. Overcoats were common and practical when rain moved in. He grabbed the camera and gear and turned back to Kyle. "How do I look?"

"Like a geek with a camera," Kyle said.

"Perfect." He used the room phone to call and arrange for Cafferty's *taxia* to pick him up, drop him in the area in question and circle waiting for him. "Got my phone, I'll stick to main streets so I don't get mugged. I'll see you at dinnertime." He slipped out the door, camera on shoulder.

Kyle spent the afternoon downloading emailed maps and marking likely locations. It would be better to be together so they could cover and relieve each other, but that would depend on circumstances. They might need to split, with one observing and one shooting from different blinds.

To that end, they needed a radio code that anyone who happened on the same frequency wouldn't find suspicious. So he made a list of useful signals, then found easy and unsuspicious German words to use. He chose German because their accents would be less definable in it, as opposed to obviously American-accented Romanian spoken in short, innocuous phrases. Also, German was a bit less known here.

Kyle didn't realize how thoroughly he was engaged until a rattle at the door presaged Wade's return. He glanced at the clock to find four hours had passed. It had felt so good to be doing serious mission work.

"Whatcha get?" he asked.

"Lots of video, some still, and a wallet."

"A wallet?" Kyle asked, confused.

"A wallet. Some punk tried to lift mine and snatch the camera. That was his mistake. I didn't let go. Then I shoved him into the wall and demanded he turn everything over to me. That included someone else's wallet. So I asked the front desk to ensure it got returned, even though it's empty of cash. I figure the pictures, ID, and the wallet itself may have sentimental value."

"We are just magnets for scumbags," Kyle said, shaking his head. "Okay, you show me pictures, I'll show you the code I came up with."

"Okay."

Wade had useful shots down streets, showing the route he'd taken. Panned shots covered the crowds to give an idea of traffic and entrances to alleys and accesses. He'd also videotaped the fronts of several buildings to give an idea of their suitability, and taken images from corners nearby so as to help calculate fields of fire down to the street.

"Very nice," Kyle said. If anything, there was too much information here. "We'll cover this tomorrow when we're rested. It's amazing how tiring doing nothing is."

Wade snickered. "Sorry, you're right, it just sounds funny."

There were more emails waiting in the morning, from Cafferty and another user who referenced him. There were leads to several ships and two sightings. The note from Cafferty said, "Just to keep you updated. We'll get you something soon. Stand by."

"Soon" was not that day, however. They ate at The Harp and decided it was decent—meat pies and thick-cut fries. They forced themselves to watch local news so as to work on the language. It was easier to recognize patterns in context— weather, politics, and traffic. They both did a couple of hundred pushups in sets of fifty, just to keep fit and burn off calories. Kyle went out and found a couple of DVDs in US format at an only mildly extortionate price, which they could watch on the computer.

The movie version of *Starship Troopers* sucked, in his opinion. He'd read the book and found it gripping. This was just fluff, and the tactics were ludicrous.

"We didn't have coed showers when I was a recruit," Wade said. "I think we should petition."

"We have leaders who can recognize a threat when they see one. No matter how bad ours are, they're better than this."

"Yeah, but this is a movie."

They fell asleep around 1 A.M., after a hefty dissection of the film. It was the only action available. They'd enjoyed it far too much.

7

KYLE'S CELL PHONE RANG.
He twitched awake and grabbed it. "Monroe."

"We have Logadze," Cafferty said.

"Roger that. Where?" *Yes!*

"He's been seen in Constanta, and is heading here by car. We know where he usually hangs out. We'll want you to wait near there. I'll email to confirm, and here's the info I have . . ." He rattled off an address on the west side of town, named landmarks and suggested two buildings. "The first one is an old Communist-built office from the nineteen fifties, now vacant. It's abandoned and has plenty of windows. The second is an old apartment block, officially vacant and abandoned but likely full of two-legged homeless rats."

"We'll try your first suggestion, then." Kyle

looked across the room. "Wade has the map up. I think I see where."

They hurried downstairs separately, Kyle by the stairs, Wade by elevator. They were dressed in casual office-type clothes reinforced with trench coats and civilian work boots, all of which they considered expendable and expected to trash. Wade had the digital cameras, a spotting scope and NVGs plus his pistol. Kyle had the Ruger in its briefcase and his Ed Brown and Colt in the pockets of his trench coat. Both carried small rucksacks of food and water, changes of clothes, PDAs with all the info downloaded, and accessories like eyepatches and gloves.

The car was running and ready by the time Kyle got downstairs, and Wade pulled out immediately.

"People drive like idiots here, anyway," Wade said, "so there's no need to take our time."

"No, just don't wreck." People *did* drive like idiots here. Not as bad the DC Beltway or Chicago, but close. Nor were the Americans familiar with the social mores that went along with driving here.

Wade ignored him. Four minutes later he said, "There it is. Where do we park?"

"Dunno. Should I get out and you catch up? No, better not risk it. There must be a space along here." He indicated an angled line of cars.

They found a space. American civilians think in terms of parking within a block at most. They were used to walking, and thought in that regard more like Europeans. It was four blocks along before they found a space.

"We want the south side," Wade said as they got out, "so we're overlooking that square."

"Got it. Let's hope it's really vacant." The building was ugly, straight sided, and brick. The roof sagged in spots, and the gutters had pulled loose.

It was also barricaded, with heavy timbers over the doors and windows on the first floor. Some had steel bars. A few were bricked up. "Ain't that lovely?" Wade commented.

"We'll have to break in."

"Around back."

"Right."

A cobbled alley stinking of urine and trash led them past windows. Those, too, were boarded. They turned into a loading area inset into the back edifice, wide enough for two trucks and with loading docks. There were no openings not covered with wood, bars, or steel. "Damn," Kyle said.

"This one's a bit loose," Wade said. "And they're bolted in place. Why don't you shoot out a couple of those bolts?"

Kyle thought for a moment. The window started about five feet off the ground. "As long as I shoot obliquely in case of a ricochet, I don't see why not." It took only a few moments to slip his pistol and the suppressor inside his coat and assemble them. "Watch for brass," he ordered.

"Will do. It's clear." It was dingy and dark in

the alcove, and the building behind had crazed and painted windows that looked abandoned, anyway.

The pistol thwapped twice, brass tinkled on the bricks underfoot. Wade bent down and scooped up the empty cases as Kyle stuffed the pistol away.

"That seemed to do it," he said. The bolt heads had been blown cleanly off, and the plywood sheet bent back as he pulled.

Then they were grunting and straining, because the plywood was three quarters of an inch thick and well secured. "Might have been easier," Wade panted, "to have brought a grappling hook and climbed up a couple of floors." He nodded up at the third floor, its windows protected by rusted bars and broken glass.

"Put it on the list," Kyle said through gritted teeth.

Then he twisted and was underneath the wood as Wade swore and pulled to stop him from getting squeezed. He stuck his hands in his pockets and fished out leather gloves, which he yanked on quickly before trying to tackle the broken sill and frame. He sought areas free from glass and heaved himself up, bracing his feet on Wade's knees for support.

He almost dislocated his spine as he bent backward inside. Then his hands touched dusty, filthy floor and he found it easiest to roll backward into a handstand, feeling like Olga Korbut.

As he collapsed in a heap, he decided old Olga

had far more grace and control. But what the hell, he was inside.

It was also pitch black. He dug for his Maglight. That let him find a chunk of pipe, leftover from who knows what, which he slid down and out and pried with. His weight opened enough of a gap that Wade was able to easily toss in their rucksacks and clamber up himself.

With both flashlights out, they were able to look around.

"Time for night vision," Kyle said. Wade opened his bag and they both pulled on goggles. With the lights and occasional bright dots through knotholes or cracks, they could see well enough. The floor was concrete, pierced with mounting holes for long-removed machinery, and was very rough. It was littered with boxes, crates, lumber, metal, and assorted cobwebs, dead birds, and junk. "Fun place."

"That gray area over there," Wade pointed. Even though everything was monochromatic green, it was a habit to refer to something halfway between light and dark as "gray." "I think that's stairs with light above."

"Could be," Kyle said. "Let's check it out."

They were stairs. Once up a floor, the light from above was soft and diffused, everything showing as lurking shadows. After that it was easy, except for the mess and loose debris on the stairs. The metal clanged softly and swayed a little, but it seemed to be no more than the vibration one would expect.

"No one's been up here," Kyle said. "Probably too cold and drafty, and no place to get a fire going, so no homeless people."

"Whatever," Wade said. "Vacant is what we want."

They pushed on to the sixth floor, and stopped at the top of the stairs. Neither man had any intention of running across floors that might give way, or showing a silhouette at a window. They were cautious professionals. "Safe up here. But I think the third floor is high enough, gets us closer to the shot and leaves us a shorter escape route."

"Makes sense," Wade agreed. "Back down we go." They slipped quietly back along their steps and down.

"Okay, open windows on all sides," Wade said once they were there. "We're expecting him on the south, but he's coming from the east. Should we each take a side and wait?"

"Makes sense," Wade said. "I'll watch east with the spotting scope. You use the rifle scope. Switch every thirty minutes?"

"Okay," Kyle agreed.

Then it got down to waiting. Kyle found a rickety, splintered table he could reinforce with some old crates. He used his knife to peel off a few large splinters and used them to wedge the legs more tightly in place. That gave him a good platform for watching and shooting. He was back about ten feet from the window, which made him all but invisible but still afforded a good view. Behind him, he could see Wade, tucked back against a pillar, shoulders hunched and seeming willing to wait like a statue.

It wasn't especially cold. It was probably over fifty outside. But the building was effectively open up here, and they weren't moving at all. Chill leaked down the front of Kyle's coat, up his sleeves and in through his boot tips. Part of him noticed and grumbled. The other part kept watch.

There were couples, business people, ragged poor, and indeterminate others. The ages ranged from ten to ancient. With the bipod out and his hand on the grip, Kyle was professionally comfortable. He could—and had on occasion—stay like this for more than a day. He had his ruck open to his left, the food and water in easy reach and easily closed and removed with no evidence left behind. A color picture of Logadze was taped inside the open top to help in recognition.

Nothing happened for two hours. They stayed still and cold, eyes alert for their target, ears straining to catch any sounds from below that would indicate trouble. Lumps and bolt heads on the table were poking Kyle through his clothes, leaving indentations in the skin and to the bone in some places. His headset was irritating his ear.

Wade came over and slid down beside him, and he rolled off the table to take the spotting scope on the east. Standing let him work the kinks out, then it was time to sprawl on the table again.

Besides people, there were buses, trucks and cars, shifting shadows from clouds, and other movements. There were also the crazed and cracked windows. It helped that there was always something to look at. It hindered in that it distracted attention from the street. The eye patch over his left eye let him avoid squinting, and he panned slowly back and forth across the field of view the window offered.

Kyle picked out several missing panes he planned to shoot through when the time came. A silenced weapon did no good if one then broke out glass that would fall and clatter to give away one's position.

It was at 10:43 A.M. when Wade said, "I think I've got him." They were using their headsets to avoid shouting.

"Where?"

"East, one block, approaching on foot, north side of street. Now crossing to south side."

"Good." He wanted to keep the talk to a minimum, and no names would be used on air. He turned his face from the microphone and said, "Pretty good intel. And they can't just arrest this asshole?" Wade was moving closer, window to window, keeping Logadze in view.

"I get the impression they're like Colombian drug lords. Everyone knows about them, but no one wants to fuck with them."

"Yeah. How's progress?"

"Coming into your field of view any time.

Navy trench coat, short, scruffy beard, gray slacks, and white shirt."

"I see him. That's our target?" He was suddenly large in Kyle's scope, disappearing momentarily as he shifted across window spars, to reappear again.

"I've got a positive match," Wade said. "That's our man."

"Got it," Kyle said without a movement. "I can't guarantee I'm going to get a shot."

"Okay."

"Because I am *not* shooting where I might hit a civilian, and I'm not shooting where it'll be obvious which direction the bullet came from, and I am not shooting outside of two hundred meters."

"Kyle, I'm on your side. Do what you have to," Wade told him.

"Right. Sorry." He resumed silence. It was easier to work that way, anyway. He could easily see Logadze in his scope. But there was no certainty he would get close enough. It was back to a waiting game.

But Kyle was patient, and trained to be more so. If this shot didn't work out, then perhaps the next one would. He rose carefully and moved to keep an open window pane between him and Logadze, skipping lightly sideways like a dancer, but a dancer poised with a rifle matched to his almost inhumanly accurate skill.

Logadze was obviously waiting for something.

Of course, innocent people waited for things, too. Girlfriends, business partners, even to kill time between buses. But this man was waiting for the transfer of a case of explosives to take out more civilians with. Kyle just hoped that information was correct. It wasn't the remorse he'd feel over a bad shot, though that was real enough. It was the satisfaction of putting a cowardly, murderous terrorist asshole into the dirt.

Kyle Monroe really hated terrorists. If they wanted to kill people, he stood ready to receive them. But none of them dared meet men like him, because they knew they'd lose. Their targets were the small, the weak, and the helpless. And those were the people Kyle had sworn to protect.

So beyond the intellectual challenge of the shot, the tactical complexity of an urban environment with witnesses, and the political intrigue and risk, was a cruel but real thrill at the thought of making this scumbucket the guest of honor at a funeral. Or maybe "ghost" of honor, he thought with a tight smile.

He was there, across the circle, and easy to see. That wasn't the only consideration, however. At much beyond one hundred yards, the little .22 rounds would be inadequate. Certainly five or ten solid hits at two hundred yards would cause enough trauma to the heart or lungs to bring him down, but that took time, allowed easier tracking of the shots, and meant he might reach a hospital in time. He might easily catch AIDS from a dirty transfusion, but that would mean years to die. Their schedule called for it to happen somewhat sooner.

So there was nothing to do but wait, and hope. If they didn't catch him here, they could try again somewhere else.

"Watch concealment," Wade said. Kyle took a quick peek, nodded, and stepped back. He was getting too close to the window.

"I'm getting photos," Wade said. "Video and still. We'll have something they can update records with at least."

"Roger that."

Just then Logadze leaned back against the wall and pulled out a cigarette pack. He shook one loose as he fumbled for a match or lighter in his jacket pocket.

Got you, you son of a bitch, Kyle thought. All he needed now was a moment's break in the crowd. Even if the .22 exited the body, it would be so slow as to barely make a mark on the aged and weathered bricks. *One shot only, then duck.* It wouldn't do to have anyone try to trace the shot back. He leaned back, left arm braced against his body to minimize oscillations.

Logadze struck a match and raised it in cupped hands. Just as he reached his face, a break in the crowd left him clear and exposed. Kyle gritted his teeth for just a moment, then let icy calm flow back through him. He was waiting for . . .

Logadze cocked his head slightly as he breathed life into his cigarette.

. . . *that*, Kyle thought, and started to squeeze the trigger.

Then the crowd thickened again. Bodies came en masse from stores and entrances. Swearing, he let off the trigger and eased from his stance. He sagged back on his legs and drew the rifle carefully out of line.

"Son of a bitch!" he said.

"Eleven A.M.," Wade said from around his scope. "I think people are breaking for lunch." His squint was still in place and he was swiveling to keep the target in view. "And he's heading into that store," he said. "I'll wait."

"Do. But I'm betting he goes out the back."

"No bet," Wade said. "Still, we'll watch and see."

"Right," Kyle agreed. Blast. Just one more second! That's all he'd needed. "I *hate* peacetime urban settings," he said. "I've tried them for one day now, and I hate them. I'd rather risk gapping an officer at his desk with a regiment of armor around him than shoot in a crowded city."

"Yeah, I'm not pursuing the idea of being a police sniper after this," Wade said. "There are distinct advantages to heavy artillery as backup."

Kyle was already dialing on his phone. "Mick, no go. He went into a store," he said as soon as it answered.

"Damn. Are you watching?"

"Yes, but there's another exit, and he may have friends inside. Or hell, he may just bull his way through to the bathroom or something."

"Right. Call me when you have something. I'll try to get someone in there to follow up."

"Understood. Out." He punched off at once, the phone letting out a *beep*. It almost sounded like a protest against his rough thumb on the button.

Letting the frustration and anger subside, they resumed their patient watch. Every half hour, they switched off, letting their eyes rest for a few minutes, red and gritty and aching. It was chilly with no heat and no movement.

Lunch was cold MREs and local iron rations of nuts and fruit. The apples were okay, but small, bitter, and tough compared to American ones. Still, it was food, and it broke the monotony.

At 7:00 P.M., dusky and chilly, the Georgian had still not come from the store. It was long since closed and locked, and the foot traffic was dying rapidly.

"That's it, we're done," Wade said.

"Yeah, I concur," Kyle said. "Let's report in. Damn." He dug out the phone again. "Monroe here," he said when Cafferty answered. "No shot. Video and stills."

"It all helps. We know he's here and we'll get another chance. Don't sweat it."

"You weren't able to track him?" Kyle asked. He was a bit miffed that they'd been left here all day.

"No. Can't explain right now. I'll meet you at the panzione tomorrow, unless things change. Oh eight hundred."

"Eight A.M. at the panzione, got it."

Hadi Kadim logged into his favorite chatroom for the evening. Actually, it wasn't his favorite chatroom. He hated it. But if he might glean a few grains, it would be worthwhile. He'd come across it by accident one night, and had been about to leave when he caught a reference to a U.S. embassy. He'd stayed, curious, and found that one of the participants was married to an ambassador. She also liked to talk.

He'd mentioned this to his mullah, who'd asked for anyone with information about the American military to come forward. Embassies weren't exactly military, but he thought it might be useful.

The mullah had thought so. A week later, he had specific instructions on what to look for and listen for, and what to say.

JulianLee has entered the room.
6 people in chat.
BLKKTTY: Julian, good evening.
LEO155: Hi, Jule.
JULIANLEE: Greetings, all. I'll be lurking while I help my son with his math.
LEO155: No prob. Crunch those numbers. Show no mercy. :-D

There was no son, and Kadim had no intention of lurking in the chat sense. He watched every conversation that passed, and saved the frame every evening. There were others who did similar things: ModevalMac worked second shift and left chat running so he could read and catch up afterward, then was actually present only on weekends. But it was best that "JulianLee" not talk too much. Watching was better. He couldn't see the private messages, but from the ones he received he concluded there wasn't any substantial content to most of them.

Much went on that was neither interesting nor relevant. But he cultivated favor by being quiet and friendly. Often, that was all that was needed.

It was more than an hour before he started making notes. One of his favorite people came online. Others found her to be an annoying chatterbox. He did, too, in fact, but she often said things of interest. She was the ambassador's wife.

Barbiemouse has entered the room.
FANCYDANCER: Barbie! Hugs.
BLKKTTY: Hi, Barbie.
BARBIEMOUSE: I am soooo frustrated and annoyed!
JAMESGUNN: Oh? What now?
Private Message from JamesGunn to Blkktty: As if I don't know already and want details.
Private Message from Blkktty to James-

Gunn: She really is predictable. I wonder what we're doing wrong this time?

BARBIEMOUSE: You wouldn't believe what's happening here now.

JULIANLEE: Oh?

BARBIEMOUSE: My husband has just been informed that a certain intelligence agency is providing support to an 'anti-terror' team here in country.

JAMESGUNN: And that's bad?

LEO155: SWEEEEEEEEEEEET! :-D

BARBIEMOUSE: Leo, you're too young to grasp how important this is. This country is developing and still trying to grasp capitalism and the modern world. Treading all over their sovereignty won't let them reach their potential. It's insulting and condescending to take such a smug, overbearing approach.

Private Message from JamesGunn to Leo155: Barbie, of course, would never be condescending to her poor, disadvantaged hosts who don't understand capitalism.

Private Message from Leo155 to James-Gunn: I'm sure she gives everyone she meets a shiny euro coin to show her respect for them.

BLKKTTY: You seem to be implying a problem beyond the diplomatic issues, Barbie.

Private Message from JamesGunn to Leo-155: You'd think an ambassador would marry someone a bit brighter than Barbie. Doesn't thrill me about our State Department.

Private Message from JamesGunn to Blkktty: Oh, please don't get her started.

Private Message from Leo155 to James-Gunn: I'm not sure she is an ambassador's wife.

Private Message from Blkktty to James-Gunn: I'm amused at what we might hear.

Private Message from JamesGunn to Leo155: Oh, she is. Unfortunately. I've heard enough to confirm it.

LEO155: I'm told they're pretty good at capitalism. High prices. Screwing tourists. Cheap hookers. Hell, I might have to book a trip.

BARBIEMOUSE: Leo, that's exactly the attitude that causes problems here.

Private Message from JamesGunn to Leo155: hehehe. Dumbass. ;-)

BARBIEMOUSE: Anyway, there's a pair of Rambo types gallivanting about the countryside trying to take shots at terrorists.

JAMESGUNN: I'm still trying to find the problem with this.

Private Message from Blkktty to James-Gunn: Private Message from Barbiemouse to Blkktty: I'm ignoring Leo and James again.

Private Message from JamesGunn to Blkktty: I am so ashamed. ;-)

BLKKTTY: I don't think the intent is to annoy your hosts, Barb.

BARBIEMOUSE: Oh, I know. They have Good Intentions, of course. It just bothers me to see our hosts' hospitality abused like this. Really, there's no reason it should be hidden from them.

JAMESGUNN: The less who know, the better. I didn't really need to know. Are you sure you should be talking?

Private Message from Blkktty to James-Gunn: she's clicked you and can't see your posts.

BARBIEMOUSE: They tried a shot downtown today and couldn't do it. I'm not quite sure who they are, but they're not impressive.

Private Message from JamesGunn to Leo155: "Not impressive"? I don't suppose Barb has ever done any shooting? Clandestinely? Against a probably moving

*target? If they'd taken the shot, she'd whine
about risk to civilians.*

*Private Message from Leo155 to James-
Gunn: Hey, didn't you tell me not to get
bent out of shape? *grins**

BARBIEMOUSE: And they're obviously not
very good, if they can't
make a 100 yard shot in
daylight. Why, when my
first husband was in the 3rd
Infantry Division, there was
a sniping competition at
800 yards.

BLKKTTY: It's likely a little different with innocent people around the target.

BARBIEMOUSE: Yes, I suppose we should all
be grateful they didn't plug
anyone on the street. But
still, it's only a matter of
time before someone so in-
secure makes a serious error
in judgment and it all comes
tumbling down. From what
I gather, they don't even
speak the language. They're
just sort of floating around
until told what to do. Really, there should be a
proper chain of command.
It just strikes me as so
sloppy and insulting to send

two half-competent people over when the Romanian SRI has very good people of its own.

JAMESGUNN: So glad to hear an analysis from an expert in the field. [sarcasm]

JULIANLEE: Now, James, Barbie is part of the diplomatic mission and is familiar with the area better than we are.

Private Message from JamesGunn to Leo155: Do me a favor and don't mention this. It shouldn't be talked about.

Private Message from Leo155 to James-Gunn: Not a problem. Dumb bitch.

JAMESGUNN: I suppose so. Anyway, I have to log out. Later.

JamesGunn has exited the room.

BLKKTTY: Bye, James.

LEO155: Later, James . . . damn, that was quick.

JULIANLEE: I suppose I should bid you good evening, too. There's chores to be done.

LEO155: Good night, Julian.

JULIANLEE: Good night, all.

Hadi resumed lurking and watching. He found chat rooms to be most unpleasant. It got very awkward when the Americans and the French got onto a kick with sexual innuendos; though rather than being offended as he used to be, Kadim was now largely bored. It seemed they had no depth, no sophistication, and made all their seductions crass and quick. No wonder they were so decadent, shallow, and lacking in respect.

But he was out again, and prayer would cleanse his soul. In that, he did respect two newcomers, Larry and Walt, who were devout Christians. He didn't believe in their savior, but they at least kept quiet when the conversations got perverse, and quietly chided the more obnoxious members. They seemed like halfway decent types, unlike JamesGunn, who was a typical anti-Islamic twit. His oft-repeated phrase of "No Palestinians, no Palestinian problem" had driven Kadim to a frenzied rage that only an hour of prayer had cooled the first time he heard it. Clearly, Allah was tasking him with patience and tolerance for such men.

For Allah's purpose, he could suffer such indignity. Allah had his own plan, and it would show its beauty and perfection when all was done.

For now, he needed to call the mullah and update him. There were shooters from somewhere in Romania under American orders. He wasn't sure of the significance, but he'd been told to report anything unusual from the dozen chats a day he monitored. Exhaling to clear his mind, he reached for the phone.

* * *

The next morning, Cafferty was waiting at the panzione. "Hi, guys," he said with a wave. "Let's talk. Problems." He stood at the back door, but inside and under cover. They hurried up the steps and through the canted kitchen door. Sam was present. He smiled and ducked into the front parlor.

Kyle bristled a little. He was afraid the problem was a perception of how they did their job.

"I hope the intel we have is okay," he said to try to probe gently. It was tight in the kitchen, and Ms. Cneajna smiled and offered them cups. He and Wade refused with thanks.

Cafferty took a cup and said, "Any pics we can clean up and use are good. The more we have on this guy, the better we can predict him. And anyone near him may turn out to be a co-conspirator. If there's someone in your pics who was in others we have, that's a good lead."

"I got about thirty minutes of vid and twenty-three stills," Wade said as they walked the twenty feet through the house to the bedroom.

"Excellent! Glad to hear it." Cafferty opened the bedroom door and waved at them while sipping his coffee. Everyone sat back down, knees almost touching in the small space between bed and chair. He pulled a laptop and a bag of accessories from his briefcase, which was already by the chair.

"So what's the problem?" Wade asked casually, as they slipped in and closed it.

"Ambassador's wife," Cafferty said with a disgusted look. "She talks too much and to everyone. She's an annoying bitch. And he's too much of a wuss to get rid of her or ignore her. She doesn't run the embassy, but she sure as hell backseat drives a lot. And I *never* want to hear about her polyps again." He shuddered and winced. "At least we know he's honest."

"Oh?" Wade asked first.

"Yeah. It's got to be love, there's not that much money in the world. So he's not taking bribes."

Wade chuckled. "Or if he is, he spends it on a mistress."

Kyle grinned and asked, "And there's nothing we can do about her?"

"Kyle, if I could designate her as a target, I would. But it would be illegal, immoral, and cause more trouble than it solved. But, *God*, I hate that woman." His face was showing lines.

"What can happen? We're not up on State issues," Wade asked.

"As I said, the ambassador can bounce you out of here. He's first and last word. It's his job to take advice and act on it. But he listens to her far more than he should. She's much harder to keep control of. And she knows more than she should. She snoops, he talks, then she talks to others—I won't say friends. I don't think she has any friends. But there's a lot of people who pity her for some stupid reason." He gulped more coffee.

"That's why you don't want us at the embassy?" Kyle asked. "In addition to visibility, I mean?"

"Yup. She was whining and complaining about you 'missing' the shot. She overheard something and is making snide comments about the CIA's assassins."

"Dammit, I didn't take the shot because I didn't want to blow cover or kill a civilian," Kyle said. "Where the f—"

"Hey, don't sweat it," Cafferty said. "I know the realities. We'll get another chance. Absolute worst case, we tell the Romanians everything we have and see if they can nail a couple of them before word gets around. Without mentioning that we were trying to do it ourselves because we didn't trust them."

"You know," Wade said, "I rather think I prefer our job to yours a lot of ways."

"Yeah, I've got a coffee habit that would bankrupt most budgets, and if I come out of this without an ulcer, I'll call it a win."

"So what's next?"

"Well," Cafferty replied, scratching his forehead, "if it goes as before, Logadze here means Florescu will be setting up something regarding a shipment."

"And we'll get a shot at him?"

"If we see him, yes. And then we have to get you up into the tourist areas to get your photos of Dracula's digs. Otherwise people might start asking about you."

"Question, and I don't mean to be rude," Kyle said. This seemed like an opportune time.

"Sure." And another gulp of coffee.

"Why are you so terse on the phone?"

"Because I'm trying to pretend you don't exist," he said. "If I'm just liaison for a military mission, then I can shrug my shoulders and say it's not my fault. But if I talk to you too much, it becomes obvious my department is running the show."

"Fair enough," Kyle said. "I'm not sure I want to see the chain of command for this nightmare."

"Yeah, it's pretty confused," Cafferty said. "Anyway, if we don't get anything else in four days, we'll move you up into the mountains and see if you can offer any help to finding them up there."

"Fair enough," Kyle said. Good. Four more days of bad food and a decrepit city, and maybe they could do something worthwhile.

"Meantime, I'm trying to stop her from hearing anything. I don't know how the info gets out, but she's good at piecing tiny bits together and blowing them out of proportion. A great conspiracy theorist."

"She listens at doors?" Kyle asked.

"Dunno. But I do have to talk on the phone and to others, and I'm not the only person in country, or even in the embassy, who is involved. It only takes a comment at lunch to set her off. And some stuff that is public knowledge gets twisted when she gets hold of it. I'll have to see about getting her some really ridiculous info to discredit her and confuse them. That's more work for my people."

"Anyway," he continued, shaking his head, "Let me see what you have, and give me a report," he laid down a microphone connected to the laptop, "and I'll get you more intel. Basic name so I can keep things straight, and talk."

Kyle nodded, grabbed the mic and said, "SFC Kyle Monroe. We departed the hotel at . . ."

Forty minutes later, with some leading questions from Cafferty, they were done. He'd split his attention to watch their video on screen, and to plug their camera into his own laptop. The photos were encrypted and emailed out, then the verbal report, then he pulled a chip from the side. He broke it in half with a heavy pair of sidecutters and held it up. He rummaged in a pocket, pulled out a lighter and scorched the broken edges until they melted. That done, he took it to a corner and pulled a very large magnet out of a drawer, then waved the two sections over it for more than a minute.

"Flash RAM?" Wade asked.

Cafferty said, "Yes. Much easier and cheaper than the old way, which was to either smash and slag a drive, or take fifteen minutes to overwrite and then reformat about two hundred times, I think. That's what the No Such Agency had set up for us. This way, it's done very quickly and for just a few dollars."

"What about security here?" Wade asked.

"Worst case, I try to smash the chip enough before anyone comes in, but this info isn't so critical. If they find it, we say he's a 'person of interest' and negotiate a swap of intel. I'm just being paranoid. Besides, there's Sam. He's the tripwire."

"Ah," Kyle said. It made sense. And likely the safe house changed from time to time.

"Okay, that's it for now. I'll work on this and try to get you another shot. And thanks. The intel is useful, potentially even more useful than a kill."

"No problem," Kyle said. He knew that. Every sniper did. But he wanted the kill because he hated terrorists, and to show the doubters that he could do it.

Then he mentally stepped back, because doing it to prove a point was dangerous. The goal here was to do a job only. Not to prove anything. Professionals didn't take revenge or show off. Professionals knew they were good. And looking back at his own record, Kyle had all the proof he needed that he was good.

They left first, out the back again, smiling at their reticent and almost invisible hostess. Kyle had to wonder what her stake was, but he trusted Cafferty, so he wasn't going to ask.

Turning to Wade, he said, "Now all we need is lunch."

"You know, there is a KFC here. It's real food and hopefully somewhat American."

"Good idea," Kyle agreed, smiling. "I haven't had chicken in a while. And it's bound to be better than their attempts at Mexican or Russian; there's corporate standards to maintain."

"We'll stop by on the way to the hotel. I think it's near there anyway."

An hour later, stuffed and sated, they sat back on their beds. They'd killed a twelve-piece drum of chicken, biscuits, mashed potatoes, gravy, and coleslaw.

"Yup, American fast food. Not healthy, not exotic, but very predictable, and damn, it was good!" Wade said.

"Shall we look at maps and dossiers again?" Kyle asked. "Or another bull session about hunting vampires?"

"Vampires. I'm thinking this whole crucifix to scare them off bit is inadequate. Who says there aren't Jewish vampires? So you also need a Star of David, a Buddhist Wheel, a Crescent, a Hindu Lion, a Pentacle, a—"

"I'll pull up a map and access an online poker game," Kyle said.

Wade chuckled and said, "Sure."

They took turns playing rounds of poker online, while looking at the city and national maps, just to be familiar with everything. They also had some tour guides and local publications. The newsstands and bookstores in the area had been very happy to take their money. As it wasn't their money, and the publications were a necessary expense, they'd been happy to spend it.

Dammar al Asfan checked his email and saw a flagged message.

Actually, it wasn't his email. It had been set up by someone who did nothing but set up free addresses for the cause, using a public machine in a café in France. But he had the username and password.

The message alerted him to another incoming message. That one was marked "spam," but he opened it anyway. It promised him generi(V!@gra at cheap prices with no prescription.

He copied the .jpg image the message was built on and pasted it into another window. From there, he saved it to a folder of a special program. That program stripped off the excess image and left a handful of letters that had been hidden underneath.

The message thus revealed made him snarl. The blasted Americans had two snipers in Romania, courtesy of the CIA. They were stalking his operation, allegedly, though they'd missed a shot at Logadze. As Logadze had not reported an attack, nor were there any news reports, he was skeptical for a moment. But this source was very reliable. He didn't know where they got the information, but the person in charge of intelligence assured him they were always correct, and so far, they had been. So he had to assume the assassination attempt had failed in the setup.

He sent a message requesting more information, then another alerting the relevant people to be especially alert. The next week was critical if they were not to suffer a setback of major proportions.

In the meantime, he'd inquire at the Serviciul Roman de Informatii through connections. Likely there was a record somewhere.

Engineman Third Class Daniel McLaren didn't actually work on engines very often. If a patrol boat or a Mk V Special Operations Boat had a problem on a mission, he's get involved, and he was responsible for maintenance and tuning. He spent more time in the water than aboard, anyway. SEALs usually did.

His swim buddy for the current mission was a Turkish combat swimmer named Tuncer Akkurt. Tunj was bronzed, which was what his first name meant, ironically, and always had a cheerful smile. That smile wasn't visible at the moment, but it was definitely there. It always was.

The two of them were in the harbor of Constanta's port, keeping low and hidden from most of the shipping, and awaiting orders to observe or pursue the *Chernomertvetz* as she came in to port this evening. Pursuit might involve boarding with others to secure her (unlikely) or to plant surveillance equipment (more likely). For now, they were cold, wet, coated with Vaseline under their wetsuits, and burdened with weight belts, flotation jackets, and vests with pistols, knives, and other gear. They were mostly above the surface, their hoods decorated with odd-shaped bits of black fabric and their faces blackened with a waterproof grease. The sum effect was such that anyone looking at them from aboard a ship would think them mere debris of the kind that floats in every port, washed overboard from ships or kicked off piers, or, more commonly, thrown in carelessly or on purpose.

Two other swimmers, one American and one Turkish, were on the breakwater, where they could use night scopes and special filters to determine probable contents of various cargo. At a signal from them, McLaren and Akkurt would try to get near enough to use a chemical sniffer to verify the findings. Nothing could be 100 percent accurate, but the closer they could get to a conclusive answer, the better. From there, there were assets ashore who would take over. McLaren had no idea who those assets were, or if they were local, American, or some other ally. All he needed to know was that his part would help the whole mission. For a professional, that was enough. That he was in foreign waters without permission wasn't a consideration. That's what SEALs did.

8

KYLE LOOKED UP FROM THE BOOK HE WAS reading and said, "Fascinating country. Pity Ceauşescu and his cronies looted it, or it could have had a lot more historical interest."

"It's getting there," Wade said.

"Yeah, I suppose twenty years or even fifty isn't that long. It just seems like a hell of a long time from personal perspective."

"That it does," Wade agreed. "Harp for dinner again?"

"I guess I can manage that," Kyle said. It would get boring eventually, but the place had a big enough menu to last several days without repeating.

Besides, it got them out of the hotel and killed some time.

After dinner, they went back to the hotel. Neither felt up to tackling the nightlife.

They were just sitting down to a mix of local and online news when Kyle's phone rang.

He stood and dug the phone out of his jacket pocket. "Monroe," he answered.

"Kyle, this is Mick."

"Yes, Mick?"

"I've got a lead for you guys. Right now."

Kyle snapped his fingers and pointed at Wade, who rolled off the bed and started grabbing gear.

"Shoot," Kyle prompted.

"There's a ship coming in tonight," Cafferty said. "Our marine mammal friends—" that would be the SEALs—"have got a probable ID on explosives from a sniff. We've decided to let this one through so you can follow it. It's big," he said, hesitating.

"How big?" Kyle asked.

"Might be a *ton* of conventional explosive, likely TNT. Not as sexy as Semtex or C Four, but plenty for a dozen small missions or one huge blast."

"What do you want us to do?" Kyle asked. This was a bit more than they'd planned on.

Across the room, Wade had the weapons bagged and was changing into local working-class clothes.

Cafferty said, "Go to the port in Constanta. The ship *Chernomertvetz* arrives in four hours. We can't imagine they'll let that stuff sit for long; it's standard to turn around fast. So they likely have an ally handy who'll clear them through customs, or a bribe or some evasion and they'll unload fast. Follow them wherever they go, report back, get photos of people and take further action if necessary."

"We're on it. Got a map and more data?"

"Yes, I just emailed your laptop. It's all there, including a phone contact for our friends. They'll give you regular updates on position and schedule."

"Will do. We're rolling now," Kyle said, nodding from habit even though it couldn't be seen.

Wade did see it and nodded back.

"Good luck," Cafferty said and clicked off.

Kyle shoved the phone into the pocket, snapped it closed, and went about getting dressed himself. He logged the laptop in with a touch and watched as it started downloading mail. A three-meg file. Lots of stuff.

"How did you know it was working-class clothes?" he asked Wade, in regard to his partner's dress.

"It's eight P.M. No way are we going out to a ball on short notice, if these guys even do balls."

"Right," he agreed, pulling on well-worn khakis. "Who's driving?"

"That depends," Wade said. "I grew up in central Illinois, flatland."

"It's hilly. I'm from southern Ohio. Better let me do it."

"Suits me. I'll navigate, take pictures, shoot if needed, and flirt with any chicks."

In ten minutes, they were stuffing gear into the backseat and scrambling into the front. "This time, we're actually using the laptop," Wade said. He was opening it to read routes and docking info. The Pakistan mission had resulted in much lost and damaged equipment, and other pieces that proved largely useless. So far this time, everything was working nominally.

So far.

"Hey, I'll take any advantage we can get," Kyle said. "What's our route?"

Wade navigated them out of the city very professionally. "Left at the third light," he'd say. "Two blocks, then right, immediate left." Bucharest was old. Even the new parts were built on ancient, twisting routes that hadn't been intended for modern vehicles.

"This is like old New England or the most cramped parts of Philly," Kyle said.

"Worse, I think. Left again up ahead. That's our route."

"Roger."

The highway was one designated as an "E," or European road. It was therefore in decent repair. They waited impatiently at traffic lights and stop signs, then powered away, swapping fuel efficiency for precious seconds.

It was quiet enough as they left town, but even this late at night, there were a few obstacles— chuckholes, horse- and mule-drawn carts and drivers in rattly old Yugos or medieval Fiats that could barely keep up—even an old diesel Volvo that smoked and sputtered as Kyle passed it. The road was a divided highway at first, a second pair of lanes obviously built alongside the older two-lane. There were quite a few intersections where "largest vehicle has right of way" was the unstated rule.

Wade got on the phone and called the number they'd been given. "Curtis here," he said. "How's it going? . . . Okay. Yes, two hours at least . . . Will you be meeting us? . . . Okay. Stand by." He started hooking the phone up to the laptop.

"What's up?" Kyle asked.

"Getting an image. We should be there in time. It takes a while for docking and clearance. Then they have to get cranes and ramps into position. But after that, they think it might be the first load off."

"What are we going to do?"

"We're going to observe from shore while they observe from sea. They'll let us know when they think it's the right load. I get the impression they were hoping to plant a tracer of some kind on it, and couldn't quite get close enough to the load."

"Damn. That would have made things much easier for everyone."

"Yeah. We'd just have to zoom in and shoot."

They passed through Dragalina, Fetesti, and several smaller, unremarkable towns, each one a delay on what was a nominal hundred-and-twenty-mile trip. It was a two-hour trip if all went well, but it was near midnight when they rolled into Constanta.

"I'm not sure we want to get too close to the port," Kyle said. "We've got radios, would you feel safe making a recon on foot? I'll circle and recon by car and be ready to roll."

"Safe, no. But I'll do it," Wade agreed. "No weapons, I want deniability, but if the radio isn't answering, you'll need to come get me." He sounded nervous.

"Take the Beretta," Kyle decided. "A magazine full of ammo might get them to duck long enough for you to get out, and I'll be ready with the AK. If they've got too many for us to tackle, just bow out early."

"Got it," Wade agreed. "But I'd rather not have a firefight here."

"Agreed," Kyle said.

Constanta was old, grimy, and broad. It had been named after Constantine, and had been a port before that. Parts had been built by the Turks, the Romanians, the Communists, Ceauşescu's regime, and again by free Romanians. The architecture ran the gamut from Turkish to baroque and to modern, and the streets were as snarled and twisted as any others in this country. They came in on the Bulevardul Tomis, past a sign for the Roman baths and then south toward the port.

The port wasn't quite what they'd expected it to be. It was bigger than they would have •

thought, and alternated between arc-lit operations and dark industrial sections. There was a rail yard that went on for miles, and docks ashore and along a breakwater. Ships were moving in at a steady clip, and others departing. Shipping companies hate port. If cargo isn't moving, money isn't being made. APM Terminals had a sign up, as did SC Socep. Workers, mostly men, were everywhere, loading, unloading, hauling, opening crates, backing vehicles.

Wade said, "It's the second pier from the south. The southernmost has petrochemical storage."

"You know what we're looking for?" Kyle asked. He'd been busy driving and had everything secondhand from Wade. He was having trouble visualizing things.

"Yes, it's a smaller, older ship. Diesel drive, no stacks, and is very low and curvy. I have the image they sent. It's grainy, but I think I can spot it."

"Good."

"It won't take long, I'm told. Ships don't like sitting in port, because they only make money when moving, kinda like truckers. So we can expect them to haul ass once they get docked."

The gate was guarded, but there was no fence. There were dark, shadowy areas, and it was toward one of those that Wade was angling in a crouch.

It took Wade only a few seconds to cut a slice

in the fence and slip in. Kyle watched him disappear, his right foot catching for a moment, then gone. He had no idea what the inside of the facility looked like, other than it was full of containers and piles, rails and cranes. Wade would have to walk quite some distance without being identified, then walk back out unseen if he were to be able to ride with Kyle on the chase.

If not, he had cash and could arrange transport back by himself. On the other hand, with a silenced Beretta, cash, and communication gear, anyone finding him would suspect him of crime or terrorism.

And that was Wade's worry, Kyle reminded himself. His was out here, ready to chase. Wade had the inside watch.

Meanwhile, Kyle sat and waited. Every minute or two he revved the engine up to 1200 or so, just to stop it from fouling. It likely wasn't necessary in a modern fuel-injected car, but it was habit and ensured the engine was responsive. He used the heat to keep his feet warm, leaving the window open for Wade. But he ensured all the doors were locked and held firmly to his Ed Brown, suppressor in place, the whole assembly tucked under his left arm inside his coat.

"Arriving," Wade whispered hoarsely in his ears. Seconds later, his shape rose near the door, disturbing and macabre despite the fact that it was a perfectly reasonable act.

Calm down, Kyle reminded himself, taking a deep breath.

"This is a job for White Man!" Wade said softly. "Gypsies and Romanians all over the place. You'll blend in fine. I won't."

"Okay," Kyle agreed. "Let me see the maps and pics." He sighed. It wasn't Wade's fault, dammit, but anything that changed his plans was exasperating.

The ship looked easy to spot; it was very rounded at the ends. The bow and stern, he reminded himself. It had a large yellow crane at the rear third. The map told him where it was supposed to be docking.

"Okay, call our friends and make sure they have my number," Kyle said. Call me to confirm, and I'll let you know what I find." It was cool enough to justify wearing a polyester ski cap rolled down to hide his radio earpiece. With the microphone dangling inside his upturned collar, it should be invisible, and he should look like any common laborer.

He took the smaller of their two still cameras so he could try for images if needed, and climbed out, adjusting his collar as he did so.

From where the car was, it was easy to walk across the rail yard. There were several other people in sight, and no one seemed to care about the fact that it was unsafe and potentially threatening. Which in this case, Kyle reflected, was good. For him at least.

There was also a sea fog moving in. That worked both ways. It would hide him, but it would also mean he'd need to get close to the ship. Meanwhile, he had to maintain a lookout so he wouldn't have to interact with anyone. He could badly pretend to be Spanish, or hope to pass off as a Brit, or even just grunt a bit in passing. But if the conversation lasted more than two sentences, he'd be obvious.

A buzz surprised him. It was the phone in his pocket, set to vibrate to keep it discreet.

"Monroe," he answered.

"This is Kabongo, on the water." The voice was clear, but there was background noise, probably a boat engine.

"What have you got?"

"They're docking and tying up now. I've got someone watching from the water, but his angle is limited."

"I'll be there soon. How close do I need to be?" He was trying to keep his voice at a mutter but loud enough for audibility. It wouldn't do to be heard in English without a believable cover story.

"Five hundred meters should be close enough. We think the cargo you're looking for is a pallet of wooden crates. Should be one of the first loads off."

"I'll see what I can do. Let me know if anything else happens."

"Will do. Out."

"Out."

Once at the docks proper, there was plenty of cover. People were all over the place, but not in concentrations except where unloading a ship.

Some sauntered, some loitered, some walked briskly. People were hanging off cranes, trucks, and ramps. Lots were smoking. It occurred to Kyle that cigarettes would help them blend in for tasks like this, and they should buy some. All he had to do was sit and hold one and he'd be presumed taking a break, whether authorized or not. He could also offer one and grunt to kill five seconds of interaction, then pretend not to speak the language. If he tossed a few broken words out and was happy to share his smokes, few would question him. In fact, he was getting the hang of this. Act as if you belong and people assume you do.

He saw *Chernomertvetz* quite far out, past a much larger cargo craft named *Yebar' Volgi*, a huge ocean freighter, and another huge ship he couldn't identify. The *Chernomertvetz* was small in comparison, only about two hundred feet long. Even from this far away in fog, she was worn and old, with rust running down her anchor ports.

Now to find a place to observe from. There were plenty of conex containers in rows, awaiting loading or removal. There were also stacks of crates and drums awaiting palletization. To skulk around anything would be to suggest an intent to steal. The best cover was just to stand out in front, shirking, leaning against the corner of a conex. It was wet with mist, but that was a minor issue. It didn't bother Kyle, and it didn't bother the men and few women who worked here, who were rough and burly and used to working in all weather.

Occasionally, Kyle nodded back at an passer-by. Someone made a fingers to lips gesture for a cigarette, and he shrugged and shook his head. Apart from that, nothing to speak of happened for an hour. *Chernomertvetz* was tied up and the only action was the clattering of hatches and planks preparing for a massive offload. The sounds were discernible with effort and observation, because a bigger, closer ship was undergoing the same preparation. Then there were several powering in or out of the harbor.

It was quite practical for Kyle to look around, surreptitiously watching from the corners of his eyes while not actually staring directly. But after an hour of even that, he was gathering more curious looks than he thought was healthy, and moved a little closer and across the way. *Chernomertvetz* was well to his left, at nine o'clock to him. He had a good view of her entire side, as cranes started swinging into place and pulling loads from her holds.

He hadn't been told, but assumed there'd be other cargo, most of it legitimate. Either it would be done as cover, or the crew really might not know what was being carried, apart from one or two conspirators. So it was no surprise to see several large containers being withdrawn. He used the camera without flash to get several pictures, trying to time them for when no observers were looking in his direction. He was point-shooting rather than risk raising it to his face. It was entirely possible people snapped photos all the time, but probably not lone men leaning against boxes, with no apparent job waiting and using a US$1000 camera set for infrared as well as visible frequencies.

After five loads of the front crane, something came up that caught Kyle's interest.

That was definitely a pallet inside plastic. It looked like wooden crates, being too light in color for cardboard, and with corners too sharp. But was it the right package? The only way to tell would be to follow it, and there were a lot of trucks along here.

It was down behind an old Mercedes box van and being stripped to load individually. That was likely a good indication, he thought. It would be easier to load the whole pallet onto a larger vehicle, which would mean cheaper. To break this up here indicated a desire to conceal it shortly, and the small enclosed truck meant they didn't want it seen.

He made a quick note of the license plate on the blunt-nosed vehicle, noted the color—dark blue—and turned casually back the way he'd come.

Steady walk, he reminded himself. To run would attract attention. But he did need to walk briskly. He stretched out his pace, being careful of his footing and trying to find a good route. He wanted one that was reasonably direct, but wasn't an obvious beeline out.

He was a good halfway out, striding through the rail yard, when two men came toward him. He quivered alert, in case they were port guards or thugs from his quarry. But they waved casually for attention. He shook an arm back and kept walking.

One of them shouted, "Ţigară?" *Cigarette?*

"Îmi pare rău," he replied. *Sorry.* It might have been a simple attempt to mooch, but they kept getting closer.

Mugging in progress, he thought. Should he run, fight, or worse?

The decision wasn't an easy one, but there were matters at stake here. He had to get this info out and follow up on it. He couldn't be dragged in locally or he'd blow the whole mission. These men weren't his friends and did mean ill. He couldn't think of a way out that was particularly safe. So he'd have to do something obvious and hope to be gone before it was discovered. He scanned for witnesses, backup, anything that might change his decision. Then, sighing, he slipped his hand inside his coat for his pistol.

In a gully between tracks, about three feet deep, wet and muddy, he saw a section of slender pipe. Perhaps eighteen inches long, one inch diameter, and thick walled. That should help. He bent and scooped it as he dropped down into the rut, then stood back up with it in his left hand. He laid it casually over his shoulder and walked toward the two probable hostiles. Would it work?

They hesitated for just a moment as he raised the pipe. Then they resumed their approach, but at a slower pace.

Kyle increased his and plastered a smile on his face. *Look at the man with the grin and the pipe. He's hoping for a good rumble to settle his late dinner. You can be his playmates. Come on, you bastards, run. Don't make me shoot you.*

Because that was the only alternative he could think of—shoot them with a silenced .45 and hope no one noticed until he was gone. Unless a passerby interfered before the fight started by being awkwardly present, he would have to take them out. And he wasn't sure they didn't have clubs or knives or even guns of their own. Probably not guns, but he couldn't risk his mission over it.

In another moment, the two had made their own calculations, and decided Kyle was too eager to meet them. They angled sharply away to seek easier prey.

Smart move, Kyle thought. *For all of us.*

9

WADE WAS WAITING AND WATCHING. AS Kyle approached, he slid over to the passenger side.

"It's a Mercedes box van, about ten years old. Last I saw, it was rolling down the access road, and should have come out there," he pointed to the second gate north. "Did you see it?"

"Yes, just a few minutes ago," Wade said.

"Carefully, then. We don't want to ride up on it." Kyle acknowledged and eased into gear. He left the headlights off, steering carefully by the lights glaring through gaps in the skyline. He coasted slowly out to where he could see the road.

"There," Wade said, and pointed. "That's them."

"I'll give them a bit," Kyle said. "Do we know what main route they have to take?"

"If they go straight, it's this one," Wade said,

pointing at the map, then zooming in with a flick of fingers. "Toward Tulcea, Braila, or Bucharest."

"Four-lane?"

"To start with."

"Okay, call Cafferty, tell him. We're going to need backup."

Wade pulled out his phone. "Curtis here. We're following them onto the E Sixty. We'll need support . . . yes . . . understood . . . We'll do what we can. Yes, sir." He clicked off and said, "Fun."

"What?"

"He says they can pick up in either town, but don't have anyone nearby. We'll have to follow them ourselves for a while. And we're supposed to do that without being noticed?" Wade asked. "I think they overestimate our chances."

"No, we can do it," Kyle said. "In theory, we should have three to five vehicles. Anytime they turn, the first vehicle goes straight, then joins the back of the pack. If they go straight long enough to get suspicious of a tail, one car will turn off and then rejoin. By varying the passenger silhouette, we'd track them for hundreds of kilometers and not be noticed."

"Makes sense," Wade said. "And how do we do it with just two Americans, one black and one white, in a late model Audi?"

"Easy," Kyle said. "Warm up the NVGs and see how the landscape looks." They were onto the highway now, staying well back. It was an easy pursuit, for the moment.

"Ah, I catch your drift. We douse the lights and follow in the dark, and occasionally put them back on as we pass side roads." He fumbled in back for a moment, then sat up again with a pair of goggles. He snugged the straps on his head and adjusted them.

"That's it," Kyle said. "Though you may have to bail out and watch for clues if they stop somewhere."

"Sure. I could use more exercise." He removed the goggles and said, "They're good to go. Want them now?" There were still some streetlights along here, but it didn't seem they'd last long. The road was narrowing to two lanes again.

"No, keep them ready," Kyle said. "I may have only a second or two to kill the lights, you slip them on my head and I'll get them in place before running off the road."

"Before would be good," Wade agreed. "What do we do if they have sentries or night vision of their own?"

"Abort, shoot our way out or die."

"Great. The Truth. Now tell me some cheerful BS so I don't worry."

"We'll pretend we're lost tourists looking at exotic rabbits by starlight. Sort of like birdwatchers, but not as cool."

"There's people *less* cool than birdwatchers?"

"Politicians, reporters, and terrorists at the very least."

"Point made," Wade nodded.

The truck was moving at a good clip. Speed limits weren't enforced much, Kyle seemed to remember. Nor was there much need. The driver of the beat-up old Mercedes truck braked hard before bends and turns, then powered through them, the box back swaying dangerously over rippling, distorted tires. He didn't seem too worried about his cargo.

"Careless driver," he said.

"Maybe it's a decoy?"

"Could be," Kyle nodded. "But that's not something we can decide en route. Maybe the guy's just an idiot with no imagination." TNT and most other explosives were quite stable. The risk of explosion was almost nonexistent. But a crash and spill would blow any cover available. "Maybe he has to be there on a stiff schedule. Doesn't matter. We're here, we'll follow them. Hand me the goggles, I'm going to shut off the lights around this bend." There was a small but obvious side road that made a convenient excuse for them to "turn off" and leave dark emptiness on the road.

Wade reached back, where he had laid out goggles, gear, and weapons like surgical tools, ready at a moment's notice. It would really screw them if they did get pulled over, of course. On the other hand, if US$25 got one out of drunk driving, a couple of hundred cash, name drops about the embassy and references to the DEA had a decent chance of getting them left alone. If not . . . no one had claimed the mission was without risk.

"Here you go," he said, as he slid the goggles into the space between Kyle's head and the roof.

Kyle grasped them and drew them down over his eyes. "There," he said. Wade grabbed them and started adjusting the head harness into place, while Kyle flipped off the lights. He'd been blind for only a second, and was still in control of the vehicle. As the curve straightened out, their quarry became visible again, taillights ahead of them.

"Going to do this for a while?" Wade asked.

"As long as we can get away with. If they don't have reason to notice a vehicle behind them, they won't pay attention when we are in sight. We should be fine."

"Until we get close and the shooting starts," Wade commented.

"Yes," Kyle agreed with a single nod.

They drove in silence for several minutes, Wade looking at maps and watching the taillights, Kyle keeping his distance steady and looking for the obvious dangers of people turning in front of them, and for the edge of the road, which disappeared at times and even the enhanced vision of the goggles didn't show.

Then the lights ahead slewed.

"They're turning off," Wade advised and grabbed the laptop back from his knees.

"I see," Kyle said. "Where are they heading?"

"Inland. In toward the mountains."

"Isn't that where they keep disappearing?"

"I believe so."

"Tell Cafferty."

"Will do," Wade agreed, and reached for his phone. "Wade Curtis here. They're heading along Route Sixty toward Bucharest . . . Yes . . . will do." He clicked off. "He suspects they'll go past Bucharest to Braşov area, and will arrange to get someone there in the next day or so."

"The next day or so?" Kyle asked incredulously. "That's a long time."

"I gather he's shorthanded and we're about it."

"Uncle Sam certainly has faith in our ability. Too much, maybe." He drifted into the turn, watching for oncoming cars, whose drivers would have no idea he was there until they wound up in a torn sheet-metal embrace.

"So we do what we can," Wade said. His voice was calm, but there was a hint of strain, and Kyle smiled. He could see adequately. Wade still was using his Mod 1 eyeballs to scan with. This had to be a bit disturbing for him.

The PVS7-XR5 night vision enabled Kyle to see reasonably well by the stars and moon. Occasional oncoming vehicles' headlights caused the goggles to shift settings, which gave them some tense moments where he was driving by feel on a narrow road, with no shoulder and a foot drop into woods at the side. Add to that driving on the "wrong" side of the road, and it was exciting, and not in a good way. Some on-coming traffic appeared not to see them, but several drivers honked their horns.

"Sooner or later someone is going to hit us, report us, or figure out we're up to something," Kyle said.

"Yeah. 'Why isn't the CIA handling this?' he asks again."

"I get the impression most spooks are computer nerds, not tuxedo-clad, stone-cold killers," Kyle said. "I also get the impression that whether this works or not, we'll be referred to in whatever news does get out as 'CIA assassins,' and that the Agency will take the credit publicly." He eased the wheel to the right, trying to avoid getting too close to the edge. His American driving instincts were pushing him to the left, to avoid the "edge" on the right. It was going to take a lot more hours of driving to get used to doing it the "wrong" way, especially under stress.

"No bet," Wade said. "As long as the Army credits us as due. And maybe throws in a follow-up mission looking for terrorists at a bikini-judging contest in Aruba . . ."

"Miss Nude Bomber, maybe?"

"Hmm . . . we'd have to search them. Carefully."

"Of course," Kyle agreed. Jokes were necessary despite the mission. Or maybe because of it.

Anything that relieved a little stress would help. Because of the goggles, he could only see the layered green world of night vision ahead and nothing to the sides. Wade's voice and the engine noise were his lifeline to reality. They'd tried the radio and given up. It was Italian pop and some obnoxious Russian stuff, neither of which they wanted to listen to.

The smaller, rougher road wove through small towns, where it would circle the town square or go through a roundabout. They paralleled the Ialomita River for some time, then turned roughly northwest.

"Near as I can tell," Wade said, "we're bypassing Bucharest to its north."

"That would make sense," Kyle agreed. "If they're headed for Sighişoara or the mountains."

"Not as fast, but less traffic and visibility, easier to find a tail—"

"Us," Kyle interrupted with a grin.

"Us," Wade agreed. "And it avoids accidents or stops where someone would see a lot of evidence. If they have trouble out here, they're less likely to be seen and can hide bodies."

"That's so reassuring," Kyle said. "Also consider that they may have a tail to look for tails."

"Joy," Wade replied and stopped talking.

Eventually, they rejoined the E60 and turned right, continuing northwest.

"Seems to agree with the Sighişoara theory," Kyle said. "If I recall the map."

"Right here," Wade said, angling the laptop. Kyle checked the road was straight, flipped up the goggles, looked at the route Wade traced with his finger, then turned quickly back to the road.

It was a long drive. At times they'd reach speeds of 150km/h or more. Then they'd hit hills or curves and drop down below 70. There were several tense instances where the truck would pass a slow-moving car right before a series of rises or bends that precluded visibility and passing. Twice, Wade leaned far out the window to try to see ahead for Kyle's benefit. They'd hit a section just long enough for bravery and urgency to overcome common sense and rip past whichever vehicle had hindered them, usually to shouts and honks about headlights.

Again they took a narrower local road, and again Wade reported it to Cafferty. "He says to be alert for sudden turns. They're likely to try to get on E Seventy," he relayed to Kyle.

"Understood." And it would be easy along here. It twisted and wove and the road was rising.

They did turn left onto another local road, and it was even rougher than the routes so far. The car crunched over loose and crumbled asphalt, occasionally skittering and skidding over gravel from underneath. There were potholes to dodge and cracks that let chunks of the road edges yawn dangerously away from the main bed.

The road narrowed and wound. Then up ahead there was an obstacle, and oncoming lights. Kyle braked hard and kept a good distance back from the slow-moving thing ahead, which resolved into a horse-drawn cart out way too late and with no reflectors or lights. It was far to the left, but there was still a considerable risk of someone smashing into it. The oncoming car whipped past and honked, whether at the cart driver or Kyle was impossible to tell. The cartman swore and shook his fist at the vehicle, then shouted something at Kyle as he powered around and back up to speed. He pulled into another curve and smiled. Everyone out driving tonight was an idiot, it seemed, himself included.

Another oncoming car flashed its lights at them as it approached. Then it was past, and its brake lights glowed brightly in the mirror as it slewed and turned. It was only a couple of hundred yards behind when it finished the maneuver. Then it started closing the gap, lights on high and a spotlight thrown in. Kyle flipped the mirror down to avoid the glare.

"Ah, hell," Kyle said. Worse profanity wasn't really needed. This had been almost inevitable.

"Police?" Wade asked.

"Dunno, but probably." The irony was perverse. Had they been using headlights, this would have been less likely. On the other hand, they might have been nailed that way, too. Sometimes, every answer was wrong.

Then the car's lights went out. Behind Kyle

and Wade the back window exploded. Cold wind started roaring in.

"Shots fired!" Wade said needlessly. "I think they've got night vision, too."

"Not cops!" Kyle said, also needlessly.

"How? Scanner? Spooks at police headquarters heard a complaint? Looking for interference?"

"Who cares?" Kyle shouted.

"Right. Want me to shoot?" Wade asked, quickly over his surprise.

"If you'd be so kind," Kyle yelled, shifting down and nailing the gas. Wade fell against his seat as the acceleration caught him. He'd been reaching for the blankets covering the rifle in the footwell.

In seconds he had it, had clicked the scope on, and was drawing it up into shooting position. He fell flat and lowered the weapon but kept hold of it as two more shots crashed by. One took out more glass and starred the windshield. The other threw sparks from the side pillar, exiting with a scream.

"Shit!" he said, yanking the rifle back up.

The best thing to do when being shot at is to move quickly, keep moving, and not sit still and take it. But the shattered and open back window was a psychological hole that made things seem that much more vulnerable. Kyle's neck and back were itching madly, and his shoulder muscles twitched in fear. He steeled himself to keep driving and let Wade shoot, and pulled the mirror roughly back into place. At least he had an idea of what was going on behind.

The fuzzy monochrome and shadows inside the car made it hard to tell, but it seemed to contain three or four people, and rifles stuck up from at least two of them. Or maybe submachine guns with long barrels or suppressors. They seemed a bit short and thick for proper rifles. But whatever they were, they could definitely shoot right through the car, and through the Rangers.

"We need police-type body armor, thin and under the clothes. Put it on the list," Kyle said.

"Sure, when we get back," Wade said. "Wonder if the embassy can get us some."

"Have to hope so," Kyle said. "But we need it now."

He didn't want to close up on the truck and let them trap him, possibly with a vehicle in the other lane, either a conspirator or convenient civilian. But he didn't want to let their tail get up close where shooting was more accurate, or ramming became possible. It occurred to him also that they might have incendiary ammo and aim for the fuel tank.

Maybe he *could* get a bit closer to the truck, he thought. It was still a kilometer or more ahead, as he came over a rise in the road at better than 90 mph, almost 160 km/h. Then he had to turn hard, because the road had a reverse camber and they were floating, drifting off to the left, where very hard trees awaited them.

The road leveled back out and another round

tore through and punched a hole in the left side of the windshield. Some scattered bits of fluffy padding came from Wade's seat. He didn't seem to notice, and sat up with the AK.

He had to shout to be heard over the roar of wind and engine. "We've got enough of a problem with the damage to this vehicle. If I shoot the driver or block, we'll have a major incident. I'm going to try for a tire."

"Makes sense," Kyle said. "Just don't take too long."

"Working on it," Wade replied, his nod unseen. "Easier with the back window gone. Get me a bend in the road so I have a better profile to shoot at. Moving," he announced, and shimmied between the seats, his thigh dangerously close to the gear shift. The passenger seat dropped as he yanked the recline lever, then he eased back a bit more.

Two more shots cracked through the vehicle, and Kyle grimaced, gripping the wheel until his knuckles turned white. Just because he'd been shot at before didn't mean he enjoyed it. But he was veteran enough to not flinch, and kept the car tightly controlled as they took a sharp bend to the right.

"Kick ass!" Wade said, and fired. The round popped through the suppressor, the bolt clacked as it cycled, and he immediately started squirming back into the front seat. "That'll teach the bastards to shoot at us!"

Though that did leave the minor matter of the

Rangers' riddled ride. Front and rear glass were missing, and there was at least one small-caliber hole visible.

"We going to keep trailing?" Wade asked over the wind noise.

"Nothing else we can do," Kyle said. "That was a great shot."

"Thanks. They survived from pity," Wade said. "It's a pity I had to be discreet."

"Right. The question is, did our boys in the truck get the message, do they know we took care of their buddies, and will they do anything to us? Or just try to get away?" There were enough small side roads that anything was possible, and Kyle was not about to drive into a potential ambush. They might be Rangers and snipers, but they were only two men, and a squad of men with submachine guns could kill them handily in the woods.

"Dunno. But I assume they know we're here," Wade said. He kept the rifle on his lap, muzzle down at the footwell. He returned the seat upright.

"Yeah," Kyle said shortly. Things always went to hell, that was a given. So it wasn't really a surprise to be driving across Romania in a car shot to hell without approval of the local government, carrying unauthorized weapons.

Not surprising, but aggravating.

The truck's driver seemed to know he was being followed. He increased speed until the whole van shimmied and tilted on the curves.

Perhaps he could catch a glimpse of reflected moon off the Audi. Or he may have had a spotter of his own with night vision. Whatever was involved, he was driving recklessly.

Kyle reflected on how a wreck would leave crates of TNT on the road, to be seized by the Romanians. If the driver and passengers were injured, they could just be left there to be dealt with locally.

On the other hand, he wasn't authorized to make that decision. "Call Cafferty," he said. "Ask him about wrecking them."

"Calling," Wade said. "Curtis here. Question. If we can harass the target into an accident, should we? . . . Yes, that's what we were wondering. Let me give you our current location while we're on air." He read off the road and approximate grid. "Yes, we'll try. We just had an encounter with a car of unfriendlies. They were encouraged to lose a tire . . . No, nothing traceable to us . . . Will do. Out." He turned to Kyle and said, "He says a wreck would be of immediate help if all else fails, but he'd prefer to know where they're going. So pursue if possible. If we can't maintain pursuit, we're authorized to shoot out a tire or otherwise cause a wreck, then find a hotel and hide while he cleans up the mess. I gather he really doesn't want us to do that."

"Roger that," Kyle said. So dammit, he'd stay on top of them and try not to spook them too much.

Every time they hit a town, he had to wonder

if the truck was going to stop, turn off, meet up with additional forces or do something totally unpredictable. Fatigue was getting to him, his eyeballs gritty and hurting from the monochromatic vision the NVGs allowed. He drifted occasionally, and took two or three seconds to recover each time. Thought processes slowing, he realized. If he reached the hallucination stage, he'd have to make a quick stop and let Wade drive. Though Wade wasn't in much better shape.

"It just occurred to me that we have to lose this car when we do stop," Kyle said. The wind roaring throughout might have seemed an obvious hint, but they'd become used to it and were still running on endorphins from the battle.

"Shit, that's right," Wade said. "Its blatantly obvious what happened and will get questions asked."

"Questions we don't want to answer, even if it's, 'We were hijacked and drove fast.'"

"Yeah, not even that," Wade agreed. "What do we do?"

Kyle realized the battle had him hyped, and the untraditional battlefield had him confused. On top of fatigue, he was barely tracking. "You'll drive when we get close, drop me off to get a room. I'll walk in with a backpack. Not too uncommon. Then I'll call and tell you where, and you follow along."

"Sounds good. But it's damned late."

"Yeah, I know," Kyle said. "Nothing we can do about that."

"Town ahead. Damn, we've come a long way."

"Probably three hundred and fifty kilometers, two hundred and ten miles," Wade said. "It's five A.M., did you know that?"

"I didn't," Kyle said. "This would be a three- to four-hour drive back home. Here it's been six already."

"How are you holding up?"

"Groggy," Kyle admitted. "But not groggy enough to change drivers. We'll swap if they stop, if you're up to it."

"Not really, but I'm probably in better shape, since I haven't been driving. Curve up ahead."

"I see it," Kyle said. "Looks like they're turning again. I see brake lights."

"I think that's E Seventy they're turning on," Wade said. "South again. I'm really wondering if this is a decoy, except Cafferty seems to think this is part of their route."

"He knows more than we do. We trust him," Kyle said. "Not much point if we don't."

"True."

Every town was starting to look the same to Kyle, and all the kilometers of forest. He was relying on Wade to keep him informed. All his attention was on staying on the road.

"Heading into Bran," Wade said. "Tiny town, tourist attraction."

"What's here?"

"An old castle, allegedly used by Dracula during the war with the Turks. You should know this, Vampire Hunter."

"Yeah, vampires." He longed to say something witty, but his brain was fried.

Ahead, the road turned and the speed limit dropped. The truck braked hard as it hit the curve, then accelerated into town.

"That's a bit fast," Kyle said. "I'd say they do know we're after them. Maybe we can scare them into doing something stupid."

"Yeah," Wade said, "or into just driving on through the day, while everyone looks at the car with the windows missing."

"Right."

Then they were in town proper, the road a long curve ahead and to the left. The truck was three stops ahead of them. Then it turned off. Kyle had already braked for a sign and couldn't maneuver quickly.

"Got them," Wade said. "Left."

"Roger." He revved up and pulled ahead hard, tires squealing slightly. He ran through two signs as he flipped the lights back off and dropped the goggles down. They were close enough now that any sign of them would be a warning.

He came to the intersection, yanked the wheel left and took the turn . . .

Nothing.

"So where did they go?" He asked, hoping Wade had seen them.

"Dunno."

"Dammit! I don't want to say we lost them!"

"I'd guess another turn, then another. Their best bet would be to zigzag so we're always a street behind."

"Let's go six blocks fast and wait," he decided.

It wasn't as easy as that. The blocks weren't necessarily square or even. But he found another cross street that was fairly straight and sat there at the intersection, waiting.

After five minutes, it was fairly obvious the truck was either stopped somewhere in the area, or had evaded and left.

"Circle the area a few times," Wade suggested. "There's not much traffic out this morning."

"Good idea. Route?"

Wade read off directions and they drove around the village then crisscrossed it, looking for any sign of the truck or its lights. After that, they returned to where they'd lost sight and patrolled street by street.

"Nothing," Kyle said in disgust. "Do we wake Cafferty?"

"I'd say so. He needs to know."

"Yeah," Kyle agreed. "Dammit, I hate to fail."

"I got some photos. Maybe he can get something from that."

"We'll see. I'm going to stop here and call."

"Okay."

From a steep graveled roadside that wasn't really a shoulder, he punched his phone while Wade packed weapons away.

"Cafferty," was the sleepy reply. It was clear he hadn't actually gotten any sleep.

"Lost them," Kyle said. There was no point in wasting time.

"Shit. Where?"

"Here in Bran. They turned, they disappeared. We were about sixty seconds behind and slowed to maintain distance."

"Dammit," Cafferty groused. "This is my fault for not having more backup. There's only so much you can do with one vehicle."

"Well, we had them and lost them," Kyle said.

"Yeah, but this has happened before. Always in that area—Bran, Braşov, Codlea, they make turns in town and poof! Gone. Dammit." He really sounded disgusted.

"What should we do?" Kyle asked.

"Get a room and stay in the area. They may show up. Can you look around in daylight? I know it sounds stupid, but they can't hide the vehicle all the time, and even if they stole it or rented it, it'll give us more of a lead."

"Yeah, we can do that. Do you have the images we sent?" he asked.

"I do, but there's nothing I can get from them. I'm having them looked at by experts, but it will take time. Later will be better. And you guys will be rested."

"Roger that," Kyle said. He realized he was

absolutely wiped out, now that they'd stopped the chase. "I'll ping you early."

"Only if you find something," Cafferty said. "I need sleep, too."

"Right, now what about the car?" he asked.

"What about it?" Cafferty asked.

"Shot up," Kyle reminded him.

"Oh, that. Dammit, I forgot." There was clear strain in his voice. "Abandon it, see if you can wreck it a bit against a pole or hillside. I'll take it from there. Hold on." There was mumbling off phone, then he said, "Call Sam when you get lodged and he will deliver another car to you. He'll be there in about four hours."

"Will do. Out."

Kyle wanted a good idea of who would have access to their room, and a certain amount of visibility made it harder for people to either sneak up or take gear out. He'd prefer a little strip motel.

It wasn't like America, though. This might be a tourist area, but it was also the absolute ass end of nowhere. Actually, it wasn't. The Afghan border was the absolute ass end of nowhere. Kyle had been there. But this was very sparsely popu-lated and not the type of place with twenty-four-hour desk staff. The hotel they chose was small, old, and seemed to be based in a large house broken into suites. But there was parking out-side, so there was a certain amount of clear space. He went in to register while Wade took the car to its grave. It seemed unfair. The vehicle had seen them through a long chase and was to be tossed aside. Their first casualty, it felt like.

Still, better the car than the people they'd lost in the past.

Several minutes of knocking got someone to rise. A middle-aged woman came to the door in a robe, then put on her business smile. Kyle didn't even haggle over the rate. Better to be thought a dumb tourist. It wasn't his money, and she was quite helpful. He arranged for two nights for now, paid her in euros and asked about somewhere to do laundry before continuing the "hike" he and his partner were on, and did she know if they could get batteries for their cameras here? Yes, his partner was just behind, having stopped to get some early-morning shots of the castle.

Once he had the key, he went straight back to the room and flashed the lights through the open curtain. Wade arrived in moments and was let in. The obvious camera cases with the backpack meant no reason for anyone to question the padded "suitcase" that held the rifles.

"There's a tub, but no shower," Kyle told him. "Make it fast, I'm about to die from lack of sleep."

"Will do."

While Wade splashed in the old iron tub, Kyle called back.

"This is Sam."

"Sam, Kyle. I've got our hotel info."

"Go ahead." Sam was reticent but alert, and sounded competent.

Kyle gave him the address and rough directions.

"Okay, I'll be there in four hours," Sam said.

Kyle bathed after Wade finished. Water cooled quickly in the metal tub, and it just wasn't efficient to get clean while sitting in water with soap and sweat in it. But it was what was available, and better than the last assignment. He scrubbed and got out. Shaving wasn't necessary, he could do that later. In fact, three days of beard made him look very unmilitary. He toweled off and headed for bed.

Wade looked up from the laptop. "Sleep until ten, then go looking?"

"What time is it now? Six? Yeah. That's when Sam gets here, anyway."

10

THEY WEREN'T WELL-RESTED AT TEN, BUT were functional. Kyle knew it was a false feeling of refreshment, but he could go another twenty-four hours at this point if he had to.

Sam was waiting in the car, and drove them to a nearby café. "Morning," he said. "Sorry things are screwed up. The boss is feeling guilty over it."

"Why him? We're the ones who lost track of the truck," Kyle said, disgust tingeing his voice.

"You followed them this far and fought off pursuit. I'm impressed," their host said.

Sam was short, shorter than Cafferty, and softly overweight rather than fat. He had freckles and reddish hair and might be thirty. What he was beyond a general factotum hadn't been said. But he sounded as if he knew what was happening.

"Still," Kyle said, "I'd like to succeed at least half the time when I'm given a location and target. Dunno about Wade."

"Oh, count me in on the frustrated side," Wade said. "I know I should be philosophical about it, but . . ."

"Yeah, we've been having that for years," Sam said with a grimace. "But we'll get there."

They ate brunch at the café, loading up on pastries and tea. Sam made a big show of pointing out sites on a map and suggesting "photo angles" for them. It was likely a meaningless cover, but it couldn't hurt. It wasn't so much the government they were worried about, sluggish juggernaut that it was, but that if someone saw three American men talking without a good explanation, they'd be suspicious to the terrorists, if they had observers around.

They split afterward, Sam heading for the bus stop that would take him back to Bucharest, and the snipers to the car, another Audi. They made another tour of the village, up and down streets, looking closely at garages or alleys that might hold a large truck. They found nothing.

"Place looks like it's frozen in the nineteen fifties," Wade said.

"Yeah. Let's go rest and think." Four hours' sleep after a grueling drive and shootout had not been enough.

They'd just entered the room when Kyle's phone buzzed.

"Monroe," he answered.

"Yeah, it's Cafferty. Got anything?"

"Replacement car. Nothing on the bad guys."

"Damn. I'm going to see about some satellite

imagery. Probably a waste, but I've got to spend the money to be sure."

"Any word from our friends at sea?" Kyle asked.

"No. Or rather, nothing new. Near as we can tell, that truck was definitely the shipment."

"Damn," Kyle said. He was saying it a lot, but it fit.

They went back to the room and napped. While being cooped in a hotel had been a drain on them before, it was a chance to rest now. Once the action started, Kyle didn't have any trouble adapting to the local conditions. They'd been up all night, and now they needed rest. With years of military experience, all he had to do was lie down and shift against the pillow. He was out at once.

He woke two hours later, head spinning slightly but in far better shape than he had been. Once fed another meal, he should be back to himself again. Wade was stirring but still dazed, so Kyle left him alone to wake up gradually. Meanwhile, he grabbed the books they'd been using for reference and resumed reading. More intelligence was always a good idea; there wasn't much else to do and he liked reading. Some people thought he read too much.

As with their last mission, they had tour guides and phrase books. While not in-depth, they were excellent for getting an overview in simple terms and for hitting the high points. They had several different ones, from little pocket-size language summaries to atlas-size map and photo collections.

Kyle leaned back against the bed and flipped open one of the little pocket guides. It mentioned the castles in the area, here and at Braşov, then others elsewhere. There were crude, unscaled floor plans that were hard to read on a page three inches high, and rough historical and "Did you know?" sidebars to provide dinner conversation.

As he read through the section on Bran Castle, a phrase in the book caught his eye. Then another one. They connected, and an idea formed. It was insane, and he had to run through it twice with the same solution to decide it wasn't as crazy as it might seem. There was a lot of sense to it. Also a lot of insanity.

Wade yawned and stretched. "Think I'm done sleeping," he grumbled deeply. It was one of the few times Kyle could recall him being less than cheerful.

"Well, then get up, sleeping ugly."

"Right. I can't say you're my prime choice of roommates, either. You snore. Off key. Without any rhythm."

"I'm white," Kyle said.

"Ah, yes. You know how you can tell if a machinegunner's white?"

"No, how?" he asked. This should be good.

"He fires a burst of six. A burst of seven. A burst of five. A burst of six."

"That's obscure," he said. The joke had to do with white men and rhythm.

"Hey, it's hard to make fun of people who are that boring."

"No argument here," Kyle said.

He picked up his phone and called again. Cafferty answered, and Kyle asked, "Any word on the truck?"

"No, nothing."

"Okay, can you tell me where you've seen it?"

"Bran, Braşov, Codlea, Râşnov, Zărneşti, and Fundata, and then it disappears. Evasive turns and then gone."

"But always in this area?"

"Yes," Cafferty confirmed. "We've seen them up there, but we're not sure where. It has to be somewhere up in the mountains, because we've kept a good eye on the town."

"We'll stay here today," Kyle decided. "Tonight we'll look around."

"Got some ideas?" Cafferty asked, probing.

"A couple. Nothing concrete yet, and I don't want to get your hopes up." *And I don't want you thinking I'm a loon*, he thought to himself. "I'll give you an update when I have one."

"Thanks."

After they disconnected, he turned to Wade and said, "I need some supplies. Back soon."

"Oh? What are you going to—"

But Kyle was already out and didn't reply. A brief walk took him past three little shops.

It wasn't hard to find a more detailed map of the area, as well as a guide and another, larger floor plan of the castle. Everything was set up for tourists, so all the books were in Romanian, French, English, and German. Some were in Italian and Russian. But the ones with English content were all he was interested in. Of course, being tourist oriented, most of them lacked proper scales and details. But familiarity was necessary, even if it was incomplete. He paid in cash and hurried back.

"Whatcha got?" Wade asked as he charged in.

"Log on, please, and do a search for Castle Bran."

"Okay. I see you have more guidebooks," Wade said.

"Yes. I was thinking about secret passages underneath."

"Secret . . . Man, you've flipped."

"You think so?" Kyle asked with a grin. "Because according to Lonely Planet, there's a labyrinth of passages concealed by the fountain in the courtyard."

"Really?" Wade asked. He looked stunned.

"Really. Abandoned and not used. Not much more information than that, which means no one goes there."

"Search engine says . . . passageways." He clicked several links into other windows and explored for several minutes. "No maps. Lots of mentions. A couple of bad photographs from people who went in a few feet."

"Jackpot."

"You really think they're hiding in the castle?"

"I'd do it," Kyle said. "It's creepy, intimidating, and the local staff are predictable. That makes it easy to be discreet. Then there's those passages underneath, that are just closed off and ignored. The staff *never* goes there, or there'd be mention and maps. No one else can get down there, and anyone who does can be easily removed and hidden. Wouldn't be surprised to find a few bodies down there when we go in."

"*When* we go in? Man, you are nuts!" Wade said.

"If there's nothing there, we've got nothing to be afraid of," Kyle said, wishing he believed it. The whole thing was creepier than all hell. But it was logical, if he could accept the logic. "If there's something there, we need to observe at the very least, snatch someone, or make a kill."

"And if we wind up as more of those bodies? What then?"

"Then zey dreenk our bllluuud!" Kyle replied in a sonorous voice, hoping he could reassure himself.

"Right. Actually, if I *were* hiding down there, I think I'd deliberately drain a few bodies just to scare others away," Wade said.

"Yes, that's possible," Kyle pondered. "Anything that will scare the shit out of people and is so ridiculous no one else will believe it. So we want a camera, weapons and IR. There's no ambient light at all for starlight."

"And body armor and a neck guard and garlic . . ." Wade added.

"So, I need to call Cafferty and tell him."

"He's going to think you're nuts," Wade said.

"Probably."

"*I* think you're nuts."

"Hell, we're both nuts to be in this job."

"Yeah, but that's a good kind of nuts. Your way is just weird."

"Right," Kyle grinned as he punched the phone.

"Cafferty," was the answer.

"Mick, this is Kyle. What do you know about the passageways under Castle Bran?"

"Under . . . nothing other than that they're sealed off."

"Yeah, well apparently you can get in. There's a kid online with some pictures, and mention of them three or four places. Everyone knows they're there, but no one goes down there."

"And you think that's where they're hiding?"

"Who'd look there?" he asked, just as he'd asked Wade.

Cafferty paused for a long moment. "Damned good point. If there's rooms or caverns, they could have operations there, not be seen on satellite or by plane, not have much chemical leakage . . . I think you're on to something."

"We're going to check it out tonight," Kyle said, thrilled at the validation of his theory, and trying to cover up his nerves. "Unless you want us to wait?"

"That depends. Can you do it discreetly, without making an incident?"

"That's the plan. I'm not going to shoot any

doors open or crack any walls. If we can't find anything without making a mess, we'll come back and let you know."

"Go ahead, then. I'll make a note of it right now. When will you check in?"

"Dunno. The phones won't work under there, I'm sure. Figure no more than twenty-four hours or there's a problem."

"Understood. Call me with anything whenever you can."

"Will do. Out."

Turning back to Wade, he said, "You know, one of the big problems is transport. We have to have a car to hide the weapons in, instead of taking them on trains or in taxis . . ."

"But we can't find parking spaces for cars like we can in America," Wade supplied.

"Right."

"We also can't add too many more men, or it becomes an obvious military operation," Wade said. "This really isn't an Army job."

"Yeah, I know," Kyle said, and was quiet again. Less screwed up than last time, but still a mess.

Wade interrupted with, "So how do we get into the castle? Try to get in on a tour and slip off somewhere?"

"That's possible," Kyle said. "I'm sure we could do it. But there's a lot of risk of being seen, or locked in. I think we should try from outside, through that entrance in the park. If we can get in, we should be able to get out, and it's outside, so we can make a little noise if needed."

"I have to wonder why that's there. I mean, it's too close and too obvious to be an escape route."

"Dunno. Maintenance for the well, maybe? Or . . ." he paused for a moment, ". . . set with traps to stop people who think they're smart. Or at least it is now if it wasn't before."

"That's a good bet," Wade said. "And if there are nasties down there, they're almost certain to have thought of that."

"So we'll take it under consideration."

"Tomorrow night, then?"

"No. Now. They could get more reinforcements. Let's get the weapons and move."

"Roger that."

They gathered up cameras, weapons, water, and snacks. They dressed and carried gloves to go with their boots, and darkened their faces slightly with paint. "Not real camo, just enough to dull our faces down, so we can wipe it off in a hurry and blend back in as civvies," Kyle said.

"Got it. Though I doubt many civvie backpackers are out this late with weapons," Wade said.

By 1 A.M., they were sneaking toward the entrance in the park, armed and ready.

"We don't want to spook the neighbors' dogs," Wade said. There were houses within a quarter mile of the castle.

"We'll just have to be slow and quiet." It occurred to him they should have asked for more backup for insertion. It was risky to walk all that way equipped as they were, but the car, as he'd noted, would be visible. The parking lot for the castle was a bit obvious. The roads lacked shoulders for even "emergency" parking.

"That's the plan," Wade agreed.

They were both wearing British combat smocks under their trench coats. BDUs would have been more familiar, but anything that might confuse others as to who they were was a plus. The rucks they wore were small, dark, civilian-style daypacks made of heavy ripstop nylon, and contained cameras and batteries, plus infrared light sources to be used once they were inside the tunnel. Kyle had his Ed Brown, with the Ruger slung under his arm inside his coat. Wade had his Beretta and the AK, stock folded, under his coat. The pistols were accessible on their belts; the rifles weren't easily deployable under the circumstances.

The forest was familiar terrain, being temperate deciduous second growth. Both men were well experienced with it. They flowed through the brush and widely spaced trees smoothly enough that had anyone seen them, they would have thought them wraiths. It was an irony they couldn't appreciate under the circumstances.

11

WITHIN AN HOUR, THEY WERE HUNCHED IN the shadows near the stone-haloed door. Kyle gestured to Wade, who nodded back and eased closer, low to the ground and under the shadows created by the sickle crescent of moon. He nodded and disappeared into the dark entrance.

Then it was Kyle's turn, through the thin trees and mud and down into the culvertlike passage.

Wade had a tiny glowstick in hand, which lit the hole brightly to NVGs. His face was ghastly in green, his goggles bulbous in front of his eyes.

"Here," he hissed. Kyle slipped closer and looked where Wade was pointing.

There was a threshold. It appeared that someone had broken in in the past and removed the bottom panel of door to gain access. The damaged door had been blockaded as an expedient fix, but it looked fairly easy to climb over. Or at least it would have been without rucks and weapons.

Shortly they were up and inside, stepping on each other and pulling each other in. And inside was totally black ahead of them.

"Let's use the IR lights," Kyle said in what he thought was his softest whisper. It echoed in the confined space into something menacing and macabre-sounding.

Wade said nothing, but in moments they both had tiny lights with filters for IR frequencies clipped to their goggles, illuminating the way ahead without letting anyone not similarly equipped know of their presence. He slipped the glowstick into a pocket.

The passage ahead was carved from stone— narrow, low, and musty. It would be a slow walk at a crouch to get anywhere. Not only was it just wide enough for one person but not two, but the rock was cold and damp.

"You first," Kyle said. Wade's AK was a better weapon if they ran into trouble, being able to put out enough fire to let them retreat. That was Kyle's rationale. It wasn't fear. He told himself so again.

Wade eased forward in a duckwalk, then rose to a slight crouch. They were both going to have very sore spines and knees before this was over, Kyle decided.

Around them, the walls turned to bedrock rather than laid stone. They were well into the hillside. Ahead, the passage widened for what was probably the elevator shaft that had been built in the 1920s. A hasty, nervous glance behind showed the space over the door to be a tiny sliver just visible with night vision. Kyle wondered briefly what it would have been like first tunneling this, then moving through it by torch or lantern light, and shivered.

The shiver was due to the cold. He told himself that.

Shortly, they came to the dead end, which had an arch over a shallow recess. Or so it seemed until they got right up to it.

"Well shaft," Wade whispered, and again it echoed off into hisses and laughs. Kyle clamped down on his guts. Christ, this was creepy.

Without speaking, they squeezed side by side and looked up and down. Across from them there were elevator controls, which the books said had been installed by Queen Marie in the 1920s.

It took only a moment to determine there was nothing down lower. The shaft above went quite high, and nothing could be seen in the low light sources they had.

Wade leaned very close and whispered in Kyle's ear, "Do those controls look nineteen twenties to you?"

"No," Kyle replied, and felt ripples up his spine. "And that wiring is newer, too. Much newer." The wires were ripped out and it was obvious the elevator hadn't worked in some time. Leaning back, there was little to see ahead in the

IR illumination. The light source was only good for about ten meters, and there was nothing in that range except elevator supports and rock. But beyond that, high up, was a faint glow that might be from a side passage. "See that?" he said.

"Yes," Wade answered.

He spoke again. "I dunno, Ceauşescu brought chicks here to screw? Had a secret torture chamber he inherited from Vlad? What do we do?" He hated to stop talking. The echoes were bothersome when he did.

"I suppose we go back and have Cafferty do a check," Wade murmured almost inaudibly. The echoes were getting to him, too. Soft voices actually resounded less than the sibilants of whispers.

"Check for what? With what?" Kyle asked. All they'd found so far was a hole, which everyone already knew existed. There was light up above. That light hadn't been on for eighty, thirty, or even ten years.

"I hate to think what you're going to say next," Wade said.

"We ground our gear and climb," Kyle said. "Me first." Then he gulped, because he really didn't want to do it, but there didn't seem to be anything else to do.

"Thanks, buddy," Wade replied.

"Don't mention it," Kyle said. It wasn't what he wanted to do, but it made sense. They had to take a look, and there was nothing legitimate up there. Add in the disappearance of shipments in this area, and the mystique involved in "Dracula's Castle," and you had a great place to hide stuff where it wouldn't show at all. Even though it had been only an administrative center and may not even have been visited by Vlad, there was a fear associated with the place, and it was far more secure than any building in town.

With gloves and boots, the elevator rails and rock, it was quite practical to do a modified chimney ascent, legs splayed in front and behind and using hands to grip. It was a technique they'd both had to do before, and the dark helped in that it was hard to notice the drop below. But the creep factor was still very much there, seeing everything in monochromatic green and for only a few feet around.

Even with gear grounded, they were still loaded down. They needed their vests for cameras, pistols, batteries for night vision, and water. Under their arms they had slung their rifles, and another pocket held spare magazines for each. They'd considered leaving the rifles at the bottom, but there was no guarantee they'd return that way, and both wanted weapons with them even if it was awkward.

There definitely was light above. Kyle paused, swallowed and waited. Was that light from something in the courtyard far above? Or was it from a level between his current position and the top?

Very carefully, he drew a hand free from the rail and tilted his goggles back, smearing his cheek with dust and moss as he did so. Below him, Wade shifted slightly but waited without complaint.

It was a side passage, about another twenty feet up, and there was a dim glow as from under or around a door. It was on the far side of the shaft.

Taking a slow, deep, measured breath, he lowered his goggles and looked down at Wade, who nodded back. He'd seen it, too. And he looked downright scared.

There was nothing to do but resume climbing. Whatever was there had been built by people, and the worst threat was bullets or stupidity. The location was a mere coincidence, or chosen for fear factor, and it wouldn't do to let it overrule logic.

So he kept telling himself.

Two minutes later, he came almost level with the passage. Straining his neck, he tried to see.

Well, there was a door there, but the light coming in underneath it glared enough to make it hard to discern much else. There was no one waiting for them, of that Kyle was certain, and that helped a lot. Gingerly, he started crabbing sideways around the shaft, taking another two minutes or more to get directly below the opening. There was a tense moment when the rifle twisted under his coat and wouldn't unsnag. He couldn't move his arm, and didn't dare try to slide backward against his other arm, because he could feel his left foot slipping slightly.

Gritting his teeth, he rolled his body to free the rifle and coat, straining to hold himself in place with one foot, a weakly placed hand, and his butt. His Camelbak sloshed water and shifted on his shoulders. He hoped it didn't rupture and spill, though it was of very tough construction.

Then his arm came free, pulling the fabric with it and scraping the rifle across his ribs. But he could climb again.

He rose until he was level with the opening, then grasped the edge with his left arm and swung into the hole. There was just enough room for him to stand and leave a bare space for Wade.

Wade slid in, panting from exertion. The sweat evaporating from him could be felt as a fog. Kyle wondered why he wasn't as worn, then realized he was. He had sweated through to the coat and hadn't realized it. It was a cold, greasy sweat.

They were almost face to face, and had to be careful of each others' goggles. Wade whispered, "So what now?" Echoes sounded.

Kyle felt for a knob or handle. There was an old style latch, and the door was heavy timbers. It was rectangular but not neat, and had heavy iron rivets holding it together. The latch moved under his thumb, grinding and squeaking.

"We really need to look first," he said as he released it. "But I'm not sure how."

Wade looked around, the goggles poking like a pig's snout. "I'll bend sideways," he said. "You hold my legs and I'll look through one of those cracks at the bottom."

"Right," Kyle said, glad it was Wade's suggestion. He sure as hell didn't want to do that.

Kyle flattened against the door, legs wide. Wade bent over and braced a hand against the far side, then raised a leg. Kyle caught it and held it, with the sudden realization that a mistake would cause them both to drop somewhere around sixty feet. He leaned as hard as he could against the door.

Wade slowly straightened back up and stood. "Hallway, doors," he said. "No sign of people in hallway."

"So let's go in. There can't be anything honest in there. Assume enemies and shoot if needed. But only if needed."

"Roger that. Wish I'd brought wooden bullets."

"Yeah, me, too."

The latch was stiff and rusty, and so were the hinges. It was lucky, Kyle thought, that the door opened inward, or they would have had to swing around it over empty space to get in. But it moved at a push and groaned. Steeling himself, he eased it inch by grumbling inch so as keep the racket minimized.

Inside was lit, but it was only due to the time they'd spent in total blackness using goggles that they could see at all. It was a bare glimmer from ahead.

Once there was room to squeeze between the

wooden door and the rock, Kyle did so. Wade followed at once and they eased it back into place. It made a little less noise, and Wade placed a hand on one of the hinges to absorb the vibration. There was good news in that; it meant the wooden slab wasn't moved very often, so no one came through this way.

And that, Kyle thought, indicated another entrance elsewhere.

The passage they were in was another one tunneled into the rock and irregularly arched. Ahead a few feet, chambers were visible to both sides. Beyond that were alcoves and the doors Wade had seen. There had been lightbulbs here at one point, hung from the low ceiling in cages. The place seemed for all the world like a freezer, submarine, or execution chamber.

Communicating with signs and expressions, the two snipers unslung their weapons from inside their coats, reattached the quick-detach slings and moved noiselessly forward. They stayed on opposite walls, clearing the area ahead and across by eye, feet placed step by cautious step with a hand running along the wall for stability and tactile input. As they neared the two side passages, they slowed to a creep.

Wade gave Kyle a thumbs-up; his side was clear of anything threatening. So Kyle returned the gesture and stepped across the bare two feet of space to the other side and into the entrance. His IR light was still on, and he dropped down his goggles.

Weapon low and ready, he took careful, measured steps, raising his feet high enough to avoid catching on any protuberances. The walls were drier this high up, halfway to the castle, and were dusty but with little mold or moss.

The side passage opened into a pit, and Kyle recoiled mentally at once, trying not to do so physically. *OhmyGod* ran through his mind, and he gulped hard as his stomach flopped.

Bodies. Rotten ones.

A shiver shook him from toes to head, then his brain caught up with his visceral response. The top layer was two recently dead adult males, local-looking and scruffy, emaciated and pallid. One had had his throat cut, the other had been shot through the head. Someone had dumped them here to hide them. The smell was just starting to rise.

Below them, however, were older, bodies reduced to mostly gristle and bone, and below that was a pit of bones, hacked and broken and still wearing moldered rags of fabric and leather. One skull had a diamond-shaped hole from a sword thrust through it. The bones were old and blackened. Even in night vision, the cut ends were dry and withered. They'd been dumped here decades, even centuries earlier.

Just what every home needs, he thought, *a pit to hide the bodies in*. He took a quick scan around to determine there was nothing else, just the bones in a chamber about ten feet across and quite some depth. That determined, he backed out slowly. He turned to keep both the pit and the main passage in sight, and skittered back to where Wade was. He nodded and waved Wade in the other direction.

Wade nodded back, his face a tight mask, lips and teeth clenched, and stepped into the other passage. He disappeared in a moment.

Kyle sweated. His eyes scanned the door, the rough-hewn corridor, and the dark shadow that led to the bone pit. It seemed to open wider and reach for him. He knew it was irrational, but he couldn't help it. He shuffled back against the heavy door and hunkered down.

Movement! He clutched at the rifle and swung it up toward the flicker he'd seen.

Then something tapped his shoulder.

Bats. It's got to be bats, he thought. Another motion flashed and he stared hard at it.

Water drops.

Right. Cave, water drops. Reasonable. He tried to let out the breath he was holding and couldn't. It wasn't the dark, or the rock, or the enclosure, or the bodies, or the mystique of the old castle and its sociopathic, larger-than-life former resident, or the fact that terrorists who wanted him dead had likely been here within the last few days and might be here now waiting to kill him.

It was all of that combined. He wasn't too macho to be afraid, and this was a jackpot of triggers. And Wade, his partner and what felt like the only human being in this world, was out of sight.

What was taking so long? Either there was something extensive back there, or Wade had run into trouble. He was shifting his feet, hesitating and wondering if he should follow, when the shadows shifted and Wade reappeared. He smiled, showed a thumb, and waved Kyle over.

They swapped places, shuffling around each other, and Kyle stepped into the tunnel.

It was only an alcove, about ten feet deep. Kyle scanned around and saw no signs of any opening. There was a slight depression at the end, about three to four inches deep at a guess, and it was wet.

Suddenly he was trying not to laugh hysterically. There was absolutely nothing here but a small depression, and Wade had taken a moment to relieve his probably considerable bladder pressure. It wasn't necessarily a great idea, as it did leave evidence. On the other hand, when a man's got to go, a man's got to go. And anyone familiar with the tunnels wouldn't bother coming down an obvious dead end that had never been put to any purpose.

Kyle had a gallon or so he needed to lose, too. He took the chance while he could, trusting Wade to guard his back.

Then he turned and walked back out, shoulders brushing the narrow walls. He grinned,

Wade grinned back, and they resumed their search much more comfortably.

Farther along, the stone had a smoother, neater finish and the walls were wider, enough for two people to pass. The caged bulb sockets were still empty, but the light from ahead was getting brighter, and there were noises.

The first one made them freeze and drip cold sweat. They stood stock still, straining to hear anything else. An eternity later, there was another one. It was a soft, low sound. Kyle leaned far over to put his lips almost in Wade's ear to keep the echoes down. "Sacks being stacked."

Wade nodded. So there was someone here, and they'd want to get a look without being seen themselves.

Kyle realized it was getting quite late. It was near 5 A.M. now, and they were a solid thirty minutes from the entrance they'd used, even allowing for the fact that they knew the route and could travel much faster on the return. They were likely even farther from another potential exit. There was no way to use the cell phones or radios in here, and they had a deadline less than eighteen hours away, which sounded like plenty, but if they had to hide here . . .

The only good part of that was that eventually someone would be looking for them, and probably in force. Though Kyle would prefer to get out on his own feet, and soon.

Two doors to the left were barricaded. Kyle

saw no reason to try to force them yet. Both were about four foot high, two foot broad, and made of heavy timbers. They had various initials and graffiti carved into them in Cyrillic, so someone had been down here since the Communists moved in. That was after World War II.

They crept forward, the passage twisting down and to the left. Wade stuck an arm out and Kyle stopped, waiting. He took a sniff and grimaced. He could smell a combination of sewer, chemicals, and mustiness. Something was down here.

Ahead, just visible around the curve, there was a sizeable cavern. It might be eight to ten feet high. It was lit from within, and that was the light that had filtered some hundred feet up and around to the entrance. Kyle had known that about caves but never experienced it: A little light went a long way when there was nothing to interfere with it.

He paused to consider the tactical situation for a moment. What they wanted to see was likely in that room, as was any potential exit. It was lit brightly by fluorescents, the hallway was not. So unless someone came into it they should be invisible in shadow.

He sank to his knees and then flattened his body for a crawl. He indicated for Wade to follow and get photos.

12

THEY GOT WITHIN FIFTEEN FEET OF THE OPEN-
ing and waited there, watching. The room
was nearly rectangular, about twenty feet deep
by forty feet wide, and had a concrete floor
painted gray. How and why someone had gone
to the effort to do that was a puzzle, but Kyle
chalked it up to the Soviet influence. What had
been down here was a matter for speculation, but
there were scars on the walls where equipment
or possibly shackles had been attached. Perhaps
being dragged down under one of Dracula's castles, shown a pit full of moldy bones and assured
that screams could be as loud as one wished and
unheard was a good way to break people's wills.

Actually, he reflected, it had done a good job
on his own will, and he'd come here voluntarily.
What poor bastards had come into these passageways, and why? Someone who slept with an
apparatchik's wife? Someone who refused to let

his wife sleep with an apparatchik? Or drug dealers and black marketeers? And had just enough echoes of screams made it into the courtyard above to maintain the legend and keep people away?

Or was it all in his mind, and this nothing but an ancient hideout like those in thousands of other castles, carved by some nutcase with too much money, and now in use by terrorists?

Movement! His field of view was limited to what was directly across from him, so it was only when people moved into that area that he could discern anything.

Six people came past, carrying crates. All were male, all likely from this area, as they were dark-haired and dressed in local style.

The digital camera Wade had didn't beep; it had been modified not to. It made no sound as he snapped a photo, then another. Assuming they got out of here without too much harm, they'd have a wealth of intel about the labyrinth and its occupants.

The men within were muttering and talking. Kyle could only half hear it, and recognized some of the vocabulary that was similar to Spanish.

One of them, tall and with long hair, was saying what translated to, ". . . glad . . . load . . . finished . . ."

Behind him, a shorter, burly one replied, ". . . take it . . . again . . . distribute."

A third, carrying only one crate to the others'

two each, said something along the lines of, "Shut up . . . carry . . . quick."

Wade crawled down next to Kyle and whispered, "Positive ID on Logadze and Florescu. Do we shoot?"

"Now's when I wish we had a grenade," Kyle hissed back. "We'll wait for a moment."

It was a tough call. They had a limited window, six targets and it was a lighted room at close quarters. They could come out shooting and trust to speed and surprise to avoid return fire, but the fact was that they didn't know what else was in the room. There might be nothing to hide behind. From here, they could shoot easily at anything in view and trust to their own skill to nail anyone who tried to get into line of fire to shoot back. Of course, one of the others might lob a grenade of their own down the tunnel. That would end things rather quickly.

We're snipers, Kyle decided. *We shoot calmly and methodically, not toe to toe, like a cop movie*. He indicated his intent to Wade with a hand, and snugged the weapon against his cheek. As soon as he got a decent shot with more than one target in the field, he'd take it.

There came the sound of scuffling sacks or crates, probably the crates they'd been carrying. The mutters continued, but more softly, and then the "squad," as he thought of them, trooped back past, heads down and intent on the job. Kyle shifted slightly and caught the first one in the scope's reticle.

The Ruger was theoretically almost silent. But in the tight confines of the passageway, the muzzle pop was a healthy crack that echoed.

"Oh, shit," he muttered, knowing what was to happen. "Back!" he hissed over his shoulder to Wade, bumping his head.

They shimmied back as fast as they could, while Kyle's target crumpled, the bullet having punched into his skull to pulp his brains. But the other five scattered and were obviously reaching for weapons, then shooting, and the passageway was a straight shot with no bends between the opening and the snipers.

Kyle realized that the best option still sucked, because it was to stand and shoot fast, hoping to disrupt their response.

He quickly raised the rifle again and started snapping off shots as fast as he could get targets. Wounds were more important than kills right now. Any hit would hopefully slow a man enough for a second shot to be effective. But any hesitation would leave Kyle and Wade exposed to full-bore military rounds that would go through both of them, or ricochet into them from the walls. They were in a bad position for any kind of defense. He hunkered down as low as he could, hugging the ground for what cover it provided.

"Over my shoulder," he said to Wade, hoping Wade would understand.

His third shot clipped an arm, and a yelp of pain sounded ahead.

Then an incoming hail of fire erupted from one of the figures, the muzzle flashes bright as he swung into view of the tunnel. The clatter of the bolt and the bangs of the rounds were concentrated by the close quarters into a deafening, echoing boom like that of a nearby thunderclap.

It took a moment for Kyle to react, and that moment was a good thing. There was nothing to do but stay low and return fire. He'd been in this position before. Sometimes, the doctrine of "keep moving" was not the best advice.

He realized that most of the rounds weren't that close. They were aimed at torso height, and that was a good two to three feet above him. Okay, so that was close, but he wasn't going to think about it even as he flinched. They hadn't hit him yet.

Nor, apparently, Wade, who took that moment to lay the barrel of the AK over Kyle's left shoulder and cap off three rounds.

After the shattering noise of the incoming fire, the suppressed bangs of the 7.62 rounds were inaudible, even though Kyle felt the suppressor dance against his collarbone. He wondered if any of the hearing damage he had was permanent, but only for a moment. That was something he had no control over, and there were more immediate concerns that required his attention.

Like that gunner, who was nicely within his field of view. He adjusted his aim slightly and commenced shooting. Four rounds ripped through throat and face, and with a gurgling scream audible between catastrophic crashes of fire, that man ceased being a threat and became a mere statistic.

The remaining four were not yet statistics. Even surprised and possibly wounded, they were returning more fire. One had what was most likely a Makarov pistol, bouncing easily in his hands as he fired toward the hole. Another was armed with what looked like a Czech Skorpion. Kyle couldn't be sure, because one of Wade's rounds shattered the weapon on its way to the shooter, and the following shot blew through his chest, leaving a bright streak and arcs of hot blood and tissue visible on the scope.

Another one turned to run, a mistake in combat and his last, as Kyle and Wade both adjusted their aim and squeezed. He was hit through the back left side of the thorax with 7.62 and right under the ear with .22. Which round was lethal first was academic; both were expertly placed shots with a bit of battle luck, and he dropped like a sack.

That left two who were reaching for weapons as Kyle rose and headed into the room. He didn't feel that staying in the obvious hole was secure anymore. The floor was slightly sunken, and he pushed off with his feet, took two lumbering, stumbling steps and rolled out, panning to the left, then right to make sure his flanks were safe. That momentarily put his back to his opponents, but dammit, someone had to clear the sides. He swung back as quickly as he could, and he was too late.

Because Wade had dropped both the remaining men with shots neatly above their blank-staring faces as they turned from a weapons rack.

Or maybe not so neatly. One had half his temple blown away by hydrostatic shock.

Kyle heaved a sigh he couldn't hear. His head was spinning and his ears ringing, his nose choked with dust and his throat itching from propellant, despite the suppressors. He was panting for breath and his heart hammered. But it wasn't time for the shakes yet. There could still be hostiles here.

Wade said something that didn't register for several seconds. He had to watch his partner's lips to grasp, "I'll cover the other tunnel. You look around." Kyle nodded and did so. First things first, he removed the ten-round magazine with its remaining single cartridge and clicked a full twenty-five-rounder in place. Keeping weapons loaded was a good habit for combat. Then he let it hang from the sling and drew his .45, which was a much better weapon for this. It was powerful and suppressed, and didn't take much room to maneuver.

He slid around the room in a sideways shuffle, looking for threats or exits. There was the entrance they'd used on one wall, the west, he thought, and the one Wade covered on the north, and nothing on the other sides except some indentations of a foot or so that might have held torches or racks at some point. But the remains of metal shackles on the walls and their positions made Kyle sure people had been tortured down here. It might have been under Ceauşescu, or Vlad, or the original owners before him. But it was ugly, and there was an atmosphere here that wasn't inspired by legend, because he'd felt it when he visited Auschwitz and that mass grave in Bosnia. Call it psychic, empathic, or just superstition, places that had this feel were places of evil that Kyle didn't like.

The six bodies were the only other occupants, and there were twelve crates, all like the ones that had just come in, as well as maps and documents on a cheap card table. There was a quickly made plywood rack that had held the weapons that were now lying with or near the corpses. There were a dozen chairs stacked in one corner and a small refrigerator, its cord dangling from a light fixture, hastily wired in and taped rather than plugged into an outlet. There was obviously no electrical code enforced here. One corner of the room had a sheet of plywood as a privacy screen and contained a large bucket and a box of sanitary wipes, its purpose being obvious. Which poor bastards had to carry *that* out when it was full?

Two radios sat next to the fridge. The antenna wire seemed to run up the ceiling. Was there an old wiring conduit? Or a passage to the surface? One unit looked to be 1980s Russian surplus, but likely had the range to reach the sea. The other was shortwave, and there was also a box with a connection for a cell phone, so there might be Web access down here. Kyle made a quick try at using the cell phone hookup, but it didn't match his Iridium.

The fridge contained detonators and timers for the explosives, stuffed behind stale sandwiches. That was a good way to store them, cool and dry. Several boxes of ammo were behind it.

He circled around again, eyeballing the ceiling of hewn rock and the floor of cracked concrete. Nothing to indicate other openings. Nodding to Wade, he angled over to the stack of boxes and examined the one by itself next to the stack.

The crates were the TNT. At a guess, there were five to six hundred pounds of it here. Unless capped with detonators, it was perfectly safe and stable even if struck by bullets, but Kyle thought about his earlier wishing for a grenade and shuddered. The shock wave would have killed their targets, certainly. It would also have painted Kyle and Wade as red ooze along the walls and likely brought the castle down. He decided he was very glad for the weapons they'd chosen for this mission. And he needed to remember that these freaks used explosives in quantity, and to not get careless.

"What do we do with it?" Wade asked, getting more photos. They'd need plenty of evidence. It was hard to make out the words. Kyle's ears were still ringing.

"Soak it in water like our fathers did with fire-crackers?" Kyle replied, too loudly. He could hardly hear himself. The quip was the only idea he could think of. "Too loud to hear myself think" had always been just a phrase to him. He realized it was accurate at the moment.

Nevertheless, the joke was ironic. TNT *was* stable. There was little to be done to it without chemical action. "I suppose we can toss all the crates down the shaft. They'll shatter and make it much harder to use. Then we can send someone to get it. Alternatively, we just beat feet now and keep the place under surveillance until Cafferty can get a team here."

"Assuming he doesn't want us to deal with it alone," Wade said.

"Dunno. Do we want to risk that other exit? Or go back the way we came? Our other gear is there," he said in reminder.

"I don't think anyone's going to find that stuff," Wade said. "As far as we know, no one has been through there in years. And none of it can be traced to us."

"Yeah, and we don't want to come out in that park down there while tourists are around. I think we've got to take the other way out and hope it's farther away, then report in ASAP and get backup."

"Okay. Hey, we got two kills and four supplemental. That should make people happy. Except the terrorists."

"Well, let's not waste time. We'll take all the

papers, then out we go. You first, shoot if needed." They had no idea if a driver waited below for them to return, or if there was another element carrying more crates. Likely not. The operation here didn't look as if it needed many people, and between bin Laden's reckless wasting of his own people on missions, the combined work of intelligence agencies, and the precision shooting of Kyle and Wade, al Qaeda had to be running short of competent people. But there were always more volunteers, with too much religion and too little compassion and stability.

"Roger that," Wade said. They stood and walked across the room, bypassing the six cooling corpses and the other crates. The explosives would have to stay where they were for now. They gathered up the maps, charts, printed spreadsheets, and the EUR 50,000 still in the bank bands revealed in the midst of it.

"Damn. Are we going to tell Cafferty about this twenty-five thousand euros?" Wade asked.

"Does he need to know about the ten thousand euros?" Kyle replied. They both knew they were joking. They'd turn it in. That might make them suckers, but it was evidence, contaminated by the scum who'd acquired it, and they wouldn't touch it.

Under the scattered pile was a fake leather briefcase, the flat, soft-sided kind that doesn't expand. They carefully folded everything in, eyes still alert for anything else that might come through those dark, staring holes in the walls.

The way out was just another passage carved into the bedrock. Beyond the room was nothing but crude steps, long and shallow, leading up the hill. There were no lights. The passage curved right and the steps got steeper, almost too narrow and steep. Then wide again. Whether it had been dictated of necessity by the geology, was intended as a trap to delay pursuit, or was simply the work of half-mad, half-blind or half-trained masons working in the depths of the mountain, it was hard to say. Along one section, the walls tilted far to the left, causing the men to lean against the side and their boots to brush the edge of stairs and rock. There was a hill east of the castle, so they were heading that way. Compass confirmed it.

This route was definitely much longer than the one that had brought them in. On the other hand, it didn't entail a climb up a greasy, moldy shaft for a hundred feet or more. It was straightforward enough, and in ten minutes they were out.

The great advantage of the infrared and night vision, Kyle thought, was that no one should suspect them of being there.

The bottom leveled out, and there were shallow puddles here and there, as if rain had leaked in. It was straight for about ten meters, then they were at an exit, the door metal and rusty, perhaps fifty years old. But the hinges had been recently oiled. There was a tiny peephole, perhaps three inches square, through which Wade peered.

Satisfied, he unlatched the door and swung it inward.

The area beyond it was thickly overgrown with weeds as concealment. A sheet of plywood protected the growth from being worn down to an obvious path.

Wade cautiously crawled out, ignoring the wetness for discretion. He was low and slow, weapon behind him but ready to deploy if needed. Kyle kept watch up high and farther back, covering the oblique. "Clear," Wade said. "There's a pile of crates here, though."

"Those stupid bastards," Kyle said, following Wade out at a crawl just in case. "What do we do about those?" It was graying dawn and would be light soon. "Hold on, first things first." He grabbed his phone and punched for Cafferty.

"Yeah, what?" was the croaked answer to the third ring. Kyle could barely hear it, but there was ringing in his ears now. They should recover.

"I'd like to report two items accomplished, Numbers Five and Three, and a sizeable amount of contraband needing immediate disposal, plus documents."

"Holy shit!" Cafferty almost whooped, awake now and happy. "Where?"

"That's the problem. Under Bran, accessible only by tunnel on foot. And we've got gear under the Queen's elevator that needs recovering. We can stay and observe for now."

"Um, yeah, you better. I'm not sure what to do about that. How much contraband?"

"Eighteen crates, approximately twenty-five kilos each. The shipment."

"And these are under the castle?"

"Yes."

"Damn. That's bad—in several ways. I can't get anyone there for several hours, and that place will be crawling with tourists in a few hours. Then there was the inquiry about your vehicle, which has been towed."

"Ah, hell," Kyle replied, though it wasn't too surprising.

"Oh, hey, I'll deal with it. You've got two items off the list. I'm all smiles here. Stay and observe as long as you can, and I'll get back with you. How's your situation?"

"We're filthy," Kyle said. "And hungry and tired. Half deaf from a firefight. We really don't want to be seen in public. There's crates outside the door here, visible to backpackers, and looks as if they were brought in by ATV." There were flattened areas and one depression that showed broad tread marks. He looked around at the forest. It wasn't as thick as it could be, and there wasn't a lot of undergrowth. The slight meadow they were in looked to be one to attract picnickers or those craving a view.

"Damn. Amateurs," Cafferty groused. "Do what you can. I'll get you covered. Let me make calls."

"Roger. Out." He turned to Wade and realized he was still wearing his goggles; Wade had removed his, leaving deep creases on his forehead. He pulled his off as he spoke. "Okay, we need one of us at each entrance, keeping an eye on things. It could be several hours, he says. If nothing happens by nightfall, I say we go back in and bring the stuff out."

"Well, the problems with that are that someone is going to miss these assholes, as unpleasant as they are, and that door takes a key from this side. So if we close it, we can't get in that way. If we leave it unlocked, anyone snooping around the crates will find it and go inside."

"Damn," Kyle replied. "I'm too tired to think straight."

"That's why there's two of us, to poke holes in each other's theories," Wade reassured him.

"Right. Well, lock it. We know where the stuff is, the bad guys do, Cafferty and his people do. There's no reason for anyone else to."

"Assuming there's anyone not plugged into those networks."

"There is that. You want to watch here, I'll trot around front?" They were both having trouble hearing, and had to face each other and talk slowly.

"I suppose. Contact every fifteen minutes?"

"Sure. Or chatter if no one's around. We need to stay awake." It had been a long night, a short day of napping, another long night and no sleep today. They'd dealt with worse, but it was still a hindrance.

Quickly, they hefted and stuffed the remaining crates into the opening, along with the plywood.

They'd be invisible from above and clearly in sight from the proper angle behind the bushes, but that couldn't be helped. Wade took the briefcase and slithered off into the sparse woods to find a spot from which he could watch the entrance and the distant road far down the mountain. There was probably a trail through the undergrowth or along one of the paths, but there was no time for that now; the sun was starting to reach fingers through the trees.

Kyle sought shadow and heavy growth to shield him as he made his way around the hill. He reslung the rifle as he did so. This was observation now, not fighting. There were noises above as the staff prepared for their battle with tourists who were interested, curious, smug, arrogant, or a combination thereof.

Kyle just had to hope Cafferty moved quickly. He didn't want to stay all day. He wasn't sure he could. Despite the trees, this was a well-traveled area. It was unlikely the terrorists would return during the day.

Still, they might have connections to the staff, and, face it: If Kyle Monroe could sneak up and get into those passages in daylight, and he certainly could, then someone else could. Heck, a Boy Scout could.

In ten minutes, the sun shouldering the trees aside to throw light at the ground, he was where he could keep track of both the entrance they'd used and the area around it.

Ideally, he'd hide near dark undergrowth or leaves in a ghillie suit that would make him all but invisible. He hadn't brought his ghillie; it was inside the tunnel where they'd dropped their packs, because he hadn't figured to need it inside, and hadn't expected to come back out a different way.

But he was a U.S. Army *sniper*, and there was no one better at invisibility. There were enough native materials to hide him and he'd make use of them. Occasional twigs and weeds he plucked as he walked, long stems of grass, a handful of leaves. All this would serve to break up his outline and cover his skin. That done, unless someone got very close or stepped on him, he should be safe.

There was a nice spot, on a slope few would want to walk, near the base of a tree. Its bark was cracked into long hexagonal scales and there were protruding roots. He slid in against it, the ground wet and cold underneath, and wiggled his feet through the weeds around it. A quick shifting of the stalks destroyed his lower silhouette, and creative arranging of a dead branch with several forks in it and some scattered leaves disrupted his upper half, which was already mottled by the British DPM camouflage he wore. Some mud on his face and more leaves on his hat left him invisible, save his eyes. He arranged the phone wires and activated it before he tucked his hands in his sleeves.

"Wade, are you there?" he asked, remembering to speak much more softly than his tortured ears thought was proper.

"Yes, and hid. There's more activity. Seems to be all backpackers. We were lucky. They come through at all hours." Kyle adjusted the volume level up enough to hear it adequately.

"Quiet here," he said. Let's hope Cafferty hurries."

"Roger that."

"Check back in a few," he ordered.

"Will do," was the reply, then it became quiet again. He could just hear birds, and couldn't hear the breeze soughing through the fluttering leaves overhead.

He knew he napped. He was dozing in and out, waking periodically as his body protested the cold or hunger, then fitfully dozing again, to awaken to some minor noise or touch of the twigs. In this prone position, he didn't shift much, and was still well-hidden. He didn't think anyone could sneak past his watch, but he couldn't be sure. He also couldn't find enough stimulation to keep him alert. The unpleasant conditions were inadequate; he'd trained in far worse. Poking himself with sharp pebbles didn't do it. Reciting song lyrics and Kipling poems would get him halfway through the verse before his brain fried out. He gritted his teeth and forced himself as hard as he could. Numb fingers needed massaging so they'd stay useful. And his entire front was wet and shivering cold.

Tourists started wandering by as soon as the sun was well up. They acted as one would expect—laughing, joking, making creepy gestures at one another. It was always fascinating to watch people, or at least it was for Kyle. The differences between people and chimps, he thought, were very few.

They came in gaggles and trickles until 10 A.M. with nothing substantial to note. Four times, people examined the tunnel entrance, saw it was barricaded and went away. One of them was a teenager who tried to climb over, but eventually his mother prevailed upon him to not be foolish. At least that's what he gathered from the few words of German he knew.

It was just after ten when a loose dog came trotting down the slope, tongue and tail wagging in happy doggie fashion. It came straight toward him, nose shifting from air to ground.

Hell, was the only thing Kyle could think. All he could do was hope the damned dog ignored him. But that wasn't likely. Dogs were smarter than people in many ways, very literal and hard to fool. This one was a mutt, but a handsome mix of shepherd, spaniel, and some kind of hound. It didn't bark or yip, but was certainly intent on finding the person it smelled. Or maybe it was the propellant or the stench of bodies it was attracted to.

Then the dog was sniffing at him. It didn't mean any harm, obviously loved people. Like him. He didn't dare hiss or shoo it away. He just had to hope it left soon. He'd even let it pee on him to maintain his cover, but he *wanted that dog to leave.*

No good. It was determined to sniff all around him. Naturally, eyes sought the dog. And just as naturally, those seeking eyes saw shape revealed where a casual glance would not have.

The dog belonged to a youth with a family group that included parents, grandparents, and possibly cousins. They were Romanian, neatly dressed and obviously reasonably well-to-do.

Even with an inadequate grasp of the language and ringing ears, Kyle heard the teen's statement clearly: "Hey, there's a man down there!" The pointing finger was an exclamation Kyle didn't need.

In moments, other eyes focused on his face, some shielded by hands to help refine the view. Then there were shouts and comments, mostly sounding curious.

But Kyle didn't dare be questioned. There was no point in hiding further, so he rose and sprinted, down and away.

It was ironic, he reflected, that tourists and locals by the dozens would now accomplish his task for him, preventing any terrorists from getting into the tunnel at this side. He just wondered if Wade was having any better luck.

The yells and occasional nervous laughs drifted away, as Kyle spoke into his phone's walkie talkie. "I'm busted," he said. "Got to find cover."

There was a vibration, he slapped the button, and said, "Yes?"

Sam said, "I'm pulling in, about ten minutes."

"Can you make it faster? I've just lost my cover and have locals looking for me."

"Ah, shit. Yes, stand by. Maybe seven minutes."

"Which direction are you coming from?" he asked. He'd started at the northwest, was now running east and past the hill where Wade was.

"From the east," Cafferty confirmed.

"Then it'll be six minutes, because I can run a mile in that time." And maybe more. As long as he was fast, most drivers wouldn't have time to notice him and the pursuit should probably forget him.

He didn't get much notice. A few passengers in cars pointed, but all in confusion, with insufficient time to decide what exactly they'd seen. Running men were unusual, but not very, so no one paid any real attention.

A one-mile sprint is not like a one-mile run. He bounded over rocks and low walls, tree roots and bushes, through hedgerows and up and down steep slopes where he slipped and scrambled. He was breathing raggedly when a blue Mercedes ahead flashed its lights and drew to the side. Then it stopped.

He piled into the back and slammed the door. "Thanks, what about Wade?" he asked.

"We'll have him in a few minutes. He's still covered."

"Good," Kyle replied. He panted and gasped, sweat pouring off him as Sam reached down into the footwell and grabbed a bottle of water.

"Here," Sam said as he passed it back.

"Thanks," was all he could choke out. Fatigue, the run across mixed terrain, and the gear he was still carrying added up to a hefty drain on his body. He shoved aside two raincoats on the seat and sat up.

"Just rest," Sam said. "We've got time."

Kyle was still heaving for breath and sipping water in between when Cafferty called on his phone, the car pulled over again and Wade climbed in the other side, clutching the briefcase as if it were the winning game ball.

"Yo," Wade said. "Good timing."

"Yeah, just," Kyle said.

"Call the boss and tell him," Sam said. Kyle did so.

"We're in the vehicle," he reported.

"Glad we got you," Cafferty said. "Sam will debrief you. And thanks again, that was a kick-ass discovery, plus two points." Kyle noted that Cafferty never said "kill" or used any other word that was obvious. It wouldn't stop professionals from divining his meaning, but it kept casual listeners from triggering.

"Good," Kyle said. "And thanks." He disconnected and said to Sam, "You're supposed to debrief us. Can we get lunch, too?"

"Yes, I can get some takeout. What do you want?"

"Anything dead," Wade said.

"Anything meat," Kyle added. The pounding pulse in his ears was dying down, leaving a faint ringing. His hearing was almost back to normal.

"Stew or sandwiches," Sam said. "They do some good beef sandwiches around here."

"And clean clothes."

"Will do. Kyle, I need your room key."

Kyle fished it out of his pocket and handed it over. Then he took stock of his surroundings.

The car was very quiet and smelled quite new. Sam was obviously familiar with the area and drove smoothly. Kyle was nodding in a doze when they got to a local safe house.

There was a back door, and they went in that way, Wade and Kyle wearing the raincoats. It was a bit warm for them, but less obvious than filthy, greasy, and torn camouflage, canvas pants, and work boots.

Heedless of company, both snipers stripped to underwear once they were in a closed room. As soon as Sam showed up with their bags, Kyle grabbed the shirt and pants he'd worn the day before—no, two days before—and Wade grabbed a pair of sweats. "Wish this place had a shower," Kyle grumbled. As with the hotel, it had a 1950s-style tub and no shower.

"Keep the drain open and splash the running water with a cup," Sam suggested.

"Good idea. So what have we got?" Kyle asked as he sat down.

"We found the truck. Abandoned. We're

working on that. Let me see the cameras, Wade, and I'll run the images."

"Here," Wade said, pulling them out of his combat vest pockets. Sam pulled out a laptop and cables, along with spare flash chips.

"I'll start on these, then go get the food. Guys, you may as well clean up now, then we can get this done and let you rest."

"Roger that," the snipers replied.

Thirty minutes later, both were clean and munching on sandwiches. They were good, Kyle decided. The bread was nutty and crusty and fresh, the beef was tasty, if overcooked, and he was ravenous. He tried not to eat too fast, gulping water in between bites. It was easy to dehydrate in the cold and not notice it.

They called Cafferty again and were all connected as a conference call.

"Pictures look good," Cafferty said, his smile almost audible. "Very good. I'm calling that two targets down. It has to be approved, of course, but I call it good. Looks to be most of this load of explosives, but I don't see any of the last shipment we think they had, so either they hid more elsewhere or they moved it quickly, which is disturbing." He paused and there was the sound of sipping coffee. Kyle suspected if he ever collapsed, they'd need a coffee IV to resuscitate him.

"How are we getting it out of there?" Wade asked. Kyle was wondering about that, too.

"Not sure yet. I might have to send you guys

in to secure it better. Could mean bringing it out, blowing the rear tunnel so it stays there, or something else. I'll have to think on that. We'll need a surveillance device planted there at once, so we can follow up on anyone who comes along."

"What type of device?" Kyle asked.

"Little camera, little phone, satellite relay stateside and someone watching it for movement. Actually, movement can be determined by computer."

"Where do we get something like that?"

Sam said, "I have something like that. Several."

"We can probably do that tonight," Wade suggested.

"Yeah, should be able to. But what if the door and the crates get discovered?"

"How many were outside? Six?"

"About that," Wade said.

"We'll have you grab those. As soon as possible. The car should carry them. Sam can come and get them from you."

"Could be trouble if we get found with that," Kyle said.

"Yeah, and I want them removed ASAP. If you get caught with weapons, I'm embarrassed. If you get caught with explosives, there's just no way to put a good spin on it. We really should involve host nation at this point, but we know there's leaks in SRI, and possibly in DGIPI, too."

Those were just alphabet soup to Kyle, but he

assumed Cafferty knew what he was doing.

"Well, if nothing has happened yet, I'd say we wait until midnight to go up there."

"Reasonable," Cafferty said. "That's as quiet as it's going to get. Sam, can you show them a place to park and make sure they have something for traction? Two by fours, chicken wire?"

"Can do," Sam agreed. "I'll go get some now." He slipped out, still on the phone.

"If we do this right," Cafferty said, "you load up, bring the car back and Sam will swap in the morning for an identical model. I'll have someone come ashore to dispose of the stuff."

"Okay," Kyle agreed. "I've driven in mud before. I'll be careful. Worst case, I'll use Wade for traction."

"Hey!" Wade objected.

"By sitting on the back for weight," Kyle said, grinning.

A few minutes later, Sam returned. "Wire and boards," he said. The call fees on a four-way satellite conference hookup had to be outrageous to anyone except a government.

"Good," said Cafferty. "I've done what I can. The pics are uploaded where they need to go. And you guys need sleep. Call me around eight."

"Roger that," Wade said. Kyle just nodded.

Sam pulled out the third flash chip of the day and sheared it, then scorched it. He pocketed them for later disposal.

Kyle and Wade stood, grabbed their bagged dirty clothes and followed Sam to the car.

Twenty minutes later, Sam dropped them behind their hotel and they walked inside.

"First a shot-up car, now the boxes . . . What's next?" Wade said.

"We don't want to ask that," Kyle said.

They lay down at 1 P.M. and were unconscious immediately.

13

TWO HOURS LATER, KYLE'S PHONE BEEPED.

"Monroe," he answered, head dizzy from exhaustion.

"Forget tonight, leave town now. Find another hotel," Cafferty said.

"Roger. How soon is now?"

"Don't run, but walk fast," Cafferty advised.

"Got it. Wade, wake up."

Wade rolled and stood. "Ready," he said. "What?"

"Stand by," Kyle told him. "Go ahead," he said to Cafferty.

"There are Romanians digging through the castle now, and I mean "digging." Someone found the boxes, reported a suspicious individual in camouflage and they responded. So they're likely inside the mountain now, and you brought all the documents. They've got bodies, explosives and radios."

"Oh, shit," Kyle said.

"Very," Cafferty agreed. "We need observers and don't have any."

"We're observers," Kyle said. "We can get up there tonight."

"Kyle, they're all over that mountain," Cafferty said.

"Yes, and we're trained for exactly that mission," Kyle told him. It wasn't false confidence. Intel gathering near the enemy was exactly what they were trained for. "We can get within a hundred meters if we have to, but we can do plenty from farther back. Photos, descriptions, report."

"You're really sure?" Cafferty asked.

"Positive. My cover was fine in daylight, improvised, until that dog sniffed me. Wade stayed hidden. Nighttime with prep, no one will know we're there. We train against people who expect us and we still get through. This is our mission, Mick." Better than trying to play spies in town, he thought.

"Okay, I'll trust you," Cafferty agreed. Kyle respected people who didn't try to overrule experts in their own fields. Mick seemed like a decent guy. "But you better slip for now, hole up and come back later."

"Will do," Kyle said. "We're rolling." He clicked off.

"I only caught half of that," Wade said.

"We're hiding now. There's locals on-site who were tipped off. We're going back tonight to observe."

"Roger that. I'm packed, you need to grab your personal items, and I'll warm the car while you check us out."

"Got it."

"And as the token black man around these parts, there are so many reasons I'm glad it was you who got seen and not me. No offense."

"None taken," Kyle said. He'd have to dig through that to figure out which of several ways Wade meant it.

Meanwhile they were still groggy and tired. Braşov was the nearest major town, but was far too close for comfort. The best bet was to drive to Sighişoara and get a room there. It wasn't too great a distance, but should be safe enough. It was also a tourist trap, and had Vlad's house, now converted to a restaurant.

"Shish kebab for dinner?" Wade asked. It took Kyle a moment. Meat. Stick. Funny.

"Right," he replied. "Turkish style?"

"I'm sure they've heard it."

"Probably sometime in the last six hundred years."

The town was old, and looked it, but in a picturesque way. It had winding cobbled streets, old buildings in stone and stucco, brick and board, with shuttered windows, and a cemetery on a hill. The whole town was quiet and slow paced.

"Looks good, let's find a room," Kyle said.

Once again they let themselves be ripped off as tourists, not really caring to haggle over the rates and wanting to maintain the "dumb Drac hunters" image. Wade secured the room and Kyle found a small shop and bought bread, cheese, meat, and fruit for dinner later. He could feel the bags under his eyes swelling, trying to shut them. He pushed on to a shop that was like a miniature 1950s U.S. hardware store, and bought two brown canvas work shirts, two fishing-style hats and a roll of burlap. Another little place had sturdy thread and needles and shoe dye in brown, black, and tan. He didn't get gouged too badly, and the proprietors seemed happy to chat with someone who almost knew their language. He tried to be charming and bumbling, with talk of needing an extra shirt to look around in the mountains, burlap to pack his cameras, and did they know the best way to apply shoe dye, and did he need polish afterward? His shoes were a mess and he might be going out to dinner with friends.

Half an hour later, he was back in the room with tactical supplies and food.

"We're going to have trouble with the car again," Wade said when he entered.

"Yeah. Hold on." Kyle dug out his phone.

"This is Sam."

"Monroe, Sam. We're wondering about visibility and the car tonight. Any chance you can run us by?"

"If you tell me what you need, yes," Sam said.

"Okay, pick us up here at twenty one thirty. You'll have to wait several hours for us," he advised.

"I can get a room, and I have a book to read."

"Good. Thanks a bunch, and we'll see you then. Out." He turned back to Wade. "I really hope that's the end of the prep. Five hours of sleep is going to feel really good."

"Yeah. Check out this news report," Wade suggested. He'd brought up a news Web site for Romania in English.

"Let's see," Kyle said, swinging it around. Then he started reading. It was a rather sobering report.

An incident this morning has drawn attention to the historic castle in Bran, Romania. Tourists reported seeing "a man in camouflage clothing with his face painted" hiding in brush near a hidden entrance that is often called the escape tunnel. Meanwhile, backpackers found crates stacked in a hole dug on the mountain to the east, near the entrance to what might be another tunnel. The crates are reputed to contain explosives.

Often called "Dracula's Castle," Bran Castle was originally built in the 14th century and added to six times since then. The "escape tunnel" exits in a park at the foot of the castle, and was used as an alternate exit by Queen Marie in the 1920s. At one time, an elevator descended inside the mountain, but it had been reported as non-operational.

Authorities have secured the two locations and are investigating. Cameras, climbing equipment and generator-powered lights were seen earlier today, along with Army soldiers. The castle remains open for tours, although some of the grounds are inaccessible. There is also a guard mounted at the top of the elevator shaft, just off the central courtyard of the castle.

Reporters were chased away from the scene late this afternoon, but some witnesses say they saw what appeared to be "shroud-wrapped bodies" and more crates like those said to hold explosives being removed through the rear tunnel.

"Yeah, we can do it," Kyle said. They'd observed under tougher conditions. Still, he was having doubts. He'd hate to be fingered as a suspect in this. "I suppose we can check again after we sleep."

"So stop talking and start sewing," Wade suggested. They'd have to work fast to get any sleep.

The burlap tore into strips and left dust in the air. They placed them in three piles on the newspapers and started dyeing them.

"We'll have to wash the chemical smell out," Kyle said.

"Yeah, I have an idea," Wade replied.

In the meantime, they used the needles and thread along with scrap pieces of leather as thimbles to tack-stitch the strips to the hats and shirts. They stripped to T-shirts and underwear to do it, because the dye residue was rubbing off. They were both dirty and dusty in short order.

But the process was familiar, and the ghillies began to take shape, or rather, lose it. When they were done, both outfits were formless piles of black, brown, and tan that should be ideal on forest floor.

"So what's your idea?" Kyle asked.

"We wash them in the tub with several handfuls of dirt," Wade said. "Should kill the smell."

"Good," Kyle agreed. He dressed quickly and stepped out to grab a bagful of earth, carefully scraping it from a flowerbed near the quiet back entrance to the building. When he returned, Wade had the tub filling and the ghillies soaking, excess dye bleeding out and running off. When the colors stabilized, they added the dirt and agitated it, rinsed, then laboriously separated the tangled strips. They looked old and smelled musty when done.

"Got to get them dry, or at least mostly so," Kyle mumbled. "Think there's a dryer here?"

"Dunno."

The hotel did not have a dryer. There was likely a laundromat nearby, but that brought up visibility of both them and what experts would recognize as camouflage. They settled for squeezing the suits, shaking them and hanging them up on the open closet door to air dry.

"Damn near dinnertime," Wade said when they were done. "Or nap time for us."

"Yeah." Kyle pulled his jacket up over his shoulders like a blanket and lay down. It was a way he'd found of taking a nap that was comfortable and easy. Wade rolled under the covers still in his clothes. Shortly after that, they were unconscious.

Waking at 9 P.M., much refreshed, Kyle called Cafferty.

"Anything new?" he asked.

"I'm looking," Cafferty said. "They've got tech crews there. They've confirmed identity on the bodies, and so have our people. So it's official now: Nice job."

"Thank you, sir."

"You deserve it," he continued. "As you suggested, it appears they took it up there with an ATV. Several trips. Must have had it stashed in the area."

"That makes sense. Whoever had the ATV took off, and they figured it would be quiet enough at night in the mountains."

"Right. If they'd made one more trip you could have nailed them safely and been done, but you couldn't know and I'm not complaining about these freaks being taken apart by Romanian coroners and then disposed of as trash. We also found some stuff in the documents."

"Oh?" Kyle had expected they would, but he was curious.

"Not much for you yet, but we found a schedule on three more shipments on their way. Our people will deal with them at sea if possible. If not, the Romanians will be waiting for them now. I told you you'd gain us a hell of an edge if you did this."

"Okay," Kyle said.

"Which means 'thankyouthankyouthankyou.' *Mulţumesc. Gracias. Danke. Taki. Merci. Tessekur—*"

"I get the idea, and you're welcome." Kyle was smiling, though. They really had done a good job under nightmarish conditions.

"Hey, this is good news. And tell Wade, too, please."

"I will. Wade, he says 'thanks' in five languages. Confirmed targets, ATVs, and documents with leads."

Wade flashed thumbs-up and a tired smile.

"So are we still on for tonight?" Kyle asked.

"If you want to," Cafferty said. "Sam is almost up there. It's your call on doing it. We're happy with what we have so far, but will of course take more."

"So we'll get you more."

"Much appreciated. Out."

"Out."

That taken care of, the snipers plotted out their return to Bran.

"I hate to say it after all that work, I'm wondering about the camo this time," Kyle said. "Dumb tourists is how we play it. I'd rather not have the weapons at all, but we need to stash them somewhere. Maybe Sam can meet us and haul stuff."

"That's a good idea," Wade agreed. "I think we should take cameras with us. Phones yes, but don't use the radios. There's no need to put out anything they can readily ID."

"Okay. You'll have the camcorder and an IR source, I can bring another flashlight. We'll each have night vision and scopes. If we get caught, we play up the vampire legend bit, and why shouldn't we be curious about men around the castle at night? That should get us thrown in jail then out of the country in short order, as rude, snoopy American tourist idiots."

"Better that than the truth," Wade said. "Rude, snoopy American sniper idiots."

"Do you hear me arguing?" Kyle replied.

"But no camo or ghillies?"

"I'm still thinking about that," Kyle said. "If we get caught in them, we're rather obviously more than camera geeks. On the other hand, if we ditch them before getting caught, they'll be almost impossible to find. On the other hand—"

"The idea is not to be seen at all," Wade supplied.

"Exactly. Take the ghillies," he decided.

They were both ready when Sam called and said, "Outside, waiting."

"Roger, open the trunk," Kyle said.

In two minutes they were in the back seat, bulky packs between them. "Weapons are in the trunk. We'll need them again. I didn't want them left in a hotel," Kyle said.

"Reasonable. I've got them taken care of,"

Sam said. "We'll meet back up in the car or I'll swing by wherever you check in next."

"Okay. We need to be dropped along the north side," Kyle said.

"Sounds good. You'll bail out moving?"

"Yes, but not too fast," Kyle said. "We want to be discreet, not put our dicks in the dirt."

Sam laughed. "I was Airborne, I know what you mean."

The road curved all the way around the castle and the hill. There was one oncoming car, so Sam slowed. They wanted it past and no witnesses when they departed.

The car whipped past, he eased off the accelerator to avoid bright brake lights, and said, "Go!"

Wade was on the left and shoved the door open. He stepped out, holding onto the door and went to a full sprint before letting go. As soon as he was clear, Kyle kicked out the rucks and hopped over himself, then jumped out running.

It worked fine until his foot caught a hole and he stumbled. He bruised and abraded his knee and shin, jammed dirt into the heels of his hands and jarred his whole body, completing it with a bang to the left shoulder and head on a downed branch.

Wade was alongside at once. "You okay?"

"Superficial, hurts, help me get hidden," he said, teeth gritted. Damn, it was painful.

Wade helped him limp up behind growth so he wouldn't be seen from the road, then walked back to get the rucks. While he was doing that, Kyle's phone vibrated.

"Monroe," he answered.

"Sam here. Looked like you fell. Are you okay? I can turn around if need be."

"Minor, I can make it. Thanks for checking."

"Not a problem. Still looking at oh five hundred for a pickup?"

"Not much after that, so yes," Kyle said for clarification. "Night is safer than daytime."

"Good enough. Call if you need anything."

He pulled up his pants leg to examine the wounds. A bare flash of his light showed cut and torn skin and oozing blood, but it could manage without a dressing tonight. It would just be stiff and ugly tomorrow.

Wade came back and stacked the rucks, then added a few weeds to break up the silhouette. "Rest a few?"

"Nah, I'm ready," Kyle said, shaking off the effects. His ankle and knee ached, his shin, knee, and hands burned and stung, but he was ready to go.

They made sure no oncoming lights were visible, then darted across the road, Kyle favoring his left leg and dragging a little. In seconds they were concealed on the other side and working their way through the trees.

It was just after midnight when they reached their insertion point, far up the hill. From there, they planned to hike down and move more slowly and cautiously as they approached the castle. Eventually they'd sneak into positions and hole up, watching, taking notes, and recording. They'd exfiltrate around 0500 the same way and be picked up. Sam would take the memory sticks, tapes, and their notes, and they'd go catch more sleep, unless leads indicated a change of location.

It went as planned at first. They hunkered down in some brush and donned their ghillies. On their faces, ears, and hands they smeared camouflage grease from a compact. After checking each other over, they flowed down the hill, shadow to bush to depression to tree, always in the dark and hidden. Kyle was slightly ahead, the shape of his face broken by a black "branch" of camo paint and several brown splotches. The small ruck on his back contained his supplies for the operation, and his garb under the ghillie was drab brown, sturdy working clothes Sam had picked up for them.

Behind and to the right, Wade had a more traditional makeup of "dark on the high areas of the face, light on the low." The layman often thinks that dark-skinned people don't need camouflage, but skin is skin and it shines in light, from oil and sweat. Wade had the additional burden of the camcorder, which had a duct-taped adaptor to fit the day/night scope. The IR capability was good for only a few meters, and they needed to be much farther away than that. The hope was that the enhanced monochromatic image, thrown through the lens gap and focused by the camera would still be good enough to be subject to analysis by experts. If not, their observations and memories would have to do.

The trees were largely evergreen, with budding deciduous scattered throughout. It smelled fresh and earthy, unlike the dank, musty smell in the tunnels. Woods were scary to a lot of people, but Kyle and Wade lived a good part of the year in them. There was no artillery or armor here, the risk of being shot at was small, and they'd had a brief chance to familiarize themselves with the area the night before. All told, Kyle was quite confident despite his aching leg and figured Wade was, too.

But these woods were rather sparse, and the undergrowth wasn't much. They'd have to be careful on the approach and keep concealment in mind for the exfiltration. If they had to depart in a hurry, it was better behind brush than sprinting across open ground.

Kyle sank carefully to his knees, to avoid exacerbating his injury further or making any noise. Wade dropped down next to him and watched the other way. They took turns pulling their ghillies out of their rucks and donning them. While coats in front, the backs were bulky and thick with fabric. But that tangle of dark and earth tones was what would hide them from almost any observation.

They stayed on their knees and crawled downhill. The castle was visible now and then through the trees. They crawled through spiky dead needles on the forest floor, around branches dropped by bushes, and through damp spots in depressions, methodically and quietly. Every few trees, Kyle or Wade would rise carefully, easing around it to judge their approach.

They could hear and see quite a bit of activity. There were four pickups and two cars, and a bank of lights attached to a generator illuminating the hole. There were people present, but no numbers were certain.

About a quarter mile back, they dropped to a low crawl, slithering along like lizards. They moved in uneven zigzags, never leaving a straight line toward the site. Straight furrows were a dead giveaway, with an emphasis on *dead*. Both men were far too experienced to make that mistake.

Kyle gingerly wiggled around a dead branch, not wanting to disturb it and make any noise. It wasn't just the humans below who were a concern, who were behind noisy equipment and wouldn't find them easily; any spooked animals might rip straight past an observer and alert him to the fact that something was out of place. Terrain involved more than just ground and plants.

Once around the branch, Kyle crept up on a slight rise. If he had figured correctly, it would give him a good view.

It did. As his eyes broke the crest, he could see the vehicles again, and easily observe the people among them. Wade wasn't visible, but should be several meters away and on a different lay of land, so discovery of one wouldn't reveal the other in close proximity. He had been to Kyle's left, and a careful search showed his hand, left out for Kyle's benefit. Kyle made a very slow wave back, and both pulled in under their ghillies, becoming effectively invisible.

Kyle had the still camera, and took an initial photo from under his ghillie, through the hanging tendrils of burlap. The shot would give a good overview to try to place later closeups against. The field of view was good, but the acuity wasn't great at this distance, in mixed light. Still, the experts could dig a lot from a picture by analysis.

He withdrew a small notepad from a pocket. The pages were waterproof plastic, not paper, and would survive fairly harsh weather. He kept a tally of the personnel and made notes for descriptions for most of an hour, alternating with picture taking. Meanwhile, he was alert for any sounds, motions, or other threats around him.

The military standard report is based on the acronym SALUTE: Size, Activity, Location, Unit, Time, Equipment. He noted each section as he acquired the information. In addition to the six vehicles, there were eleven people, nine males and two females. Two were in coveralls and handling human remains. The rest were in police-type fatigues with filter masks and gloves. Two were using laptops, one inside a car and the other across a hood. Three were photographing and examining items brought from inside the mountain. Three more were seen intermittently, bringing items from inside. There might be more in there, as a cable led from the generator through the door. Location was obvious, but he wrote it down for record as "east tunnel entrance, Castle Bran, 0123 hours" and the date.

The bushes around the opening had been dug out, as had the tunnel entrance. It had obviously been buried after being originally built and left as an emergency escape route. That combined with the hideout underneath and the secret staircase inside, plus who knew what else, made this a place needing a lot of investigation for historical purposes. But science wasn't why Kyle was here. He made notes as to how the entrance had been partially cleared by the terrorists, and how it had been opened up since.

A careful look through the telephoto lens at the personnel didn't help much. There were unit badges on the uniforms, but not clear enough for him to determine. Perhaps Wade was having better luck with the spotting scope.

No one inside the circle of lights should be able to see them, and that left only the two working at laptops and one of the photographers who'd chosen to stay out of the actinic glare. He noted their positions in a sketch. Soft fog was falling into the low areas, and it hindered his observations.

The crates of explosives were not in sight, so at least the six outside had been removed. Photographers were taking pictures of one of the communication devices on the ground, set against a meterstick for scale. It wasn't a radio, and was probably some kind of encryptor or antenna booster for the cell phone, because he'd seen it attached to that cable inside. The report said the bodies had been removed, but examiners were going over several small items with gloved hands, indicating possible blood. It could also just be a precaution against bacteria, however. One woman was making notes and checking an item with a magnifying glass, turning it different ways. Kyle took a photo of that, and of each other item he could see brought out.

He had four memory sticks, so he could get 200 photos. Also, the digital camera allowed him to delete unwanted images when he acquired better, clearer ones of the same items. It kept him busy comparing and shooting. It lacked the Hollywood glamour of their last operation, but was likely as useful long term and much safer. On the whole, Kyle liked a challenge but preferred not to get shot at. It was part of the job, but not one to embrace. Soldiers who got off on that didn't live long.

Two workers came out carrying what appeared to be a body. Kyle zoomed in closer and tried to see.

It wasn't quite a body. It was body parts. He didn't recognize the specific bones in question, but the blackened skull and sheared long bones, along with cracked and dusty ribs with desiccated flakes of skin still attached had almost certainly come from the pit he'd discovered. In the available light and through the camera eye, even despite the mist, he could tell this was decades old at least, more likely centuries. Which poor, forgotten bastard had that been, and who had taken a dislike to him? Likely that would never be known.

The only good part for Kyle was that above ground, outside, he had no fear of corpses. He'd seen more than his share.

A sharp sound made him freeze, even though he hadn't been moving at the time. He went into a trained, reflexive brace and replayed what he'd heard. It had been a crack and a swish, as of someone walking through the woods. Then it came again. *Patrol*, he thought.

The only thing to do was stay motionless and trust his camo. The only real risk was that his boot soles might be visible. They were a paler tan and might glisten in the now condensing dew.

One of the keys to good concealment was attitude. It wasn't a psychic power, or at least not to Kyle. He'd heard some who thought of it that way. To him it was an attitude, a sense. Being too alert caused one to quiver and stand out to an observer even if it was only at the unconscious level. To blend in, one had to be part of the scenery. So Kyle closed his eyes for a moment and tried to think like a pile of leaves.

The footsteps were clearer now, even over the hum of the generator. He thought he heard voices, soft and low under it. They were quite close, likely within twenty meters. But there was no urgency or caution to them, as there reasonably would be if Kyle or Wade had been ID'd. The worst thing to do would be to anticipate trouble and move. That would not only reveal them, but might be perceived as a threat and earn them incoming fire . . . and not only was neither man armed, that was exactly the type of engagement they wanted to avoid. Facing nothing worse than arrest and damage to their professional pride, he knew Wade was doing exactly what he was: holding and waiting.

Movement to his left alerted him, and again he didn't react. Boots came into view and moved down the hill. In a few seconds he could see legs, four, then torsos, two in Romanian mottled camouflage. It was the older type and likely passed down from military to police. Two men carrying shortened AKs strode down the hill, talking back and forth. They turned to Kyle's right, the north, and kept walking. They were obviously trying to keep spectators out of the area.

Kyle heaved a slow, quiet sigh. They'd been within four meters of him and not seen him or Wade. Score 2 for the snipers. And keep them in mind during the exfiltration. He was able to get photos of the Romanians from behind and to the side. They probably weren't relevant to the operation below as far as useful data went, but he had the opportunity and took it. Too much data could be sorted. Too little was a problem.

The guards came by about every half hour, it

seemed, taking the same route. They were obviously there to chase off tourists and weren't taking a serious look for anything. Still, it didn't hurt to be prepared. Kyle improved his camouflage by covering his boots with a few twigs. He used enough to break up the outline, not enough to make it obvious something was covered. And he tensed up every time they came by. Wade fixed his own camo, and flashed a smile as he did so, barely visible under his ghillie.

They took more photos, made notes, waited for the guards on each circuit, and ignored the cold, dampness, prodding twigs and needles, and crawling insects. It was 0347 when Kyle checked his watch. They'd like at least an hour to exfiltrate and be rolling at 0500, to be clear of any daylight or early traffic. He eased out his cell phone and punched for Wade.

It was odd to be calling someone only a few meters away, but it was safer than trying to get his attention now. He kept sight of his partner, who looked back when he felt the vibration. A quick flash of thumb acknowledged receipt, and then they were crawling back, progress measured in mere centimeters per minute.

Kyle got his NVGs back on and scanned the terrain ahead. It was clear, and they were out of line of site of the work party. A thick, spreading bush ahead of him offered good concealment. He angled cautiously around it, pausing every few movements. Even detected movement could easily be overlooked if it didn't continue for long.

He judged the distance to be far enough and rose to a high crawl. Wade moved closer, and they took long, plodding "steps," knees and hands lifted high to avoid disturbing growth. Another couple of hundred meters and Kyle decided it was safe to bunch up.

In moments they peeled off the ghillies, wrapped them as padding around the cameras, and stuffed them in their rucks. Securing the straps, they shouldered them and began to walk, bent low still, meandering through the trees and across contours. Kyle fished out his phone and punched for Sam. "We're almost to our point," he said.

"Roger," Sam replied.

Then they were heading down toward the road, still alert for the patrol or others they hadn't seen yet. They ducked and darted under the canopy and over the deadwood.

They were only a hundred meters or so from the road when Kyle saw movement and froze. Wade keyed off his act and likewise stopped. Slowly, they both sank down where they were, to minimize profile.

The movement was a person. Then a second one came into view. Young men, dark clothes, civilians. They were trying to be discreet as only untrained, overeager, self-absorbed teenagers could. Kyle cursed silently. His mind ran through options.

If the kids, who were obviously going up to spy for themselves, went past the snipers without seeing them, no problem. The patrol could handle them. If they saw either of the Americans, then they'd have to decide how to respond. They could act authoritative and try to bully the kids into submission, and Kyle liked that option, except he was clearly a foreigner. The kids might just bellow for help or try to fight. That wasn't discreet.

He could try to disable them gently, say by wrapping them around a tree, or knocking them cold, or wrestling them down, gagging and lashing them. But that would make a certain amount of noise and would definitely be considered a hostile act by anyone responding.

That left one of two options, which would likely be effective but were not very military.

The boys were heading straight for Kyle, would likely pass within two or three meters of him, so the odds of them seeing him approached certainty.

One of them spoke in surprise and Kyle was able to extract, "There's a man up there!" from it. It had been a slightly louder than conversational voice, because the teen had been nervy and working at caution, so overcompensated when jarred.

Right. Stand and walk. "Stay there, partner," he whispered, not using Wade's name where anyone might hear it. Word of foreigners at the castle wouldn't be that unique. A black man accompanying a white man, however, would be rather easy to find after word made the news.

As Kyle stepped forward, the other boy said something like, "Who are you?" and moved aside. That left a clear gap between them. Kyle intended to walk through, smile, and look triumphantly guilty at getting a glimpse of the castle before these kids had, and just keep walking. If he did it right, they'd stop, stare, and either walk away or get jealous and rush in to prove they were as good.

He was just between them when the second one, to his right, said something involving "camouflage face." That was one of the keywords from the news report. Both of them tried to close and grasp at him.

In a perfectly conversational tone but with his arms thrown out and waving wildly, Kyle said, "Boogaboogabooga!"

They stepped back for just a second, gasping, and Kyle took off in a sprint.

Noise behind him was Wade, who said something like, "I veel dreenk yoor bluhd!" as he also dug in and raced. They turned parallel to the road and headed east. Kyle unpocketed his phone once more and said, "Sam, we're blown. Pick us up on the roll," as soon as it was answered.

"Three minutes and closing," Sam said. "Windows are down for gear. I'll make a pass each way, about two minutes apart."

"Roger that," Kyle said. "Stay on air." He clutched the phone and resumed dodging as a dog nearby started to bark. There were houses here and there, with perhaps three dim lights showing through the curtains of early risers. He really didn't want any more witnesses.

Behind him, he heard the youths shout in confusion, and behind them came shouts that had to be from the patrol.

Actually, Kyle thought, it might work out well. The two guards would catch the kids, and be unlikely to split forces over allegations of two men already leaving. They'd prefer to believe they were competent and that no one had gotten past them, that their captives were trying to be clever, and that all was well. They'd congratulate themselves over a simple collar and never suspect their perimeter had been broached going in and coming out.

He saw the illumination of lights ahead on the road. There was a car behind coming up the hill, and he raised the phone. "Is that you?" he asked.

"I think so," Sam said, sounding tense and amused. "Slowing."

"Roger."

Wade bounded in alongside, then they were both running straight at the road then parallel along it in a rough gully. Kyle was cautious for his feet. His right leg was hurting like hell now.

"Cross over," Sam said.

"Wade, go," he pointed. Wade was on the other side in two seconds, and as Sam rolled past, he tossed his ruck through the rear window and dived in behind it. The car picked up speed and moved far ahead of Kyle, then over a ridge.

Kyle kept going at a run. He was doing a lot of running on this mission. He figured it would be another five hundred meters before Sam turned. Two minutes. That would put him well away from the castle grounds.

He dodged obstacles of rock, timber, clumpy grass, and holes. There were pieces of the edge of the road missing, that had tumbled off the side and into the ditch he was running through. He grimaced as his ankle twisted slightly on uneven ground and sent shocks up his shin.

But then there were lights ahead. He raised the phone and said, "Ready."

"Wade's in front, you take the back," Sam advised him.

"Roger." He turned and began running back the way he'd spent so much effort coming from, so he'd be pacing the car.

It came alongside and he shoved his ruck through. Hands clutched at it and took it, then he was diving headfirst through, hands on the ledge, then the seats, then tumbling in, his wounded leg scraping and stinging. But he was in.

"Stay low," Sam said and gradually sped up. They rolled right past where they'd had their little dustup and kept going. Kyle took deep, slow breaths as the sweat poured off him, trying to calm his nerves and twitching muscles, aching leg and itching skin.

"Okay," Sam said, letting out a breath of his own. "I see two men around twenty years old and two Romanian police. Is that a good thing?"

"That's a good thing so far," Kyle said. He explained what had happened.

Sam nodded and said, "Likely they won't go looking. Okay, there's baby wipes to clean up with and your spare clothes are in the bag in the footwell. Get neatened up and I'll drop you at the hotel. Sounds like you did great until the punks showed up."

"Yeah," Kyle said. "I think I may take up drinking again."

"Romania does that to people," Sam said.

14

TWO HOURS LATER, THEY WERE ENSCONCED in their room and cleaned up. Once again, everyone was on their phones in a conference call. Wade and Kyle both gave verbal debriefings, reading their notes verbatim, then giving detailed interpretations. Wade proceeded to shred the coated pages into tiny pieces they'd scatter among various trash cans and outside. Sam had taken the memory sticks and they were being processed already.

"So how did we do?" Kyle asked. He hoped the information had proven useful. It had been a rough task to acquire it.

"Well, there's good and bad news," Cafferty said.

"Yes?"

"The good news is, the photo interpretation people confirm your kills from yesterday. The less than good news is the Romanians discovered your packs. They've got the bodies, the explosives, the other bodies, and the commo gear. That's not necessarily bad, as long as they don't tie it to us."

"What's the bad news?" Wade asked.

"Someone got a photo of you, Kyle, in profile as you ran that first day."

"Ah, shit."

"Not your fault," Cafferty insisted. But he obviously wasn't happy about it. "They haven't ID'd it yet, but it does mean if you get spotted somewhere else it might bite us in the ass."

"Damn!" Kyle said. He was seething. That damned dog! He was totally invisible and had been sniffed out by a mutt. And a friendly mutt. He liked dogs, he couldn't be mad at it for being a dog, so he was mad at the situation.

"The real bad news is really not your fault," Cafferty said, bracing him.

"Right. Hit me, then." What had Murphy done now?

"Ambassador's wife heard some of the news, and some of my report, and a few other things, and is on the warpath."

"Oh, fun." Kyle couldn't think of any profanity that fit.

"My problem, not yours," Cafferty assured him. "But it's a bitch, and so is she. More relevant is that the bad guys know we're after them. On the other hand, they know we can dig them out. I'm still trying to assess this."

"What next, then?" Wade asked.

"Stay hidden I have a deportation order for my two snipers, from the ambassador. Luckily, you aren't my snipers." He sounded sarcastically gleeful at that.

"How much trouble is this going to cause for you?" Kyle asked. The internal politics of this were a nightmare he couldn't begin to grasp.

"He won't ship me out yet. I'm too useful. And your bosses and my bosses pulled favors higher up. He's not happy, though."

"I can understand his position, a little," Kyle said. He wouldn't like some chairwarmer like Wiesinger running operations without his clearance. And the ambassador did have other issues to deal with. From that perspective, Kyle was a really small fish with annoying habits.

"A little? I grasp it perfectly," Cafferty said. "But I have to do my job, you've got to do yours, and he has to deal with it. At some point, he'd be replaced if he got in the way too much. So rather than do that, he just makes my life a living hell."

"You know, I think I prefer my job," Kyle said.

They waded through the pictures, Kyle and Wade adding notes from memory to go with some of the less intuitively obvious ones. The mental wringer added to the physical stress had them almost hallucinating by the time 9 A.M. rolled around. Kyle thought of that old Army ad campaign and winced. "We do more before 9 A.M. . . ." Yeah, as if that was a selling point.

Still, it had been a very productive couple of

days. He couldn't complain about the accolades they were getting. Cafferty, and presumably others, were very happy.

Kyle would be happy to get a good day's sleep. So it thrilled him no end when Cafferty said, "I think we're done for now. You should be secure where you are. Keep the phone handy, and Sam will stay in touch. Now get some sleep. I'm going to need you again and I want you functional."

"Yes, sir," he said, with Wade in parallel. They grinned at each other and crashed back on their beds.

Kadim woke to the alarm and rose. It was far too early, before even morning prayers, but this put him on the same schedule as the Americans, some of whom seemed to keep chaotically odd and later hours.

He had almost missed vital data, he realized shortly after he logged in. The chatroom was busy and moving quickly.

JulianLee has entered the room.
7 people in room.
FANCYDANCER: Hi, Julian
LEO155: hi
AUSSIEWALT: Julian, long time no see
JULIANLEE: Yes, it has been a while, Walt. Peace.
AUSSIEWALT: Peace to you. Did you know this is Lent for me? Or is that just a greeting?

JULIANLEE: I hadn't known. What did you give up?

AUSSIEWALT: Caffeine

JAMESGUNN: I gave up self-restraint for Lent. For six weeks I'm denying myself nothing.

FANCYDANCER: *LOL@James*

BLKKTTY: -)

LEO155: I gave up sobriety one year.

AUSSIEWALT: Leo, if you stayed drunk for 42 days, you'd get the punishment you deserved from the act itself. :-)

Barbiemouse has entered the room.

BARBIEMOUSE: STEAMING MAD!

BLKKTTY: Hi, Barbie

FANCYDANCER: What's wrong, Barbie?

JULIANLEE: ??

Private Message from Leo155 to James-Gunn: Right, nutcase in, old artillery puke out. ciao.

Leo155 has left the room.

JAMESGUNN: Good luck, Walt. I live on caffeine.

AUSSIEWALT: I only have a little, but I enjoy Coke and coffee. Thanks.

Private Message from Blkktty to Fancy-Dancer: do we really want to know?

BARBIEMOUSE: You wouldn't believe what those IDIOTS have done now!

Private Message from FancyDancer to

Blkktty: She needs help. Letting her talk in here can't hurt and might let her feel better. Private Message from Blkktty to Fancy-Dancer: bites tongue* Yes, I suppose that's true. I'll try to be nice.

JAMESGUNN: Barbie, please do me a favor and do *not* discuss foreign service operations in chat.

AUSSIEWALT: What are we talking about?

JULIANLEE: Barbie has some issues with government policy, I understand.

BARBIEMOUSE: No, it's not the policy. Well, yes it is. But those two CIA hired goons almost blew up a historical site yesterday. I can't say which one, but if you do a Web search you might find it. And they left several people dead and blew their cover, and it's going to turn into a diplomatic *mess* that my poor husband has to help deal with.

JamesGunn has left the room.

FANCYDANCER: he works for State dept, right?

BARBIEMOUSE: in some capacity. And this is in his lap.

Private Message from Blkktty to Fancy-Dancer: he's the ambassador.

FANCYDANCER: the ambassador???

Private Message from FancyDancer to

Blkktty: OOPS! I didn't mean to blurt that out!:-[

AUSSIEWALT: <u>here's a link to the story</u>

JULIANLEE: Thanks, Walt. Barbie, is it that bad?

BARBIEMOUSE: Maybe not. If we can get them to stop or at least talk more before running in shooting, it would be a good mission. But as it is, it's verging on criminal.

BLKKTTY: maybe you should report it to the host nation.

BARBIEMOUSE: Maybe I should.

Private Message from Blkktty to Fancy-Dancer: I was being sarcastic. Now it's my turn to be embarrassed. :-/

AUSSIEWALT: Castle Bran? That's one of Prince Dracula's HQs.

FANCYDANCER: I've got a performance early tomorrow. Got to go.

Private Message from FancyDancer to Blkktty: I know you won't, but please do NOT tell Barbie I'm a stripper. It'd be all over the net. Tryout at a nice new club tomorrow. Better music, less smoke, richer clients.

Private Message from Blkktty to Fancy-Dancer: good luck. Hugs. I won't say a word.

Private Message from FancyDancer to Blkktty: Thanks! :-) Hugs back, gone.

FancyDancer has left the room.

AUSSIEWALT: Good luck at your . . . shoot, missed her.

BARBIEMOUSE: Yes, it's a Dracula site, but it's also a very important historical building otherwise. And it's being used by terrorists and Rambo military types as a battlefield. They both need to think about their priorities. Or at least the military does. I sometimes wonder which group is worse?

AUSSIEWALT: I have to get to church and help them set up for the evening service. Good luck.

JULIANLEE: be well, Walt.

BARBIEMOUSE: Take care. Hugs.

Aussie Walt has left the room.

BLKKTTY: Got to chase my kids back to bed. Back later.

BARBIEMOUSE: sigh. And I really need to talk.

JULIANLEE: I Don't know much about things like that, Barb, but I can be a friendly ear.

BARBIEMOUSE: Oh, there's not a lot to say. I really don't know that much.

JULIANLEE: Well, I'm staying in chat for now. You just ping if you need me, okay?

BARBIEMOUSE: Thanks, Julian

BARBIEMOUSE: I suppose I really should call the host nation.

JULIANLEE: Will that improve things? If these men mess up, wouldn't it be better to deny them?

BARBIEMOUSE: . . . that might be true. I don't know.

BARBIEMOUSE: I suppose I should get it out of my system. But I can't name names or places, okay?

JULIANLEE: Okay.

Yes, it was just fine with Kadim if she said anything at all. He'd send the saved chat in its entirety to the mullah, and then it could go where it was needed. Perhaps a sufficient incident would get the political resolution that was needed. If not, it was better that soldiers get killed rather than children or civilians. If the military wanted a solution, they'd find one. Civilians really didn't have any power, and the politicians didn't care.

Kadim was proud to do this small part for his people and the world. There was definitely good to be seen in the outcome.

Two hours of chat and instant message yielded a lot of talk from a woman who was obviously stressed. Her husband would do well to take her home. Or at least keep her out of such troublesome affairs, which wasn't equipped to handle. On the other hand, she was the source of the information. It was a moral quandary for Kadim, but he would pray to Allah to calm her soul and to resolve it in His way.

BRAN, Romania: Investigations continue in this historic little village today. Two days ago, a "man in camouflage clothing" was seen hiding near an abandoned entrance to Bran Castle. At another, previously unknown entrance to the east, investigators found several crates alleged to contain explosives.

The Romanian government still has not made any comments, but witnesses claim to have seen several shrouded bodies removed, possibly as many as twenty, along with other crates similar to those found to the east. The area is being patrolled, and investigators are at work around the clock.

Bran Castle, a 14th-century fortress, may have been used by Prince Dracula in his war against the Turks. There are rumors that the bodies being removed are remains of some of his victims. While he is often attached to the vampire legends, Dracula is not known to have drunk blood. He did, however impale prisoners on stakes and torture them at length.

Other reports, from sources close to the operation, say that the bodies are those of dissidents and the crates were explosives to be used to create terror in this still developing nation.

Al Asfan pored over the new report with interest. So there were definitely two CIA operatives specifically tasked with harassing his operation. They'd taken out the chase car for the delivery, then apparently killed—because they hadn't reported in—Florescu and Logadze. That angered him until he broke out in a sweat and gritted his teeth. Worse yet, most of the new load of explosives was now in Romanian government possession, and they'd lost some very expensive communication gear. On top of that, the most secure operating location anyone could have ever dreamed of had been exposed.

He'd told those idiots that driving directly into Bran was stupid. One never headed straight for a safehouse, but detoured around the long way. Instead, they'd drawn an arrow straight in, and either been seen or deduced.

It was time to close up here and move on. There was a good place on the French Riviera where he could stay quiet for a while.

In the meantime, he should see if those CIA infidels could be taught a lesson. There were local assets who might trace them. The ideal result would be to leave them dead, publicly and creatively. Barring that, enough attention would perhaps make the Romanians stick them in jail. So far, there were questions about the men who'd abandoned a car in Bran. A few more questions should suffice to get them taken in.

With a mean grin, he reached for the phone.

15

KYLE'S PHONE BUZZED. HE WAS FINALLY GET-ting used to that and not suffering what was known as "beepilepsy"—reacting with a jerk when it vibrated.

"Monroe," he answered.

"Kyle, it's Mick. You need to get hidden in a hurry. The police are looking for two Americans, one black and one white, wanted for questioning regarding the incident at Bran."

"Shit," Kyle replied. He couldn't think of much else to say.

"Indeed. I'm going to try to shift notice away from you. We still don't want to come out if we don't have to." Kyle translated that as, "At a certain level, you're expendable to maintain security." It should by rights piss him off, but he understood it. He believed Cafferty would dig them out if they got caught. He also believed

that the man would milk it as much as possible
for favors and position first.

"What do you want us to do, then?" he asked
for clarification.

"Move again, you rent a room, Wade needs to
stay out of sight. There are enough young American males here that you won't immediately attract suspicion."

"Will do. We'll check in when we can."

"Good luck, and I'll try to distract them. We'll
get you another target yet." Kyle doubted that,
but they did have two so far.

They waited nervously until well after dark.
Then Kyle settled at the desk and headed for the
car with most of the luggage. He returned for the
rest and cleared the route ahead of Wade, who
kept his hat on and collar up to reduce visibility.
They encountered no one on their way out the
back, and were shortly on the road, Wade
sprawled in back with his face mostly covered.

"I could nap like this," he said.

"Sure, then you can handle the next early call
alone."

Kyle drove out of Braşov and onto E574 toward Sfintu Gheorghe. That was another small
town that should have enough tourists and hotels
to help them stay hidden. After that, he wasn't
sure what to do. Likely, Cafferty would try to
draw attention away from them and onto some
other suspect. Then they'd be able to depart. He
wasn't sure they'd get much more done on this

mission. Still, a ton of explosives and two terrorists was a good tally. But it irked him to let the bigger brains go.

Ten minutes into the trip, Kyle was sure they were being followed. "I've got the same Dacia sedan behind us as two blocks after we left," he said to Wade.

"Cops?" Wade asked.

"I doubt it," Kyle said, trying to see past the headlights in the mirror. He'd caught the vehicle once or twice at stops, but couldn't get much more at present. It had stayed a car or two back so he wasn't sure how it was manned, but was now following within a few lengths. It was obviously intended to be intimidating.

"We don't have weapons in the car, do we?" A ripple of adrenalin went through him. They'd wanted to be prepared for a police stop, and shooting it out with the police wasn't anywhere on their agenda. It wouldn't have helped any situation.

"All in the trunk that I know of," Wade said.

"Shit."

Kyle had done quite a bit of off-road driving, both stateside and in Bosnia. He'd done plenty of miles on road. He'd even done the usual teenage "stunt driving." But this was combat driving against a possibly armed enemy. He was fairly sure he could find a way to get lost if they got to another town. But that wouldn't solve the problem, and would leave an enemy loose, which he hated to do. The ideal solution was to turn the pursuit around.

He just wasn't sure he had the driving skills for that. The ideal outcome was to disable the pursuing vehicle and stun the driver for capture and interrogation, then follow up against enemy infrastructure. That meant no more than a smashed bumper for Kyle and Wade's car. Any major damage or disabling of their car would bring the government in. That was a far less desirable outcome, because it would mean a capture of a mere flunky who might get away, and their capture and the resultant incident.

The only thing that came to mind was to try to cause a crash for the pursuer, quickly get control of them and get information. Kyle didn't think of it as torture, because he intended a simple punching and beating of someone who helped terrorists blow up innocent people. After that, they could be left for the police or Cafferty. The other option was to see if they had a radio or cell phone and threaten them into contacting their leadership, so Cafferty or Kyle could trace them.

Frankly, he had no idea what he was really doing, but couldn't think of anything good. So he jockeyed for favorable position for the crash. After that, he had only guidelines.

First was to get them close enough and fast enough that he could cause a minor accident. Kyle didn't know college physics, but he did know some ballistics. Faster velocities greatly increased energy, and in this case would also reduce response time. So he needed to accelerate and act fearful until they caught up, make sure the road was quiet, then lock up the brakes.

He started with some gentle acceleration. He wanted to appear to "discover" the possible threat and run away. Let the enemy, who likely didn't know exactly who they were, get overcautious.

It worked. Within a couple of kilometers, the tail had matched his speed and closed distance. They had him right where he wanted them. He edged the speed up a bit more and looked for a good spot.

Actually, it was hard not to edge the speed up as they got closer. He didn't like tailgaters, and this was not the place for it, with the road bumpy and uneven and occasionally pulling the car toward the edge. He used that, since it was going to happen anyway. Let them think he was scared and fleeing.

Right then, he found exactly what he was looking for. The road curved to the right, leaving them on the outside. It wasn't banked, and there was no other traffic visible at the moment. "Impact," he warned Wade, and stood on the brakes as he left the turn.

It appeared the pursuit wasn't in the mood for a wreck. The driver braked hard himself. But he was in the curve, and started to skid. The lights bounced as the car shuddered and slid on the loose pavement. Then it angled off the road, still at a good clip, and plowed through the weeds. It had almost turned on its side when it slammed into some trees.

At once, Kyle pulled half off the road, there being no shoulder, and put the emergency flashers on.

"Get weapons, cover them, stand clear of the car," he ordered as he popped the trunk release. Wade rolled out the door and reached for the rear. In a moment, he was down into the growth and Kyle threw the car into reverse. He wanted to conceal the other vehicle from anyone coming the same way they had. Anyone traveling the other direction should see nothing, if all went well.

Wade was good. Kyle had known that, but the man continued to demonstrate it. They needed to keep control of the situation, and Wade did it through the expedient of shooting the headlights out of the vehicle with the AK. The occupants had a good look at him, then it went dark. He had his little xenon flashlight out, which they'd not needed yet, and used it to blind the occupants. They knew he was armed with a suppressed and highly illegal weapon, was aggressive, and had backup. That was an excellent start to an engagement.

Kyle slammed into park so fast the transmission made the ratcheting sound that says it's been abused. He twisted out, seat belt clattering against the rear door, and reached into the trunk for his Ed Brown. It was right under his ruck, and the suppressor was in the same case. By the time he'd bounded down the slope to the Dacia, he had it mounted. That put him right at the driver's window with the gaping hole pointed through the frame—the window was down.

"Get out and lie down!" he snapped in English, thrusting the big pistol forward.

"Okay!" the driver said, eyes huge and nodding agreement.

Score 1. The enemy had admitted to knowing English. That made it much easier.

"Wade, get on the phone," Kyle said. He wanted to ask questions and move quickly. Wade pulled out his phone and Kyle turned to his prisoners. There were three, all locals, males in their 20s. They were facedown and clearly not prepared for a military engagement.

A shot went right past Kyle's head and scared the hell out of him. He dropped, rolled, and prepared to return fire. Then the driver was on him and wrestling for the .45. He could hear Wade shooting, the suppressed fire in contrast to the appalling reports from someone's pistol.

Then he ignored all that. The driver was trying very hard to cripple and kill him. Kyle was underneath, his attacker astride a leg, and they both went for the obvious knee to the balls at the same time. The attacker got the better of it, because he could let gravity do some of the work, and Kyle had to clench against the incoming blow. His own strike was weak. The hand that ripped at his Adam's apple had ragged, long nails, and he coughed and choked. He managed a nice clip against the driver's forehead with the butt of his pistol, which stunned his opponent just enough for Kyle to break his grip. But then they were both tangled up again.

He didn't know what this guy ate, but he probably didn't own a toothbrush. His breath reeked. He tried desperately to roll over, but they were against the car and couldn't. Up and down, trying to get position and control, they struggled for several seconds. In a fight, that's a long time.

The muzzle of the AK appeared, and Kyle was glad for the support. But the driver grunted and heaved, twisting them both into a ball again. Wade backed out.

"Alive!" Kyle said, hoping it was neither too soft nor a shout. The others weren't helping, so he presumed in the back of his mind that Wade had killed them. But they needed at least one alive, and that was a problem, because the driver didn't need one of *them* alive.

They were both getting banged about by the car, fists, the pistol, and several broken, rotten but still sharp sticks underneath. Kyle was aching and sore all over. Finally, though, he got a foot against something and pushed. That turned them both over, and he was able to butt his head down against the man's large, angular nose. That momentary stun let Kyle wrench his hands free, and he delivered a hefty smack across the eyebrows with the pistol. The eyes under him crossed and rolled up.

Wade was moving in muzzle first, and Kyle rolled back to rest. His shins had been kicked, his groin kneed, his ribs punched. His throat and head had taken a lot of damage, and he was abraded all over from sticks and grass, as well as muddy and filthy. He rasped for breath, and took a full minute to cough and clear his throat of phlegm and dust.

"The other two are dead," Wade told him while he recovered. "One had an old Tokarev, the other a cruddy old Czech revolver he never got to use."

Kyle just nodded. He couldn't believe he'd been so overconfident. Even idiot punks were dangerous when cornered. After all, they had no reason to expect to live, so they'd fought accordingly. They would have done so sooner had the wreck not stunned them.

"Let's talk to the driver," he said. "And quickly." He wiped his lip and his hand came away bloody. He'd bitten the inside of his cheek and banged his lips and teeth. Nothing loose, but shredded and cut.

Wade tapped the man on the forehead with the muzzle of the AK, and he recovered with a wince and a jerk.

"You talk and you don't die," Kyle said. Part of him was glad for the fight. It now meant he had zero qualms about smacking this asshole around for intel. Chasing them had been one thing, but these guys had been armed, so they'd been sent to kill.

"I don't know anything!" the man said at once. It was too quick to suit Kyle. He swung the suppressor right between the man's legs and blew a round into the dirt.

"I think you do," he said. "Shall we bet?"

"I got only a telephone call," the man said. He was wide-eyed under his welted and bleeding brow and matted shaggy black hair.

"Cell? Mobile phone?"

"Da, yes," he agreed, nodding and wincing.

"Where?"

"Here," he said, and reached for his pocket. He stopped when Wade raised his chin with the suppressor.

Carefully, Kyle reached into the pocket. There was only the phone in there. He flipped it open. "Standard phone," he said. "Maybe Ca . . . our friends can trace it."

"Maybe," Wade said. "Yes, I'm still here. We had a mixup. In control now. Send backup. Stand by." Kyle had forgotten that Wade had had his phone live. "Can you trace a call on a standard cell? Or the number? Roger." Wade looked over and said, "He says to find the number first."

Kyle turned the phone around and said, "Which number do you call?"

"Number five on list," the man said. "Is who sends us orders."

"And the others?" He looked over the list.

They were all family members or friends, it appeared. Number Five was labeled with a little factory icon for workplace.

"Such nice people you work for," Kyle muttered. He read the number off for Wade.

"He says it's another cell number, but not far from here. He's seeing if he has a way to check it."

Kyle realized their prisoner shouldn't be hearing this, and that they were exposed if anyone happened by and wanted to help the people with the flashing lights and open trunk, or had heard the fight. They were in a very bad position if discovered.

"Into the car," he said. "We'll talk while we drive."

It took another few minutes to go through all the pockets and the car. There had to be stuff they were missing, but two cars whizzed by while they were doing so, and Kyle was frantic to get away. Getting caught now would ruin a lot of plans.

It was rather obvious, Kyle thought as they dragged the man up the bank. The car had been crashed, shot, left with two bodies and a third one dragged away. They couldn't very well stick him in the trunk; modern trunks were easy to open from inside and all their gear was in it. So he'd have to ride in back with Wade. They didn't have cuffs, he might try to attract attention, and there was the risk of a fight.

The mission had officially gone to hell, Kyle

decided. It had taken five days this time? Not a record, but only because there were some missions in hell from the word go.

He did most of the handling, because Wade was still talking on the phone. "Yes. Got it. Okay, we're about to roll, we'll need Sam to meet us. Roger, staying live." Wade lowered the phone and said, "He can get the call traced, but he needs time to set things in motion first."

"Okay," Kyle said. He shoved the punk in back, Wade piled in and jammed the suppressor into his belly, and Kyle slammed the trunk before getting back in front with his pistol. It felt good to sit.

Wade said, "He has to call someone else to get the serial number on the phone and set up to trace it. Once that's done, we call the number and they can ID it within a local area."

"Right. What do we say on air?"

"Dunno. I leave that to you."

"Right." Kyle built speed back up and resumed driving, though with no destination now. Driving was just a cover. "Find out what more he knows."

"Right. So," Wade said, turning and prodding with the AK. "Who is this boss?"

"I don't know."

"And how did you meet him?"

"Sorin introduced him by telephone. I never met him."

"And you take money from a man you've never met to drive around, cause wrecks, and shoot at people? You must be a loser." Wade called up to Kyle, "Should I smack him around?"

"I think he's too stupid and cowardly to know," Kyle said. "Too much of an idiot to know what he's doing. Bet he drinks most of his income. I'm surprised he's literate."

The ploy didn't work. The man kept silent, lips tight.

"Well, when we do find out, I can just shoot him and roll him out the door," Wade said. "Or just roll him out the door and hold his foot, let him drag to death. Should be fun. I've never seen that one done."

"That's true," Kyle said, getting into it. "We grenaded that one asshole across a cliff face. We dropped that other guy out of a helicopter. We crushed one under a tank. Fed one to sharks. That was kinda neat. Then there's the one we drowned in the toilet. Think his head will bounce and concuss him to death? Or just grind away until his brains smear?"

"Dunno." There was silence for a few minutes, and it was obvious the man was bothered. His kept pulling his eyes away from the door, but soon they'd dart back again. "Fuck it," Wade said, shifting quickly. "He won't talk, let's give it a try."

"Sure, how fast?"

"Oh, hundred K should do fine," Wade said. "Better than a good belt sander."

"He's in Tîrgovişte," the man said, believing they meant it. "But I don't know where."

"Pity," Wade said with a snarl. "That means you just gave us information for free and we'll still grind your head off. Ready, boss?"

"Ready. As soon as we hit this straight."

"I DON'T KNOW!" was the insistent response. "I know they smuggle drugs, but I never was told names. I wasn't supposed to."

"Drugs, yes," Kyle said quickly. "And the DEA sent us to deal with it." Better to use that story than to let anything slip. On the other hand, this cretin was even more of a mercenary. There was no cause for him, no end goal. He'd kill someone for a few lei just because that was his job. Kyle's teeth clenched as he gripped the wheel. It was morally right to smear this scumbag. But it wasn't his job to deliver that justice. When they found a terrorist organizer, however . . .

The phone buzzed and Kyle stole a glance at it. "It's Sa . . . another element," he said. He clicked the button and raised it. "I'm here."

"Where is 'here'?" Sam asked.

"On E Five Seven Four, now heading back to Braşov and then to Tîrgovişte. We're going to try to scare out this punk and nail him."

"Okay, it might work, though we can only get a rough estimate on the phone's location."

"Yes, but we have a prisoner who's deathly afraid of having his face ground off as we drive.

You don't mind if we waste him? The government's okay with it? Right. We'll hide the body so no one has to ask any questions." Most of that was pure bull, but Sam should figure out what he was doing and ignore the extra chatter.

"Clever," Sam snickered. "If you've killed a couple already, it really doesn't matter actually. Though we don't endorse it and officially forbid it. I'll head in that direction. If time permits, I'll take your prisoner and we'll see if he'll tell us more. Though as we can't use force, it might take a while. Meanwhile, please do keep him alive."

"Thirty minutes and dump him in a river. Understood. We'll meet you there," Kyle said. He clicked off. Over his shoulder to Wade he said, "We don't need him. If he won't talk, grind his face so it's not recognizable and we'll chop off his fingers before we dump the corpse. The local cops won't know and the government just doesn't want anything that can be traced."

"Got it."

The prisoner spoke. "Domnule, sir, I have a family," he said weakly.

"Good, your widow can marry a man, then." Kyle was trying to sound as callous and casual as possible.

"I really don't know any more," he insisted. He was quivering and squeaking in fear.

Then Wade wrestled him face down on the seat. The man might be 140 pounds and Wade was in much better shape. It took only a few seconds.

"Say when," Wade said.

"Straight road, no witnesses, any time."

And Wade pulled the door handle.

The man screamed and flinched hard enough to make Wade jerk as air rushed past.

Almost, Kyle thought. "Just so you know," he said. "This isn't about drugs. The man you work for blows up children on buses in Israel. He's also killed people in Egypt, Spain, and France, and some of my buddies. You picked the wrong people to play with, and you're going to die very slowly because of that."

Wade was good. He gave about five seconds for that to sink in, then knelt and thrust the man's head out the door. He started leaning forward, weight on the man's neck.

"I KNOW AN ADDRESS!" came the shriek. Wade yanked him back up into the car.

Kyle exhaled as quietly as he could. He was sure Wade did, too. Because no matter how much they hated these assholes, they couldn't really torture someone like that. And this poor bastard was just a flunky who likely didn't endorse terrorism.

"So tell us," Kyle said.

"I . . . I," the man stuttered, forgetting his English.

"Wade, grind his face off, I'm sick of this crap."

"I'll have to show you!" he insisted. "I don't know the name, but I visited there once."

"Man, this is getting good," Kyle said with mock glee. "First you know nothing, then you know a phone number, now an address, I wonder what else you know?"

"That's all! I swear!" he insisted.

"Likely true," Wade said. "This little coward just pissed his pants all over our back seat."

"One more reason to get rid of him. But let's see if he knows where this place is. And you better not be lying," he said. "If we don't find him in Tirgovişte, we'll find an even more painful method."

– 16 –

THE MAN WAS QUIET AND WHIMPERED OCCA-
sionally all the way to Tirgovişte. Wade took
no chances and kept the AK's suppressed muzzle
in his guts. It was about 120 kilometers, near a
two-hour drive with the local road conditions,
and at that rate, Kyle was abusing their bodies
and the car with road vibration.

"Okay, we're entering Tirgovişte, where to?"
he asked.

"North and east corner," their prisoner said
quickly. Kyle used one hand to pull up a map
and kept the wheel steady with the other and his
knees. The town was about 90,000 population,
not huge, and the roads were sized accordingly—several large arteries and lots of small
ones that didn't matter.

The phone buzzed and Kyle answered. "Yes?"

"Sam here. I'm entering Tirgovişte. Where are
you?"

"Stand by," Kyle said, and found the name of the nearest large street. It was a "Strada" named after somebody "escu," like so many others. He picked an intersection nearby.

"I'll be there in ten minutes. Want to transfer your prisoner?"

"Sure," Kyle said. "See you." He disconnected. "Man, that's a bitch," he said.

"Oh?" Wade asked.

"Yeah, Sam is coming to get him."

"Sam?" Wade asked, playing straight and sounding scared.

"Yeah. That's rough. Tough shit, kid. You're all Sam's now."

"Sam?" he asked, unsure and sounding bothered.

"Yeah. I would do exactly what you're told if I were you. Sam will kill you if you try anything."

He had no idea what Sam actually planned, but cowing the man into submission couldn't hurt, and might make him more pliable.

Shortly, they saw a car flash its headlights. A wave indicated Sam, and they pulled in behind him. He was heading toward the river.

Then they were along the river on a quiet street, and side by side. Sam leaped out, opened the rear doors of both cars and helped Wade shove the frightened lump of a prisoner into his vehicle. Heavyweight cable ties appeared, and they lashed him at ankles, knees, and wrists. He was dumped unceremoniously into the footwell and mostly covered with a thick blanket. Wade said, "Good luck, kid. Do what he says and you might survive."

Kyle almost burst out laughing.

They departed a few minutes apart, giving Sam the lead. He rolled into a housing area and down several streets. Periodically, he'd pause, then drive on. Kyle took a moment to look around. The houses were small, mostly with tiled roofs. There were little flowerbeds and fences. Nice Old World neighborhood, straight out of a book. Who'd think to look for a bomber here?

The phone buzzed and Kyle was waiting. "Yes?"

"He's not sure which street it was, and I think he's telling the truth. It's somewhere around here, he says, but he's not certain."

"Terrific. What next?"

"Let's try that trace. Stand by and I'll call the boss."

"Roger, then call Wade." Kyle left the phone live. "You still awake back there?" he asked.

"Sure am. Are we on it?"

"Going to try the trace and see what it scares up."

Sam came back. "Okay, he's ready. Call him and we'll see what happens. Switching to Wade now."

"Got it," Kyle said. This was nerve-wracking. He had no idea what technical tricks were needed to pull this off, and he still felt as if he were responsible. He urged calm on himself and grabbed the prisoner's phone. How many phones and radios did he have here? Cameras? Weapons? This was nothing like the movies.

It was a bad idea to do all this talking on a phone while driving. But that was pretty far down Kyle's list of worries right now. He dialed the number next to the work icon and waited to see what would happen.

"Da?" was the answer, in a voice that was male, adult and not much else.

"I work with your employee, and we have problems," he said. "We've been ambushed!"

"Who is this?" So, the man spoke English with a Middle Eastern accent. Even better.

"This is Frankie," he said. "From the ship."

"You are most unwise, Frankie," came the reply, just as Wade said, "They've got it, Tirgoviște as he said."

"No, you're unwise," Kyle said, deciding to apply some psych warfare. The guy had to know there were problems. Kyle wanted to see if he could scare him up. "We're coming to Tirgoviște to splatter your terrorist fucking brains on the bricks. We call it Excedrin Headache Number Seven Six Two. Adios, Motherfucker." He disconnected at once. No need to let the man get any response in. Act tough, in control and most people would believe it.

"Got it localized pretty closely," Wade said. "Within a couple of blocks . . . half kilometer south of us."

"Right. Now to see how fast we can get there."

"You'll have to nav," Wade said. "I'm busy."

"No problem." A few blocks wasn't great, but perhaps they'd catch him on the way out of somewhere. They were closing in, and Kyle would be scared if he knew people were shooting his henchmen, stealing his explosives and tracking his phone calls.

And Kyle found it amusing how many allegedly brilliant people assumed cell phones were secure because there was no wire. This was the second time. And last time had been a satellite phone that hadn't been able to tell them much other than within a few miles. This time, they had it down to mere blocks.

Al Asfan tried not to panic. He forced calm into his mind and told himself it was all Allah's will. Allah would not let him fail. The road might be rough, but it was all part of a plan, and he was one of the slaves of Allah.

Still, it was a frightening course of events. He'd have to leave at once. While he'd like to call back and insist he wasn't afraid and challenge this arrogant American to meet him, he really didn't know who the man was, how many he had with him, or what the stakes were anymore. He was losing assets and people and needed to withdraw. Only a fool refused to retreat. He was no fool. Leave at once, head for France where the Arabic community would protect him, and regroup. This all would come back in its time.

He needed to hold things where they were

until he could get to his other hideaway. From there he could arrange travel and call in favors to slow pursuit. But it was time to leave now. Rafiq bin Qasim, Allah bless him, had tried to hold out in Pakistan and had died because of it, when the Americans had slipped agents into the area. Al Asfan would not make that same mistake.

If he'd known the same shooters who got bin Qasim were the ones after him, he might have been even less confident. As it was, he grabbed an already packed bag and headed for the car. He left the cell phone behind. It was obviously betraying him, and he had another.

The Americans spread out two blocks apart, though "block" here was slippery. The roads wound and crisscrossed. But they were in approximately the right area. Now they had to wait and see what happened. Kyle had a picture of al Asfan onscreen, and assumed Sam did, too. Of course, in the early light, and with considerable time since the pictures were taken, it wasn't going to be that easy to identify the target.

"I may have something," Sam said. As before, they were using satellite phones with headsets, and stayed live. The cost per minute was horrendous to Kyle's budget, but not even a blip on the chart to Uncle Sam.

"What?" he queried back.

"Male of approximately right age and description with a large overnight bag. Looking around, may be nervous. Getting into a Mercedes model echo five zero zero, dark brown. He is facing east. Starting car. Driving."

"Where should we intercept?"

"Identify target first," Sam said. "Then we'll follow if we can," he warned. "Let me find a good cross street. I can follow him a few blocks."

"Intel first, then shoot, roger," Kyle said, as both acknowledgment and for Wade's benefit. "Camera ready." He caught Wade's nod and turned back to the map window on the laptop. The scale was small and the language a bit awkward, but he found the street Sam named. "Yes, I can get there. Rolling," he said, and gave the engine gas.

Wade had the camcorder ready, as it had the best resolution for night, and any frame of its video could be enhanced. It was effectively an autowinding still camera the way they intended to use it.

The question was, did they have the right target, or was it just a similar-looking businessman on his way to the office early? That could lose them the whole lead. Kyle began to see why espionage could be addictive. It wasn't as heady a thrill as shooting, but it was plenty exciting, and the high went on for hours. This wasn't even his part of the gig, and it was a rush.

He reached the intersection and said so as he shut off the lights. Sam replied, "About twenty seconds, start filming."

"Roger, start filming. Wade?"

"Filming to the west, waiting for target," Wade said. All the talk and confirmation might not be necessary, but it was better, in Kyle's opinion, to be redundant. Any errors could thus be caught.

A car came from the west, and the driver was a single male. Kyle ducked so Wade could get a good pan, even if windows did interfere with visibility. "Got image," he said. "Comparing," and he reached for the laptop as he scrolled back to a good shot. Sam rolled past the same intersection.

"Want us to wait?" Kyle said, worried that it might be the wrong man and they need to do another search.

"ID him if you can. Follow me if not."

"Roger." He looked expectantly at Wade, who was squinting at the image on the viewfinder and looking hard at the laptop.

"Probably him," Wade said. "Ninety percent certain, and I don't think I can do better without daylight."

"Probably him!" Kyle repeated. "We're following."

"Roger that," Sam said. "I will turn off when you join the tail, and take up position behind you. He shouldn't have seen me as more than headlights yet."

"We're still just tailing?"

"As long as we can," Sam said. "If he IDs us, go for a shot. Can you do that while moving?"

"Can, but it depends on the environment.

Even if you aren't worried about witnesses, by-standers complicate shooting."

"Roger. We'll do what we can."

"How's your passenger?" Kyle asked.

"Oh, him? Quiet. Apologetic. Apparently, he's not thrilled to find he was helping terrorists. And he seems scared of us."

"Good." Kyle was just as happy. If the man had ethics and morals, it would be nice to get him back to his family. Though likely the Romanians would want to deal with him first.

"How are you doing on fuel?" Sam asked. "I can get another couple hundred kilometers."

"Ah. Not good," Kyle admitted after a glance at the gauge. "Maybe half that."

"Right, when you get close, you fuel up, I'll take the lead. But that means when we swap back he'll know he's probably being followed by you. And I'll be getting low. So if he's not where he wants to be by then, you shoot."

"Right. Can you clarify the rules of engagement again? Just for my benefit."

"No problem," Sam said. Then his voice took on a dark tone. "If we can't trace this guy, you're to kill him, by shooting, wrecking, whatever you can do. Avoid collateral casualties as much as possible. We want the body identifiable, and we don't care if there's witnesses. Just wipe this rat-fuck son of a bitch off the face of the Earth, and we'll handle cleanup and publicity."

"Understood," Kyle said. That was encouraging and scary. Encouraging in that they'd nail this dirtbag. Scary in that Kyle and Wade could very likely wind up as pawns for politics thereby. But hell, no one had claimed the job was safe when they took it.

They were on open road again, and heading back toward Braşov. They had a good distance between vehicles, though that had worked against them last time.

"Wade, be ready to shoot," Kyle said.

"Ten rounds of match grade in each pocket," Wade acknowledged. "I can be out either side window in five seconds, or shoot out the front or back glass faster."

They were again climbing the Transylvanian Alps. Despite the dark connotations attached to the name, *Transylvania* meant "across the forest." It really was pretty terrain. With the sun rising to the east and burning out pockets of mist and dew, the first blush of spring on the trees and the road a crumbled charcoal line, Kyle decided it really would be a nice place to visit. The mountains were high enough to be fun, not so high as to be work. They reached around 2500 meters.

And even here, there were bomb-throwing scumbuckets. There was nowhere on Earth, from the most productive, most desolate, to most idyllic these trash didn't pollute. Kyle had met troops from several dozen nations, including Iraq, the former Soviet Union, China, and Vietnam. Some of them were officially threats or enemies, and yet in every case, they could look at each other soldier to soldier and recognize patriotism and the willingness to serve. They could all sit down to a drink together and be comradely, even if they might have to shoot at each other later. Business was business. And despite everything different about their cultures, soldiers all hated terrorists. They were undisciplined, unprofessional, and cowardly thugs.

And Kyle was really hoping to catch this one.

As they cleared one rise, he saw a small village ahead. It was after 8 A.M., and business was in swing. He grabbed the phone and said, "Sam, I'm gassing up. Shift it in gear."

"Stand by," came the response. Behind him, he could see Sam's car accelerate. Ahead, al Asfan was starting to pull into the village traffic. This was where it was risky. He could turn, go straight, catch them in traffic and lose them. But so far it had gone well. Kyle eased over to the side so Sam could blow past him. "I've got him," Sam acknowledged. "But do hurry."

"Roger."

But Wade had to stay hidden when around Kyle. Black man and white man together. That's what people were looking for. Wade tucked down with a blanket as Kyle pulled neatly into the gas station and popped the fuel door. The attendant was right there as Kyle waved a wad of lei at him. "*Umpleţi repede, vă rog,*" he said. *Fill quickly, please.* The man grinned and complied, and pumped away.

Gas, or petrol, was hideously expensive here. It also wasn't of the highest quality. But it wasn't Kyle's car or money, and he was in a hurry. He handed over the cash and waited impatiently for change, because it would be suspicious to leave without it. He wasn't going to waste time haggling, however. He nodded, said, "*Mulţumesc*," and started rolling. The attendant gave him a quick, quizzical stare and a glance in the back, but Wade was hidden. He might think someone was asleep, but he didn't seem overly suspicious.

"Stay down for now," Kyle advised. "No need to be seen."

"Roger," Wade said, muffled under his cover. It had to be stuffy down there.

"Sam, I'm rolling."

"Straight through town and keep going," Sam said. "We're just leaving now. He's starting to look at me in the mirror, so hurry."

"Shortly," Kyle said. He didn't want to run anyone over or otherwise attract attention. There were goats in the village, and school children, and dogs. He passed a small school, some houses, and then saw fields pocked amongst the trees again with another stop sign ahead. Far in the distance were several cars and one of the ubiquitous horse-drawn conveyances so many farmers still used. The sun was well up and bright now, and visibility was excellent barring a faint haze that was still burning off.

"You can get up now," Kyle told Wade as he floored it, and drove like the maniac he'd been at sixteen. He piled up behind a little Dacia, waited for a break in oncoming traffic, and rocketed around, revs at five grand and foot to the floor, on the wrong side from his American perspective. Then he jerked back in and braked hard to pace the next vehicle. Over another rise, he saw clear road and stomped it again, running up to 160 km and beyond, the car bouncing and careening on the rough pavement. Then he had to whip back in behind another vehicle, a truck this time.

He slammed against the seat belt as he braked behind the cartful of something, whatever one hauled with horses this time of year, then dodged quickly around. Sam was clearing another rise and the target was ahead of that.

"Arriving," he announced, blasting up the hill with his foot through the firewall, heedless of the gravel flying. It was quite enjoyable.

"I see you," Sam said. "I'm turning as soon as you see him."

Kyle cleared the crest and saw their target down below, heading toward Braşov for certain. "Got him," he said.

"I see a road to the right. I'm pulling off and will follow about two minutes behind. Good hunting."

"Will do," Kyle said.

Hopefully, al Asfan was much more comfortable now that the car following him had pulled off. They'd find out soon.

The downside was that Kyle had to keep him in clear sight, which meant creative dodging and weaving. Everyone drove like that here anyway, but it did stand out the third time he got honked at for almost going nose to nose. Sooner or later, al Asfan was going to catch on.

It was on the edge of Braşov that he finally twigged. He stared steadily into the mirror for several seconds, then nailed the gas from his formerly quick pace to a breakneck one. Kyle was about two blocks behind, just close enough to see the reaction.

"He's seen us, we're going to shoot," he announced.

"Understood, good luck," Sam said. It was only a friendly comment, of course. Luck didn't enter into it. Wade was a professional shooter, and if they got a field of fire, they'd take it. But they would have to get in close and be quick.

Traffic built up in a hurry. This was another decently sized town, with a few main routes and a lot of convoluted smaller streets. Kyle was hoping to get close before al Asfan turned off. So far, however, he seemed to want to stay in public, possibly thinking that would protect him.

He would be disabused of that notion very shortly.

"Wade get ready. I'm about a block back."

"You got it."

A few moments later Kyle saw him in the mirror as he sat up in the rear, legs across the seat and into the passenger side footwell. The rifle was along his body, held close where it would be less visible, the suppressor near his face. That wasn't the safest way to hold a rifle, but there wasn't much safe about what they were trying to do.

Meanwhile, al Asfan had definitely figured out he was being pursued. He drove faster and even more recklessly than was the norm here, and ducked between two other cars.

"I'm not sure if he's trying to lose us or keep someone between us as cover," Kyle said.

"I'm watching," Wade said. "If I think I have a shot, I'll yell and take it unless you say not to."

"I trust you. Take the shot," Kyle said. Wade wouldn't risk hitting a civilian, and he had already proven he could take shots at moving cars.

"Will do," Wade said. "If we can get a drive-by afterwards, I'll make sure we finish it."

"If our cover's blown, yes," Kyle said, as he braked hard and slewed through the tail end of a light and cars stopping for it. He was momentarily on the right and it felt both normal and weird, with his American background and his experience here. "If we're still covered, we'll risk letting him survive. They can always find him in hospital. No offense to our planners, but I'd rather walk out of here." He gunned the engine, yanked back into traffic and ignored the honks and shouts.

"Got it," Wade agreed.

Al Asfan couldn't mistake their intent. If they were observing, there should be another car or a stationed spotter. That they came through traffic indicated their purpose was to stop him physi-

cally. He seemed to lack the fortitude for that engagement, because he tried to cut farther into the
flow.

Cursing, Kyle accelerated again, then braked,
slipped into a space that was barely big enough,
then back out. But if he could prod him into a
wreck, they could cruise by and ping him
through a window, with no one the wiser. Con-
versely, if they got in a wreck, they'd lose him.

It was hard to decide who had the advantage
of traffic. Al Asfan was having to break trail, but
he had a largely unsuspecting crowd around him
who didn't react until after he wove. Kyle had to
deal with traffic that, while slow or stopped or
recovering, was already scared and chaotic. But
sooner or later, one of them was going to make a
mistake, and if he played it right, Wade would
get a shot.

Al Asfan still didn't seem to realize he had
snipers on his tail rather than spies or cops. He
stayed four cars ahead and looked happy there.
On the other hand, four cars was a respectable
distance, and far enough to get them stuck at a
light. Kyle needed to get closer.

Only he couldn't. Traffic was snarled and tangled, cars halfway between lanes. He eased between two other cars, ignoring their honks as he
rode the white line. There might be four lanes
here, but there were no turn lanes to speak of,
and he didn't want to be stuck in the right hand
lane when someone decided to turn. The light
ahead was turning amber, and he needed to get

across quickly. He revved up, honked and pushed forward.

It worked. The cars on either side assumed him crazy and shifted over a few inches. That's all it took, and he was through as it turned red, ignoring louder honks from the cross traffic.

Their quarry was already through the intersection, and a car behind him was trying to back into a parking space. Kyle cursed and shifted over, forcing another car almost into traffic to avoid hitting him. At this point, he was willing to swap a few fender benders. Three car lengths and closing. If he could offset the car to some degree, Wade would have an oblique shot.

"A few more feet and I have him," Wade said. He was hunched over the rifle, one leg braced on the seat, one in the floorboards, one elbow over the back of Kyle's seat. That left the suppressor right alongside Kyle's face.

For just a moment, there was space ahead, even though the car beyond that was braking hard. If they wrecked, Wade would likely lose the weapon and smash into Kyle, the airbag tossing them both at the roof. But screw it, Wade needed a shot. Kyle maintained steady speed and said, "Shoot!"

A pop like a balloon on steroids blew past his ear. The driver's window on al Asfan's car exploded, and he swerved.

"Nice!" Kyle shouted, louder than he expected. He couldn't help grinning, either. That had been a sweet, sweet shot, and they had their score.

"Not nice," Wade said, snarling. "I fucking missed."

"Dammit," Kyle said, elation turning to depression. That was twice they'd missed now. The two they'd gotten had been sitting ducks. So far, their intel gathering was far outweighing their shooting and stealth. And some of that was luck.

Worse yet, now that he was being shot at, al Asfan was ignoring all traffic laws. He blatantly drove on the wrong side, cars ahead screeching and swerving to miss him. Kyle was momentarily blocked by another car, and that driver, a middle-aged man, looked over in shock.

Then he pulled out a cell phone.

"Dammit, diversion!" he yelled, hoping Wade had an idea. Wade seemed to. He pointed the muzzle in the general direction of the man, who braked hard. That let Kyle slip over into oncoming traffic.

Oncoming traffic was heavy, honking and swerving. Kyle fought for control of the car and himself. Wade leaned out and fired again. He'd been trying for a tire, but missed it by a hair and threw asphalt from the road. Kyle couldn't fault him. Shooting between two moving cars was rough, and he'd made the last tire shot handily. But that driver hadn't known he was being shot at. This one did, was evading and in front, and Kyle was avoiding wrecks and trying to catch up. On the whole, it was a god-awful situation.

The terrorist seized a break in traffic and dove across to the left, then down a side street.

"Not again!" Kyle shouted and dodged back into their lane, clipping a car which didn't brake hard enough and missing the turn because of a truck.

"No way to stop or slow down," he said. "I'm going to zigzag out of the area and we'll get clear."

"Roger," Wade said, tucking the rifle back under the blankets. "I don't see anything behind us," he reported.

"Got it," Kyle acknowledged. He changed lanes, steadied out, and prepared to turn left.

He didn't get the chance. Two police cars screamed across and blocked him. Two more were behind, lights flashing, sirens silent. Then police were tumbling out with weapons.

17

"DAMN. CALL CAFFERTY," HE SAID. "SAM, We're busted," he said into his own phone.

"Dialing," Wade said.

He didn't need to speak Romanian to understand the shouts as, "Get out of the car slowly with your hands in sight!"

"Do it," he said, just as Wade spoke into the phone, "We're pinned by police, help."

Wade continued, "I'll leave the phone connected until they take it away. Kyle, I'm complying, phone in hand."

"Then reach the phone out first and slowly," Kyle said. He'd seen weapons from this side before, several times. But there was no cover and no way to shoot back now, and he'd heard that Romanian police were very eager to shoot sometimes. There were also hi-tech guns disguised as cell phones. The combination was bad. He felt a hard knot in his stomach as he reached and opened the door using the outside handle. "Be very helpful," he told Wade. "Might get us a bit better treatment." Though Cafferty's warning about the police hereabouts was bright in his mind, and he wondered if they were to get an obligatory thrashing before being tossed into a cell. Could even State get them out of this? He extended his own phone, still live for Sam to listen in.

He continued his progress as his brain whirled. Wade was stepping out, one foot at a time, phone held high so it was obviously not a weapon. Kyle waited for him to finish, then followed, hands open and clear.

The car's hood was hot but not painful as he was slammed down onto it. The cuffs, however, hurt moderately. Hands were plucking at his clothes and voices were shouting at him. He caught glimpses of batons, pistols, and tear gas, and wondered which they planned to use.

"*Sînt American*," he said clearly. "*Sînt armuri în automobilul.*" *I am American. I have weapons in the car.* They were going to search, anyway, so he may as well admit it and be helpful. Police, like soldiers, liked to have control of a situation. And unless one's goal was to fight them, it was safer to let them have it.

"Are you carrying any weapons?" he heard behind him in heavily accented English.

"There are none on my person. Oh, a knife in my pocket," he added hastily. He'd forgotten that the knife he carried as a "tool" could be perceived as a weapon by others.

His pockets were emptied onto the hood, he was felt down for anything hidden, then placed on his knees. Wade was already in that position, he saw, but then they were turned in opposite directions to prevent communication.

The police found all the weapons. It took only a few minutes before the .22, the AK, both pistols, the suppressors, cases, ammunition and their knives, flashlights, pocket tools, and cameras were all laid on the ground. A crowd had started to gather, but was chased away with a few curt words. It gradually built up again until it reached a level the police considered unacceptable, then was chased away again.

"Who are you and what is this?" A man in a gray suit, presumably a detective, asked him.

"I am Kyle Monroe. I am an American. I would like to talk to my embassy before I say anything else, domnule," he replied. He wasn't sure what if any rights he had here, but there was no need to talk unnecessarily. At the same time, he didn't want to be rude or evasive. They might have the legal right to smack him around for answers. And they did need to talk to the embassy.

"Why did you shoot? Who are you working for?" the man asked. He was neat-looking and appeared confident and calm despite the agitation around him, but clearly wanted answers.

"If you call my embassy and ask for Mister Mick Cafferty, he can explain everything," Kyle said. *I hope*. They'd been told they wouldn't be abandoned, but the government was notorious for changing the rules partway through.

"Spell that name," the detective asked curtly. Kyle did so, grateful that they seemed to want answers more than to bust heads.

"We will discuss this at the station and there you will answer my questions. You are under arrest and in much trouble."

"Da, domnule," Kyle said. He could hear Wade being questioned and harassed further over. Perhaps they'd heard stories of American street gangs and drug dealers. There was a drug trade here, after all. Heroin.

A van pulled up and the doors were thrown open. They were shoved rudely but not viciously into it. It drove away at once, swaying them off the plain metal benches they sat on. There was a single dome light for dim, shadowy illumination, and not much else. It was a steel box.

"I hope he doesn't brake hard," Kyle said. He could see them being slammed around like bugs in a box.

"Know how to get cuffs around front?" Wade asked.

"No."

"Like this," Wade said, rolling on the metal floor and forcing his wrists past his hips, then tucking his feet through the cuffs one at a time. "Gives leverage in case there's an 'accident,' and lets you scratch your nose."

"Thanks," Kyle said, dropping and rolling

and yanking until he, too, had his hands in front. It had hurt a bit, the cuffs cutting in, but he did feel better with them in front. He was restrained still, but not helpless. "And how often have you had to do this?"

"Let's not go there at this time," Wade said.

"Fair enough." He spent time examining the cuffs. They were well-worn but solidly built, and there was nothing to be gained by unfastening them, anyway. All it would do was annoy their captors, if shifting them to the front wouldn't have done so already.

Shortly, the van stopped and someone opened the doors. Figures waved them out into a dark, dank basement and through a steel-barred gate into a concrete receiving area. The staff were all male, mostly smaller than the snipers but with attitude and control to back them up. They may not even have known why these two were here.

Again Kyle and Wade were searched, finger-printed, photographed, shoved around like sides of beef, then dragged down a passage and tossed into a small cell with a sink and toilet, both slimy gray with mold. They were separate from any other prisoners, but the noise indicated there were quite a few in the building.

"Well, we're not hurt yet," Kyle said. He was still worried about abuse and torture. Enemies he could face bravely enough. Being cooped up was a different threat entirely. The room was a con-crete box with a barred door. There were two concrete benches, shelves really, to sleep on. Both were filthy and dusty.

"So we sit and relax and wait," Wade suggested. "We both need sleep."

"I suppose."

It seemed Kyle's responses had put off any further questioning for now. They were left in the cell. They swapped jokes and war stories. Kyle started to wonder about food and water. Then he stopped wondering, because they obviously weren't to get either anytime soon.

He untensed enough to use the toilet. He hadn't gone in hours, and was puckered and wound up tight. Between the arrest and political incident, and not getting their target prior to that, he was very worried. If there was a dead terrorist to ID, they were in a much better position than if not. There were two others they could claim as kills, but that might not improve things. Results aside, few nations approved of operations in their territory without their oversight. After all, the people being disposed of had their own home countries which would be disturbed.

There was just no way this was going to end well, he thought.

He sat on one of the benches and leaned back. It was cold, smelly, drafty, and dank in there. The lightbulb above in its cage, glaring into his eyes, reminded him of the non-functional ones in the castle. He had a quick flashback to the burial pit and shivered. They certainly knew how to hide people in this country.

He really hoped Cafferty could do something. He was their only link, and if he decided to deny them, it would fall on Robash, who would have to deal through State, which wasn't happy with them.

He looked across at Wade, who was pretending to be calm and not succeeding. There was an uncharacteristic twitch to his left knee.

"Scared?" he asked.

"Trying to sleep," Wade said. He didn't deny the inference and didn't crack a joke. He was scared, too.

Sleep was the only thing that would pass the time, and they'd need to be alert when questioned. Hopefully, they'd have a representative with them when questioned. He thought that was considered normal procedure in most of the world, and hoped it held true here.

He twitched awake, gasping in pain. He was still sitting up, and his head had flopped sideways. Added to the tight muscles, it caused him an excruciating cramp. He rubbed it, then his gritty eyes. Then he muttered to himself and lay down. If he could sleep, he should. Wade was already out, breathing evenly but tossing fitfully.

Kyle had never felt hopelessness in this measure. There was nothing to give him any hope at the moment. He wasn't religious, his only friend in this hemisphere was next to him, and he had

no idea what the government would do. As he
drifted back into a disturbed doze, that colored
his dreams.

It was some time later, hours at least, when noise
came down the hall.

"Someone's here," Wade said. They were both
awake but lying, staring at nothing.

One of the guards was clanking keys in the
lock. "*Veniti*," he said. *Come*.

"Better something than sitting here. Maybe
we'll see a phone or a judge," Kyle said.

"*Linişte. Vă plimbaţi*," the guard said curtly.
Silence. Walk. Kyle picked up his gist.

They preceded the guard down the hall, not
cuffed, and wondering what was next. The passage was scrubbed but ugly cinder block, and
would have been foreboding had not Kyle seen
the holes under Bran already. On the other hand,
there were definitely people with guns here, and
he was definitely at their mercy. Movies aside,
trying to break out of a police station, with no
map, no communications, and no idea of where
they were was suicide. It made him feel even
more helpless, and he didn't like it. He glanced at
Wade, who was silent and had a firm set to his
jaw. He was scared, too.

They waited while the guard clanked open another heavy door. He waved them silently
through into what was a normal office hallway.
They blinked at the much brighter and more

modern lights, and stood waiting. The guard motioned them forward and pointed at a door.

They entered and were in an office. A Romanian in a suit awaited them, along with two men in Romanian leaf-pattern camouflage, similar to U.S. Woodland pattern but splotchier. The ranking one didn't come across as a cop but as a government authority figure of some kind.

"Captain Monroe, and Lieutenant Curtis," he said with a nod. His English was accented but clear.

"Uh, yes," Kyle agreed. The ranks were wrong, but he wasn't going to object just yet. The names were right and this man was obviously from the government. He knew who they were and was going to want answers.

"Mister Cafferty spoke with me. I am a little annoyed that the U.S. chooses to run operations in my country without consulting."

"I can understand that completely, sir," Kyle said. He felt relieved, though. Cafferty knew they were here, and they were speaking to an official, not a local cop. And being out of the cell and in an office, not an interrogation room, was a good sign.

"So you will finish this in cooperation with DGIPI." It was a statement, verging on an order.

"Ah, yes, sir," he said. Then he said the thing he was afraid would get them back in jail. "But I must consult with my government first." He also wanted to know who exactly the DGIPI were, but that could wait a few minutes.

The man, who had not yet identified himself, stared coolly at him for a second that seemed endless. "With yours, and not with mine. You forget which country you are in." The obvious threat was left unsaid.

"But," he continued, "You are obviously disciplined and professional, judging from your accomplishments so far. We shall all discuss this. Then, we shall hunt terrorists. You will come with me." His face betrayed nothing.

With that, he turned and headed out, two of the men nearby picking up the case that held the Ruger, a rifle case that apparently held Wade's AK, and a box that sounded like it held pistols, from the clattering. That left a cardboard carton full of clothing and other gear. The police stood aside and pretended not to see what was going on.

"That's a hint, I think," Wade said, nodding after the mysterious spook.

"Yup. Forward," Kyle said.

Out the door, down the steps. It felt partly like freedom, and partly like a step toward a firing squad. Outside was dusky again. They'd been in jail all day and not fed.

They were led to a car with an open rear door. It was a large, black BMW sedan, and they climbed in without urging. It was away from the station, and the official had told them they were involved in the operation. Given that, their property accompanying them, and Cafferty's name mentioned, it should be safe. But the specter of the cell followed them and would for a while. They sat silently.

In a few minutes that seemed oddly compressed, the car stopped and the door opened. In the growing dark, they went where directed, up steps into another office. It seemed the Romanians liked steps. Their chaperone and his soldiers flanked them. Others waited inside.

Then they saw Mick Cafferty, sitting in a chair. He looked grim, until Kyle realized it was fatigue. The man was gulping a cup of coffee, and it probably wasn't his first. He smiled when he saw them, and it was an ugly smile on that lined and worn face.

"Glad to see you gentlemen," he said.

"Likewise, sir," Wade said, while Kyle was still shifting mental gears.

"How are things?" Kyle asked.

" 'How are things?' " Cafferty repeated, eyebrows raised. "We've annoyed our hosts, killed people on their soil, chased terrorists through their streets, allowed a shipment of explosives we knew about to come in without warning them, admitted to espionage and deceit . . ."

"That bad?" Kyle asked. Maybe they were all to be back in jail soon. Or just deported on the next plane.

"That bad. But you got two who were confirmed and scared up another, plus the explosives, which were secured. If we didn't have that to show, it would be bad. As it is, you impressed several bureau chiefs, including Dvidiu Pavenic." He pointed at their escort.

"Really?" Wade asked. Both snipers were still in shock.

"Really," Cafferty nodded. "There's new respect for our ability. We got you in, you tracked these bastards right under everyone's noses, and pulled them out."

"And the secrecy wasn't embarrassing?" Kyle asked.

"Not publicly. If you'd made a scene at any point and the press had caught on, that would have been embarrassing. But as long as it's quiet and our hosts get the credit," he hinted, "we can finish this."

"Hell, we knew we'd never be allowed to boast, anyway," Kyle said. "And I don't care about credit. General Robash knows what we're doing, and I don't crave to have hit squads bent on revenge. Anyone who wants the credit can take it."

From behind him, Pavenic said, "That is a very professional attitude, Captain. I like how you think, and I like how you shoot."

Kyle turned to face him. "And I like your honesty," he said. "With Mister Cafferty to approve, we're at your disposal." He wasn't quite sure he felt that way, but he knew they were under local command now. Still, that meant backup for any operation, and no need to worry about local issues. They could just shoot as they were told and let someone else take the blame. As much as Kyle liked independence and the trust placed in Wade and him, he could use a break.

"Yes. It's a pity Mister Cafferty didn't know to come to us first. But of course, he couldn't have known."

"Sir?" Kyle asked.

"Like yourself, we are a counterterror unit," he said, though Kyle had never thought of himself as a "unit." He was a soldier who took the shots and gathered the intel he was told to. Target acquisition was largely not his problem.

Pavenic continued. "We are a small platoon within DGIPI. And we all know our people, so we know there are no leaks here." That might not be entirely true at all times, but it likely was in regard to terror. No one competent wanted to shame themselves in front of their buddies, or get them killed through carelessness.

"And there was no way to know that," Cafferty agreed, "But I am very glad it turned out this way."

"So are we," Kyle said. It had likely made it much easier to get out of incarceration with the equivalent of the FBI interested.

"Then we are all happy, and happier still when these filth are shot, eh? Every nation that shoots a few makes it that much harder for the rest to operate and find homes. We shall get your property, and discuss what we are to do. I will return." He left, as did his henchmen, though

Kyle was quite sure there was one posted outside the door.

As soon as the door closed, he took a glance around and asked Cafferty, "How bad is it?"

"Well, it could be better," Cafferty admitted. "We're on probation, and if we don't have something else to show, it's not going to be good."

"So you still need us to pull off a shot?" Wade asked.

"That would make things better," he admitted, drinking more coffee. "There are other ways, but that's cheapest and simplest."

"No pressure," Wade said, but he was grinning.

"None," Cafferty smiled back. "We told him you were officers. It made a better appearance that we required that status for a mission, rather than 'mere' NCOs."

Kyle nodded. "I thought that might be it. Understood, sir."

"Is there a temporary pay raise with that?" Wade joked.

"Sure is," Cafferty said. He leaned back, fished a European five-cent coin from his pocket, and dropped it on the table. They all chuckled.

"You're lucky," he added. "High profile prisoners are harder to have accidents with."

"Yeah, I was worried about that," Kyle said. Hell, there were American cops who would have shot first or applied a club. He didn't imagine it was any better or worse here. Police were charged with the peace, but were also human beings, subject to prejudice and attitude.

"It was very tense," Cafferty agreed. "But I made calls, the ambassador made calls at the behest of State and DoD. We got someone over there. I hope you're both okay?"

"Hungry, thirsty, tired. And not thrilled about working with the locals." It was true, he had to say it.

"Well," Cafferty observed, eyebrows raised slightly, "it *is* their country. And I'd rather work at this level with Mister Pavenic than let the word leak out. DGIPI is known for their . . . vigorous attention and forthright approach."

Kyle looked at Wade, who nodded back. They both understood the implication. The government as a whole wouldn't hear of this, except as statistics. And there'd be no due process. DGIPI would bury the bodies deep and erase the records.

"Then we'll do it their way," Kyle acceded. There was nothing else to say.

The Romanian counterterror chief returned a few moments later. He was smiling faintly, and the smile became a grin when he saw the nods from the Americans. "Excellent," he said. He spoke a quick, fluid sentence to the captain with him, and the weapon cases were placed on the table. "Your tools, gentlemen," he said.

"Thank you, sir," Kyle said. He and Wade both dived in to assess the weapons.

They had been well dusted for fingerprints by

the police, and some powder still drifted from ports and wells. But someone, likely with the DGIPI, had wiped them down with oil. They spent a few minutes stripping and cleaning with long-practiced fingers while they discussed strategy. The Romanians drank tea and Cafferty chugged coffee. What he really needed, Kyle thought, was a caffeine IV. He looked up from his work as a tray of sandwiches on dark bread arrived. He was grateful for that. His hunger was severe. It was decent roast beef with butter, salt, and mayonnaise. It would go a long way toward reviving him.

"We have posted guards at the borders, airports, and the port. While that doesn't prevent him from leaving, it does make his task harder. We were hoping to drive him underground," Pavenic said.

"That's where we found him last time," Kyle said.

"Perhaps not literally this time," spook said. "Nevertheless, with his photograph on television, he seems nervous. We are hoping to shortly get reports on his whereabouts."

"Assuming he comes out and is seen," Kyle said.

"Yes, there is that. However, we were able to trace his car to its owner. The owner also had a satellite cell-phone relay station, and several maps and charts. While not conclusive evidence, it was enough for us to question him further. He was hesitant at first"—Pavenic sounded rather pleased with that, and smiled a very cold smile. Kyle had an American's belief in due process, but a soldier's hatred of terrorists. The latter ruled and he wasn't very bothered by the probable torture that the accessory had suffered—"but he eventually told us what we wanted to know. It appears there was some kind of contact missed, because al Asfan was not in his hotel when we arrived. But we know where he is, approximately."

"Oh?" The question was asked simultaneously by Kyle, Wade, and Cafferty.

"Yes. He had another hideout in the Carpathians and tried to get there. He apparently figured out it was occupied and is now trapped. The road in that area is blocked, and we have the area monitored. But that still leaves a lot of mountain and forest to search. He could slip out at night, and we do have to let other vehicles through from time to time. We need to find him quickly. We will have the Army search, but he may be dug in quite well. As you have taken two of them so far, it seemed polite to invite you along. Besides, it allows me to keep an eye on you both without worrying over your whereabouts." He smiled again, with some humor.

"Oh, I'm in," Kyle agreed. "We both are." He looked over at Wade, who nodded slowly with a big grin. "There may not be enough left of this asshole to bury after everyone gets a shot," he said.

"There is a problem here?" Pavenic asked with a cold, feral grin.

"No problem," Kyle said. "Should I leave him alive for the rest of you?" he joked.

"That's rude," Wade chided. "I just may get the first shot."

They all chuckled together. Kyle asked, "Do we get to meet our counterparts?"

"As we have time," Pavenic said. "I shall be leading. Our sniper is Sergeant Tibor Dobrogeanu." He pointed. The man stepped forward and nodded.

It was pretty obvious who he was. He held a ROMAK-3 rifle, well cared for and customized to fit him. It had been customized the professional way, with duct tape, files, and spray paint. Only amateurs prettified their weapons. Experts went for function. Dobrogeanu was tall, blond and very lean, and looked very confident. He'd make a good, lanky Southern farm boy, and Kyle knew without asking that he could shoot. He was reaching out a hand, and Wade shook it, then Kyle. His grip was firm but without any attempt to prove how strong he was.

At once, the rest of the team was running through, gathering gear and piling it around. They nodded or shook hands at a run. Pavenic yelled orders, grinning and gesturing flamboyantly. Periodically, the team would respond with "*Da, domnule!*" in shouted unison.

Cafferty came over, sucking coffee, and said something to Pavenic. The CIA man looked like hell, Kyle thought. His eyes were sunken, his skin waxy. Whatever stress the snipers were under, this man looked as if he were fighting a war by himself. Or perhaps avoiding a war.

The two exchanged nods, then Cafferty came toward Kyle and Wade. He nodded with a faint frown and directed them to a corner for a bit of privacy.

Once there, he asked, "How are you feeling about this?"

"At least it's like being soldiers again—outside and shooting," Kyle said. "Woods, hills, support. I like it. It's much more our mission than the espionage stuff."

"Kyle, you got two so far. Another has been arrested and we're working on a fourth. Stop beating yourself up."

"Yeah, I know," Kyle said, frowning. "Still, we got found."

"Everyone gets found. That's why we have State, and why I've got a bank of favors I can draw on. Hell, it'd be a miracle if you hadn't been caught during this. We warned you at the beginning."

"I suppose," Kyle said. He did recall the emphasis. He just hated to be less than perfect.

"I trust Pavenic, but keep in mind he's very aggressive. You're on your own as far as orders go. I have no authority and you're volunteering to work with him. If there's any roughing up and it gets reported to the UN . . ." he tapered off.

"War crimes charges?" Wade asked.

"Could be," Cafferty said. "So you make the calls. I've got to slide out of here. But good luck, thanks for everything so far, and we'll talk again in a day or two."

"Right," Kyle said. "I just wish I knew more about this."

"So do I."

He turned with a half grimace, half smirk, and trudged out.

Meanwhile, Pavenic came over and asked, "Is there any equipment you need?"

"Yeah," Kyle said. "Our boots, some clothes, weather gear of some kind. Whatever radios you're using, or we'll use ours." He paused to think.

"Preferably our own stuff, if it can be gotten in time," Wade said. "We had all we needed at the hotel."

"I will see to it," Pavenic said. "That should only take an hour or so."

While they waited, Pavenic briefed them. It wasn't as bad as Kyle had anticipated. Pavenic laid a large map out across a conference table and used a wooden pointer. He waved it like a rapier, jabbing it when excited.

"Al Asfan was seen here as he left Braşov. Our informants tell us he has a facility of some kind in the mountains here." He jabbed the map over the Carpathians, near Comănesti. "We have a helicopter observing, and there is something there. So we will investigate."

"Flying in?" Kyle asked.

"We are flying nearby. I do not care to land on top of explosives," Pavenic said. "I am crazy, and vicious, it is said and is true." His men snickered. He smiled. "But I am no fool. We will approach a few kilometers on foot, quietly. The helicopters will maintain watching, and I have called Army units to patrol the lower elevations. They will stop and inquire of anyone, and shoot anyone who does not stop. The police are likewise blocking the road."

"But this is a large area," he continued, "and if al Asfan thinks we follow, he may leave on foot or by vehicle and manage to escape. So we will leave at once. I would like him by daytime." His expression said it would be by daytime or else.

Loud but cheerful voices came from the outer office, and in a few seconds, one of the operatives clumped in. He was dressed in urban casual; raincoat, jacket, shirt but no tie and sturdy shoes, and was carrying all their luggage. He looked like a cartoon gunbearer for a safari.

"We don't really need the cameras," Kyle said as he smiled. He reached out and helped the young man untangle from his burden. "Those were mostly for cover, anyway." Wade stepped in to grab other bags.

"This way you don't have to fish for them later," the man said.

That was true. "It's appreciated," Kyle said. "But we'll have to do a check for anything we left." He was thinking of notes or possible small items forgotten behind furniture.

"There is nothing left in the room that is not the hotel's," the man assured him with a grin.

"I'll take your word on that," Kyle agreed. The man was a professional at this; he'd likely gotten everything.

"Captain Monroe," Pavenic called, and Kyle turned, still holding the betacam. "Here is your new rifle." He came over with it extended at port.

Kyle took it. It was another ROMAK-3. The ROMAK looked a bit like a Dragunov, but had been built up from the AK action. It wasn't impressive, because Eastern Bloc theory was for the sniper to support the infantry squad, not be a force multiplier by gathering intelligence and disrupting operations by shooting important targets. It was what Kyle would call a designated marksman's rifle, not a sniper's rifle.

But this one, like Dobrogeanu's, had a Dragunov stock fitted to it, proper windage drums on the iron sights and a decent-looking long scope with tritium reticle. It was also, he discovered when he checked the ammunition, chambered in 7.62 NATO, not $7.62 \times 54R$ Russian.

"Not bad," he commented softly. This might shoot well after all.

"It will shoot as well or better than you," Pavenic said.

"Want to bet?" Kyle asked with a challenging smile.

"I will trust you, Monroe. But if we get al Asfan first, you will buy the dinner."

"Deal," he agreed. It was a win/win proposition. Either he or Wade bagged another bad guy, or they assisted. If it all failed, there were a lot of people higher up to take the blame, and both nations would pass it off on each other. It was much more like the military he was familiar with, and would be a more comfortable shooting environment. And if he had to buy dinner, he had cash for the purpose. Uncle Sam's cash.

18

WITHIN ANOTHER TWENTY MINUTES, HE and Wade had gotten dressed, equipped, and armed. They were in British DPM smocks, canvas pants, and boots. They wore their tactical load-bearing vests with Camelbaks, knives, holsters, and ammunition, plus compasses and radios. They carried their ghillies rolled up, and each had their weapons. Wade had the AK104 and his Beretta, Kyle had the ROMAK3, the Ruger, and his Ed Brown. He still liked something for quiet shots, and there was nothing quieter than the Ruger, but the ROMAK allowed him heavier shots if called for.

They were issued headset radios. They weren't too dissimilar from the kind they'd used before, but Kyle decided they'd take their cell phones, too. "We can avoid interception with those," he said.

"True, and it can't be a bad thing."

Then they were in vehicles and driving for the local airport. Kyle and Wade were in a Mercedes SUV with Pavenic, who had ditched his suit for a camouflage coverall and an AK. It seemed he wanted to keep an eye on them after the car stopped. He hoped it would clear some before it was time to shoot. Kyle couldn't really blame him. It wasn't a long trip, but visibility was poor from the back seats, and the driver was as aggressive as any local, plus had government authority to flout the laws even more. It was a nauseating drive, made worse as the amphetamines kicked in. Kyle didn't approve of drugs, but he'd heard pilots took these to stay alert on long flights, and they'd had little sleep the last week. After being stuffed with sandwiches and water, he'd felt better, but sleepy. Now he was awake and things were spinning. Things kept spinning even after the car stopped.

They flew out by helicopter. This was something Kyle had heard about but never done. He had flown in helicopters often. What he'd never done was fly in a French Puma built under contract by Romanians using their own engines. The design was older than Kyle, and this craft wasn't the newest of the fleet. Still, his hosts were offering it, and the pilot had to be good enough to fly it, and so, hopefully, was good enough to land it. There was no need to create a fuss and it wouldn't matter. Kyle climbed aboard and took the outside seat. Wade was directly across, Pavenic next to Kyle with Dobrogeanu next to him. The others filled in and stuffed their gear.

"How many on this mission?" Kyle asked just before the engines started. He'd seen a number of personnel running through the headquarters, but wasn't sure who was support, operations, pilots, or just home station staff.

Pavenic indicated a helmet and headset. Kyle squeezed it over his head. It was a tight fit. As soon as he had it secure, Pavenic said, "Sixteen of us. I want to limit the number in the area to avoid bumping into each other. Between mobile phones and radios, we should easily be able to call the Army for assistance if needed."

"Okay," Kyle said. He preferred more lead time, and he didn't think it was possible to have too many troops. But it wasn't his operation anymore, if it ever had been. He was just the guy who made the shots.

Across from him, Wade gave him a nod and a thumbs-up. They'd be fine.

The chopper was in decent repair. They rose quickly through fairly smooth air and headed toward the mountains. Helicopters always shift a bit through air currents, the density affecting lift. Every time it buffeted or dropped, Kyle had an image of them being taken out by a missile. It wasn't as if Stingers or their equivalent were unknown among terrorists.

He realized a lot of it was nerves, and much of it caused by ghosts from the past. He'd not thought about Jeremy or Nasima for some time. He'd been too busy out here to dwell on them. That was likely good, but they were still present in his unconscious. He thought for a moment about Jeremy, young and eager and funny in a refreshing way, different from Wade's cynicism. Then Nasima, who'd been a civilian guide, but very bright and with a dry wit.

Just thinking about them calmed him down. That was a first. Perhaps he was coming to terms with things at last. God knew it had been long enough, and one couldn't live in the past forever. But pain was part of life, and he needed to deal with it. He just wondered why it was always coming to him on his way into action. Was it fear for himself? Concern for Wade? Or just caution for mission safety digging a bit too deep? Analyzing the emotions kept him busy and did lower his stress level, even if it made him morose. He took the harness offered him and strapped it on without much conscious thought.

The pilot took his time. If they'd known where their target was, faster would have been better. As they didn't, there was no reason to hurry. He felt out the buffeting winds and settled over the trees, then gradually lowered. They were no more than twenty-five meters up when the signal came.

It was a respectable rappel, and the trees were an obstacle. The snipers had done rappelling, and did refreshers often. Wade was far more current than Kyle. Adding the height and dark to the fatigue and nausea, Kyle almost lost dinner. He gulped back and clamped down on his stomach. It was a standard descent, and he snapped the carabiners around the rope, checked it, and leaned out the side.

The rotor wash was rough, but he slid below it and things steadied out. With cool, fresh air to help, he was soon much more comfortable. The dizziness was gone, the nausea retreated a bit, and he was himself. He looked around and realized he'd been hanging for several seconds. It was time to catch up.

They slowed as they reached the tall pines, feet spread to kick away from limbs and trunks. This was when it was dangerous, with limbs to stab and blind, tangle and catch. Kyle wove and twisted his way through the timber until he could see the ground a few feet below him. He dropped the last few feet gratefully, then unsnapped from the rope and unfastened the harness. He jogged over with his stuffed ruck to form up with the others. Pavenic was waiting, smiling.

The helicopter powered away to drop another squad of six elsewhere, and a four-man element at a third point. They'd advance in three different directions, hoping to catch al Asfan at one of several likely spots. This group was heading straight for the "facility," which looked on photos to be a small barn or large shed.

Pavenic spoke quietly, everyone in a huddle with one man on watch.

"We will split into pairs, one leading, one behind and to the side for support. Minimize radio talk. The target of this sweep is three thousand, one hundred meters that way," he pointed up the mountain they were on, then checked his compass—"at ninety-one degrees." He double-checked by GPS. "We shall start at a slow walk, then crawl upon suspicion of threat. Understood?" He repeated it in Romanian, even though most of the team did grasp English. The snipers nodded, his own people whispered, "*Da, domnule!*" quietly but firmly, and they were on patrol at once.

These had to be the darkest, dankest, creepiest woods Kyle had ever been in. The hanging limbs and shadows were spiderlike and black against the sooty gray sky behind them. Midnight was near, and that's when al Asfan was likely to make a break for it. Anytime from midnight to five was the best guess.

Of course, that assumed the man was competent and trained in this environment. One had to always assume the enemy was both genius and fool, and allow for both possibilities at the same time. And no enemy ever reacted to plan, no matter how many plans one made. One followed the plan until things went to hell, then discarded it to fight by one's wits. Abandoning the plan too soon or too late was what caused one to lose.

"Going to take a lot of luck," Kyle said as he looked around. "Well, we know we've gotten two and the explosives."

"Hey, looks good so far," Wade said. "We'll find him."

"Not sure about that," Kyle said. "But if anyone does, it'll be us. Pride is at stake."

"Good enough," Wade said.

They advanced up the large hill, amplified eyes alert for anything unnatural. Night vision does take considerable practice to use, but an experienced professional can find many things that would escape a newer soldier. Various materials will reflect differently and show outlines even behind camouflage that would be effective in daylight.

It was a hill by American standards. Not like the Rockies, but perhaps like the Appalachians. Still, it was cool, becoming chill, and damp with the spring weather. Nice weather for hiking for fun, not nice for crawling in weeds. But then, there were no nice conditions for crawling in weeds, except Arabia, where there were no weeds. And there was the sand.

They spread apart to allow different angles for shooting or observing. This time, there was no risk of the government finding them; it already had. This time, they had backup. It made Kyle much more confident, and he reminded himself not to get cocky. Amateurs could still be good observers, and just because much of the enemy's operation was amateurish didn't mean there wasn't a vet or two among them. They hadn't created as much havoc as they had by being unintelligent, just by being prejudiced and stupid.

So Kyle made a conscious effort to avoid rushing.

Nothing happened for the first kilometer. They came to a dirt trail that they'd seen in the photos, which was one of their landmarks. It came from the left, north, and curved to the east. The plan was to secure the area and then advance up both sides. So they examined the area for any fresh traces, smells, any sign of human activity. The DGIPI pilot would call down his observations. Until then, there was nothing to do but wait and be alert.

Pavenic called through and asked, "Report?"

"Nothing," Kyle said. "Clean, undisturbed."

"Good. We continue." The phrasing was simple and obvious to them, not so to anyone listening. It was well to assume the target had radio gear.

They had the easy part, continuing as they had. The Romanians had to cross the rutted path. That would take a few minutes, but there was no reason not to advance. They couldn't get far ahead at a crawl.

Another five hundred meters of tangled weeds and uneven ground passed, trees reaching down to caress them. Kyle was used to it. He'd spent much of his life in the wild. But it might be making their quarry nervous, as he was not from terrain like this. It was dark and foreboding, and a shot might come at any time. Combat didn't start when the enemy shot. Combat started when one hit the ground.

"As discussed, down," Pavenic ordered. Kyle dropped slowly to his knees and into a crawl, the nerves in his hands reaching out for warnings. He wore thin Nomex flying gloves, which kept off bugs and allowed good movement. He could feel feathery touches of leaves through them, and the ground. It was safer and less visible down here, but also slower, and it hindered their own views of their surroundings.

Forward and up they crawled around trees and shrubs, every movement careful. Neck back so as to see, with the NVGs dragging the head down and straining muscles. Hands and knees soaking up moisture and cold. Sweat beading under the arms. It reassured Kyle, because it was familiar.

"Possible sentry," Wade hissed through the phone.

Moving very carefully, he reached to his own phone body and pressed to transmit. "Where?" he asked.

"Appears to be a hasty position, under a bush. Do you see me?"

Kyle squinted to the last position he'd seen Wade in, then scanned forward. "Barely, but yes." There was a shape there, and a part of a boot. It wouldn't be visible to anyone ahead, but from here it was just discernible.

"Twenty-five meters ahead, left of the large gnarly tree, I think it's an oak. Spreading bush."

Kyle examined the area. One side of the bush did have a bit more hollow underneath it, where the natural debris and fallen leaves had been removed. He changed his angle slightly to the right and took a good look. There was something there that was probably human. Under the branches and leaves it stood out at the correct angle.

It looked as if the person revealed had used starch and/or an iron on their shirt. That flattened the nap of the fabric and created a reflective surface. To their night vision, it may as well have been aluminum foil. The guess was confirmed when the person shifted restlessly into a new position.

"Question is, who is that?" Kyle asked.

"Dunno. We have to check on whether or not it's one of ours," Wade said. It shouldn't be, on this side, but one didn't fire unless one was sure. Unless the target shot first.

"Calling." It took some time to move his hand to the radio controls, and Wade waited patiently while he did so. "Monroe here," he whispered inside his coat, eyes still watching. "We have a potential, IFF." He hoped that was clear. Identify Friend or Foe.

"I understand you. Where is the target?"

Kyle gave approximate grid coordinates. "Up slope from us. If anyone is on a slope, have them wave down and report."

"Wait . . . Do you see response?"

"Nothing here," Kyle said.

"Then you are clear to go."

"Understood. Out." It took another full minute to shift his hands and contact Wade again. "We're clear to fire," he said.

"Roger."

That wasn't all there was to it, however. There could be other enemy, presuming this *was* an enemy, within range. So it was necessary to secure the area first, then try to arrange a silent kill.

"I will traverse left and set up for shot," Kyle said. "Secure and observe."

"You will traverse and shoot, I will secure and observe," Wade repeated.

"Moving," Kyle said.

"Moving, roger."

It took nearly twenty minutes to shift to a spot with good visibility of the enemy's face. Kyle didn't recognize it, but he was armed and he wasn't in uniform, so he was a target. And the AK he held was ready. The first shot had to disable at the very least, to let them stay alive. That wasn't a problem. It would be better, however, to get a kill, so there would be no incoming fire to create a problem. The only reasonable way to do that was with a silenced, subsonic weapon. The 10 22 wasn't powerful enough for a reliable, instant kill. But fifty meters was a long range for any pistol, even an Ed Brown.

Just then, Pavenic spoke in his ear, "We are prepared to attack a perimeter position." He was speaking in clear, so he anticipated starting at once.

Kyle shifted as quickly as he dared. If they could get inside silently and set up, then they could have easy targets at the backs of their enemies as the DGIPI attacked frontally. That would roll all these guys up.

It took twenty seconds to shift the radio, while he cursed and sweated, expecting them to open fire any second. What was needed here, he decided, was some kind of radio that could handle internal squad communications, communications up a level, and a frequency for command. All of those should be selectable by voice.

But he did reach the control and brought his attention back to the task as he said, "Hold, hold. Do not fire."

"Holding fire, understood," was the response.

"Curtis and I can get inside, then we can roll up the entire perimeter," he said.

"How long do you need?"

"Another twenty minutes," he said. He could bag this guy now, and then they'd get past him.

"Hurry if you can," Pavenic urged him.

"Roger."

He continued his lateral movement and picked a log as his shooting position. Logs often crumbled when stepped on, but all he intended was to rest his arms on it. He elbowed along, dragging the rest of his body as silently as possible, the ROMAK dragging behind him from a sling over his shoulder in case he needed it.

He felt movement, and froze. It was just a small nocturnal animal of some kind skittering past, but he paused to ensure it hadn't attracted attention. A measured minute later, he resumed his creep and eased up against the dead limb. It was starting to rot and was slimy with fungus, mold and moss, but that wasn't something he worried about. It was cold to his forearms as he gingerly checked its stability. It didn't shift, and he was satisfied. A quick mental check of his condition and surroundings assured him he was well-masked and still unseen. Now to set up and shoot.

Slowly, he drew the pistol up under his body and secured the suppressor. In five minutes, it had grown in front of him like a metal log, lying atop the limb and pointing forward. He hunched and shifted, twisted his head and hands until it was where he wanted it. The only practical way to sight it while wearing NVGs was to extend it at arm's length, dead center. It was odd to see a single sight picture with both eyes, but that was the nature of the goggles, which focused one incoming image for both eyes.

There were the guard's eyes. He wanted to put this round right between them. For ease of function and consistency, he had stock 230 grain ball ammo. With his sight settings, it should be only two inches of drop at fifty meters. And the sight pattern barely cleared the suppressor's body. So he would lean way down, hold there, and place the front sight blade halfway between the bushy eyebrows and the combed hairline. The wind was negligible, and the heavy projectile wouldn't need any windage adjustment.

Right there, and as long as the man was holding still, squeeeeze.

With a thump that might be mistaken for an animal against a log, the .45 bullet erupted from the suppressor. Kyle could just see the flash with night vision. Anyone else could, too, and he tensed in case of fire. But the only response was for the enemy guard to jerk his head back, then slump forward. The shot had been dead center on the bridge of the nose.

"Go, Wade," Kyle muttered into the phone. He eased back from his brace, letting his eyes scan over the pistol for any potential targets. He relaxed his grip and prepared to shift for any new threats.

"Roger," Wade replied. Kyle saw movement from the corner of his eye as a "bush" rose to its knees and crawled forward. Wade was moving unnaturally but slowly. Several minutes later, he stopped just to one side of the corpse, his Beretta out and ready. He shifted in until the suppressor nearly touched the skull of the body, and fired an insurance shot that popped softly. It never hurt to make sure a corpse was really dead.

"AK, radio," he muttered back. "Cell phone. We need to hurry in case he's expected to check in."

"Got it. Is the other side of the road manned?" While Wade dealt with that question, he radioed Pavenic and said, "We have removed one sentry. Stand by and we'll clear the road. I think you can advance on our side safely."

Wade reported back right then. "I see what's likely a position, well dug in. I identify a rifle barrel. I cannot take a shot from here. I can spot for their sniper."

"Roger," Kyle said, then switched channels again. "Wade says he can perform terminal guidance."

"Please do," Pavenic replied. He sounded quite pleased. A few moments later, Dobrogeanu came on air.

"I am ready," he said.

What they were about to try would be dangerous against professionals. Against these amateurs, it was a different story. The big threat was that the enemy would not react predictably. An expert, upon being alerted, would call that fact in, then commence suppressive fire until reinforcements arrived. A frightened neophyte might shoot wildly, alerting everyone, call on the radio, or panic and do something really stupid. Either way, the other sentry had to be removed. It was just a case of how responsive he'd be.

Wade came on air and relayed his observations. "Fifteen meters left of the road. On a line horizontally, just above the water-filled ruts near the large pine with roots extending into the roadway."

Dobrogeanu replied back, "I see a pile of brush with ten centimeter limb running sideways from a pine tree. There is a light color boulder about two meters downhill."

"I see it," Wade said. "From that boulder, target is one boulder width higher, one meter left of the tree, just under the limb."

"I sight something in that location. It appears to be dull fabric." Dobrogeanu sounded confident and eager.

"Confirm target," Wade said.

"Confirm. Target acquired."

Pavenic came back on air. "At my order, Dobrogeanu will fire. All others will hold fire. Ready. Fire."

The ROMAK pop-cracked, and the animal noises stopped suddenly, leaving things silent. Hopefully, nothing else would happen and they could now advance.

From uphill there was a loud whisper. Someone was looking for the perimeter guards.

"Damn," Kyle said.

"I have a target," Wade said urgently.

"Shoot," Pavenic said.

The suppressed AK104 was no louder than a rock thudding on a tree. A third enemy dropped dead. But again, the local noises stopped.

"Well, we're known now, I think," Kyle said.

"Yes, but we have position."

Kyle didn't answer. It was true. They were military against amateurs, and even a defended position wasn't going to help the amateurs. But that didn't mean the professionals wouldn't take casualties.

The six of them progressed up the hill. Kyle really wished for more backup in the form of the Army. He knew there were disciplinary problems and potential leaks, but he still didn't like the low numbers. It was simply a matter of the number of people needed to cover the area.

On the other hand, there was no way a common Army unit could move that quietly en masse. They'd need an elite unit, anyway, and that would take time. As it was, the perimeter could be secured by any conscripts available until better forces came along. But it still left them as sixteen men spread across a large chunk of countryside, and only six on the advance.

Sure enough, there was response. It was a trained response, too. They might not have the experience of the snipers or DGIPI, but they knew how to move and were doing so in a coordinated fashion. Several figures were moving, low to the ground and hard to discern; they sounded heavy, which indicated equipment.

"They have night vision," Kyle heard from Pavenic. Someone had observed one of the enemy.

"Roger." So hold very still and try for a shot.

For long minutes, bare shuffles could be heard. The high ground was the tactically better, and these men had it. Also, they had hard cover in their positions, and possibly body armor, too. They'd be hard to dig out.

But waiting was something Kyle was used to. All they needed was to wait for daylight, then saturate the area. That it came down to a standoff at night was a good sign.

Nothing. For half an hour they lay and waited and watched. No obvious targets revealed themselves. Kyle asked Wade and Pavenic, who inquired back the other way. They shifted around to get different perspectives, aware of the fact that they were known this time, and that their targets were also adept at cover. If these troops had the mindset of many Muslims, one would expose himself to fire, and his buddies would return it in force against the attacking position. While that was always a risk, it wasn't one to be taken without support.

And it was too late now to retreat, or try a drop directly on the facility. They had to be sure their target was actually here, or risk pouring force here while he escaped elsewhere. With men this dangerous, "probably dead" in an explosion was not sufficient. A body or at least photos were needed. If the building was booby trapped, they'd have only estimates as to al Asfan's presence or lack thereof. That wasn't good enough.

Which meant that someone, very likely Kyle Monroe, was going to have to fight through or around these troops, and try to get a visual on al Asfan.

They knew there were sentries ahead. The sentries knew there were attackers. It was a standoff, and it favored the attackers, but it wasn't the best scenario. With that many people on the hill, al Asfan could more easily slip out, even with IR or night vision scans. He was willing to waste his troops to escape, and they were willing to be wasted, most likely. But that also meant a substantial hole in his network when this was done.

If nothing else, that was a nice consolation prize. But Kyle wanted this bastard's blood. So he sat and waited patiently for a signal.

The tableau was broken when Pavenic said, "Monroe, we have contact with Target Primul."

"Where and how?" he asked at once, quivering and even more alert, nerves bristling. Had they been seen?

"Through the captured mobile phone."

That made sense. If the man wanted to get hold of them, that was the logical way.

"What does he say?"

"He says he wants to talk to one of you directly. He thinks there's six snipers, for some reason."

"Disinformation from Cafferty," Kyle said.

"Ah, yes. You have your own leaks, despite your mistrust of us." Pavenic sounded a bit put upon.

"Not my department," Kyle said. Nor was now the time for a debate over the merits of one nation over another, the reliability of personnel and the relative risk of known and unknown leaks. Now was the time for shooting. "Give him this number."

A few moments later, Pavenic replied, "I have done so. Please do keep me aware of your discussion."

"I'll try to connect through the radio," Kyle agreed. He could hold it up and let it transmit from the earpiece. It might be audible. Or . . .

was there a way to connect them directly?

No, he decided, after a few seconds of study. With a few cables, it would be possible. But not with materials on hand. His pondering was interrupted by the phone buzzing.

"Yes?" he answered.

"Sergeant Kyle Monroe," al Asfan said, barely above a whisper.

Sergeant. Not "Captain." So this guy did have some decent intel. Kyle wasn't that surprised. It wasn't all that unlikely, with the leaks they'd had, that someone would get his correct rank. It was a bit odd that the terrorist would make an issue of it. One never gave away intel advantages, unless it was part of a psy-war ploy. So this character didn't know as much as he wanted to, and was trying to impress them with the little bit he did. Still . . .

"Yes, may I help you?" He neither acknowledged nor denied the name or rank. Hopefully, he didn't sound surprised, either. In truth, this stage of an incident like this called for a professional negotiator. But they didn't have that option, time was short, and there was a real risk this asshole could blow something up. Best to keep him busy here, if he really was here. He wouldn't make the mistake of using a traceable phone again, so was either using a satellite cell, or had some way to spoof his signal. Actually, they knew he'd done the latter.

"I intend to see you dead."

"Of course you do," Kyle said. "Actually, seeing it shouldn't be hard. Just wait until I die from old age and come to the funeral home."

"Don't play stupid. You know I control this situation. I could make some other phone calls and have some bombs set off."

Hell, you might have arranged that already, in case you die. But I sure as hell won't say so. Kyle had little idea what to do at this point, except he was sure the things shown on TV were wrong. Meanwhile, he'd managed to get the headset mic next to the cell's speaker, and hoped it was being heard.

"What is there to talk about?" Kyle asked. "Or are you just trying to postpone the time when I blow your head off?"

"I just wanted to tell you that there's explosive in the building. Attacking it will cause it to blow up. Also, several other bombs will be triggered if I don't send orders not to."

"Okay, you have bombs. We knew that. You want to kill kids. We knew that. Is there anything important?" He wanted to goad this man into talking more, so they could glean intel.

"I am explaining to you why I control the situation. Don't be a fool, or much blood will be on your hands."

"The only blood on my hands," Kyle said, "is going to be yours. Sorry, jackass, but 'Waah! Waah! Look what you made me do!' doesn't impress me. If anyone else dies, it's your fault, and it might get you to live a bit longer. That way I can watch the expression on your face while you bleed to death." He intended no such thing. Revenge was dangerous, and Kyle could create such thoughts himself, if he really wanted to. The fact was, he hated killing, despised having to shoot people like this, but there was no way anyone had found to reach them otherwise. And given they choice between killing them or letting them hurt others, Kyle knew which he preferred.

"I have just sent an order," al Asfan said tightly. "People are going to die because of your arrogance."

"Hell, if my word can cause death, I've got every right to be arrogant." He figured that would shake things up. He also *did* feel guilt over any pending deaths. If they'd gotten this guy earlier . . .

No, that wasn't true. Kill one, and the next idiot stepped into his place. "The War on Terror" might be a good political name, but the reality was there were always people wanting to tear civilization down, and there had and would always be a need for men like Kyle to deal with it. Bin Laden was in hiding or dead, and the bombings continued. Bin Qasim was dead, and the bombings still went on. But if they kept taking out the brains of the operation, and the demented whiz kids who built the bombs, eventually they'd trim it to a manageable level.

Until next time.

"I had hoped to reach you and talk like a man," al Asfan said. "I see I was mistaken. Another bomb has been ordered."

"I do hope it's France," Kyle said. "Everyone hates the French." He was taking a guess there, but playing on current politics. He really had to convince this nutcase that he didn't care about bodies, that he, too was a sociopath. That would mean al Asfan would have to find another way to antagonize him.

There was silence. That might mean it was working. Of course, the guy could also be ordering several dozen bombs around the world as a "fuck you" gesture.

Likely not. If he had all those bombs, he would have been setting them off. That he'd ordered all that explosive meant he intended to. But most of it had been captured.

So tweak him again, Kyle thought. "Why don't you come here?" he prodded. "Afraid?"

"Afraid of being shot by cowards who hide in shadows? Why, yes, I am. Are you afraid to meet me like a man?"

"Not at all. I'll give you my map coordinates and you can come meet me."

Best case, he'd get in, bag this trash, and nothing else would happen. That seemed unlikely, but he had come here to deal with this, so he might as well. But he didn't want to sound eager. Nor could he sound impressed by the threats toward civilians, or they'd never stop.

"You and DGIPI and your five other gutless snipers. No doubt you'd wet your pants upon my appearance, but then you'd attack me, like so many rats. I prefer a better way."

"So do I," Kyle said. "I advised them to just bomb the shit out of you from the air, but they want to be reasonable."

"Of course you will not bomb me, because the retribution would be horrible," al Asfan said smugly. "We know you are a nation of cowards."

"Yeah, whatever," Kyle said. "Is there anything important to discuss, or should I get back to hunting you? I even have a terrorist hunting call here. *Allahu akbar!*"

"One more mindless insult, and you shall cause another bomb to go off. Many more people will die for your ego." He was shaking now, audible through the phone. It was dangerous to tread on religious ground with lunatics, and not something Kyle would ever do with decent Muslims around . . . but there weren't any here and it was helping to infuriate his enemy. Al Asfan's threats were very repetitive. That was a good sign. It meant he had no other refuge.

Always the way with terrorists. They built the bomb, placed the bomb, chose the victims and the reason, but someone else "made" it happen. It was appropriate for five-year-olds. But from terrorists, wife beaters, or rapists, it drove Kyle into a frenzied rage. Which is why he was here.

"Right. You set off your bombs. I've got work to do." He deliberately held the phone down underneath and cycled the bolt on the Ruger. Then he disconnected.

Because there was no more intel to be had from this source at present, the enemy obviously feared snipers, and cutting al Asfan off denied him control of the conversation. He should be well stewed by now.

"Did you catch all that?" he asked Pavenic and Wade.

"*Da.*"

"Yup. Guy's nuttier than a box of granola."

Pavenic continued, "I recommend we press on. He made no threats against us, and we can secure this area. I suspect he is here, or he wouldn't be trying to distract us."

"I concur," Kyle said. "Fast or slow?"

"As dictated," Pavenic said. "After all, we would prefer not to take casualties to filth like this. We shall continue slowly and go to the fast attack if circumstance changes."

"Roger. I recommend we pick a probable target and saturate it. That will split their attention among all of us, and we'll have Wade and Dobrogeanu spot for additional targets."

"That should work," Pavenic said. "Do you have a target?"

"Wade does. Wade?"

"Target, individual with rifle. Reference, large pine to one o'clock, just above a ridge of rock . . ." Wade read them in until everyone had acknowledged some kind of target, either the man, or the spot where Wade said there was a man. The volume of fire should be sufficient to ensure success. Of course, there were quite a few others in these woods, and God knew how they'd react.

Still, battles were like that. It was time to bring it on.

"On your order," Pavenic acknowledged.

"Roger. Stand by on my order. All elements take aim. Commence . . . fire!"

The sound wasn't that of shots. It was one disciplined, controlled roar that shook the hill. Through his goggles, Kyle could see a rifle slump down into the dirt below the position. *Scratch another asshole.*

It also had an effect on the other enemy. They opened fire, just as wanted. Kyle hadn't left any traceable signature with a suppressed .22, but the larger rifles did have muzzle flash. Flash suppressors attenuate the blast somewhat, and more important, divert it from the sight plane of the shooter. But large-caliber rounds always have a nimbus of fire.

The return shots were chaotic and ragged, but there were a lot of them. Then there was the glare and bang of a grenade. Wade was shouting another target reference, but Kyle couldn't make it out clearly in the din. So it came down, as it usually did, to two groups of people shooting it out, each hoping for the other group to make more mistakes.

Kyle was about to deliberately make a mistake. They needed to get through this line and find their real target. There wasn't time to discuss it, and the mass confusion offered a chance. He wasn't about to let al Asfan slip away yet again, so he took immediate action on his own authority. His headset spoke, someone reporting himself wounded. So the enemy weren't totally incompetent. Or else they'd been very lucky. Other shouts came, both directly and through the radio. Most were Romanian. A few were fractured English, from Pavenic. Some sounded as if they might be Arabic, and one was probably Russian.

He unfastened his ghillie by ripping the buttons. He wasn't going to be hiding, and it would slow him down with what he had planned. He wrapped it around the ROMAK and dropped it. It wasn't as safe as pulling the firing pin, but he was in a hurry, and as tangled as it was, it would take time for anyone to get it, even if they found it.

That done, he stood to a crouch and ran forward, dodging from tree to tree. Taking cover and concealment was not something he needed to think about; he'd had fifteen years of practice. At each position he scanned ahead for threats, then rose to dart forward another few meters. He kept a close eye out for the perimeter guards, and saw one, cuddling the ground and trying to look invisible. That was probably the smartest thing he could do, but it wasn't going to help here. Kyle swung the Ruger and tapped two shots past the helmet and deep into the collar. The man convulsed and probably yelled—Kyle wasn't sure. But as the man arched up, another bullet through his throat made it academic. There were major blood vessels in both locations, and even if he didn't die at once, the battle was over for him.

Kyle was panting up the mountain. Even though he'd practiced the method, uneven movement took more energy than a straight run, and it was uphill. Adrenaline coursed through him, making him warm. It would also make his shots a bit less accurate. He kept scanning ahead for other threats, but it seemed to be clear along this line. Then he saw one far to his left, focused on something farther downhill.

He knelt, raised the Ruger and got a sight picture just as his elbow met his knee for stability. A squeeze and it was over, the round catching his target right below his helmet line, almost through the ear. The man dropped and spasmed as he died, and that was it.

Except for the grenade he'd been holding, which detonated a few moments later, blowing him and large chunks of landscape around. Still, that meant no more grenades—at least not from that source. Another banged farther away.

It sounded as if the fire below was slacking off. That was either an indication of success or of lines stabilizing again. But that wasn't his concern. If he'd moved properly and the reports were correct, the facility in question should be a bit farther up the hill.

He slowed slightly, both to reduce the rasping

tear of cold air through his throat and to keep better track of his surroundings. Ahead, the terrain appeared to level out, with mist starting to fall. That was probably where he wanted to go.

Wade spoke in his ears, "Where are you, buddy?" It was the cell phone.

"I'm closing on where I think the cabin is. Get them to encircle closer if you can."

"Will do. I'll be along in a few."

"Roger."

He topped a slight rise and entered a meadow. Ahead, he could see a rude lodge built of clapboards and blocks. It was of good size, perhaps ten meters by six. But that didn't mean that was all there was to it, and even that space was enough for plenty of people or explosives. He kept walking, slowing his pace slightly and making sure he kicked brush and weeds. It wouldn't do to surprise a man who was a raving paranoid and liked blowing up children. If he was here, Kyle wanted to let al Asfan feel he had total control of the situation. Then Kyle, or possibly the others, would exploit that imagined superiority.

Closer still, he could see signs of light within. A few slight gaps around the door glowed with a dull yellow, as of a flashlight or low-power bulb. That also was a good thing for Kyle and his people. Any target would be illuminated.

But that meant he had to go in and check. Al Asfan might already be heading out. And Kyle was damned if he would get away again. It might let the man feel competent and worthwhile. Or be taken as a sign from Allah. You could never tell how a nutcase would interpret things.

Worst case, al Asfan wasn't there, a flunky shot Kyle or blew him up, al Qaeda set off a bunch of other bombs and went public. Tough for the CIA, the army, the president, Romania, the United States, and whichever poor bastards were within bombing range.

And, tough for Kyle, who would be dead with nothing to show for it.

He really didn't want to do this, but the opportunity had come around, and he was going to take it. And when he got back, he'd have a polite discussion with General Robash, who'd hopefully have a less than polite discussion with others, to the effect that snipers weren't Delta, and weren't spies. They watched and shot.

Kyle moved back to his knees and crawled through the wet grass. In seconds, he was sodden from dew. But the dense air, mist and tall growth should reduce his visibility and sound. A few burrs, jabs from sticks and thorns, and the wet chill were minor things to trade for tactical advantage.

He kept a good scan going. Nothing threatening was apparent, and he reported that to Wade. "I'm about fifty meters out," he said. "I won't speak again until I know what's there." He didn't want to be given away by the sibilance of a whisper.

"Roger that. Good luck," Wade said.

"Roger and out."

He wove through the grass, lower and more cautiously. But he didn't want to take too long. There were no positions visible, a careful scan across the woods showed nothing in the way of people, though there was a fox or something similar trotting at some distance. The building had no windows.

Controlling the buzz in his head, his throbbing pulse and cold sweats, he stood and stepped straight toward the door, through knee-high weeds and boulders. He hesitated for just a moment at the door, studying the weathered, grainy planks.

19

THE HANDLE WAS ON THE RIGHT SIDE. IT turned easily enough, and he pushed, half afraid of a blast or shot. The door had swelled from weather and stuck slightly at the top, but gave to a bit more force. The dim light within was still far brighter than that outside, and he blinked against it. His glance took in crates, dust on a badly cracked floor and cobwebs. He held the rifle in close and eased through the opening.

To the left was al Asfan. He was standing, smiling, and held a device in his hand, with wires running to a backpack. Kyle took that as a warning, and made no sudden moves. Adrenaline should have been ripping through his body, but he'd exhausted all he had already.

"Please sit, so I can keep an eye on you," al Asfan said. His smile wasn't there anymore, just a smirk. "I have no reason to trust you."

Kyle sat on the floor and said nothing. He ignored the chunks of concrete poking him and waited. He wasn't sure what to do under the circumstances, so he would wait until something happened he could deal with, then react accordingly. Al Asfan was wearing that pack, the thing in his hand could be a detonator, and Kyle wanted to know a lot more about the situation before he tried to shoot. It might be a switch that triggered on release. He had no reason to trust, either.

"Remove the headset slowly," Al Asfan said. Kyle sighed very softly. He'd hoped he might get a word out. Still, his silence would be a broad hint to Wade. Eventually. "Now lower the rifle slowly."

Which assumed Wade could get up here in time. So he'd stall and hope. In the meantime, he'd keep an eye out for exploitable mistakes, and curse himself for being rash. He lowered the rifle muzzle first. Caution and stealth. And they shouldn't have split up. An Army of One, he thought to himself.

Bad idea.

"This is a mercury switch," the terrorist said. "Attack me, tilt it just a little, and it will connect. I use them to avoid having people handle my bombs." He smiled a little.

"How special for you." No fear. At least not visible. He looked the man over. Work jacket, pants, boots. A bit muddy. He'd been outside. A Browning Hi-Power tucked into his belt. The backpack. The wires. The switch.

"It is special," al Asfan said. "Few can do it well. I've counted five bomb-disposal experts among my score."

"Not bad. I'm up over thirty terrorists and their buddies," Kyle replied. He wasn't going to accede anything to this jerk.

"You should watch your words." That while shaking the switch in his hand. Kyle cringed inside and felt his anus pucker. He forced his eyes away from the stubby tube and back to his opponent's eyes.

Was that a real switch? He thought. It wasn't smart to shake it, if so. But then, this man was insane and stupid, and he'd only stirred it around in the air, keeping it vertical. So assume it was real, for now.

"Hey, I call it like I see it," Kyle said. "You wanted to compare body counts, so I gave you mine."

Again the twitch of the switch. Again Kyle kept his face clear, though inside his guts were ice, his stomach flopping and acidic. He might get an ulcer from this, if he survived.

"I will not kill you yet," al Asfan said. "Perhaps I will not kill you at all. But I do require your silence and stillness while we deal with your assistants. Then we shall leave this place. Would a ransom be paid for your survival, hmm?"

It was very unlikely the current administration would back its troops that way, he thought. It was always bad policy to pay a ransom. They might send a team from Delta, if it was deemed worthwhile—assuming this jackass intended for him to stay alive. The best way to help that was to play along.

"Very likely," he said conversationally. He wanted to be loud enough for Wade to hear, but not obvious. "We're not the easiest people for the CIA to replace."

"Isn't it interesting how often the CIA makes such critical mistakes?"

"Yes, but we also get a lot of things right. Those don't get heard about. Like your buddy bin Qasim."

"He was shot by Delta Force in Pakistan," al Asfan said. "I watched. And that is why I moved to Europe, where such cowardly tactics are harder. Witnesses might see such skulking and object. That is the weakness of your world."

"I killed him," Kyle said, pushing. "Through the head and chest with a three oh three Brit. And if I'd known you were there, I would have hung around to get you, too."

That got a reaction. The man snarled, his face in an ugly, screwed-up mask. "Then I am glad to meet you, so I may send you to hell!"

"No problem. I'll be waiting when you get there and spend eternity blowing your ass away," Kyle replied.

A growl and clenching of his other fist was the only immediate response. This man didn't like being outmaneuvered, out-talked, or out-flanked. He really wasn't very bright. But he was dangerous.

Kyle stared at the mercury switch for a fraction of a second. He thought about a shot at that hand, hoping the energy imparted would destroy the switch. But from what he recalled of the subject, it wouldn't take much of a connection to cause it to trigger. If he managed a head shot, it would be dropped and trigger. A center of mass shot wouldn't kill fast enough, and the switch would be dropped and trigger. Frankly, he couldn't think of anything to do that would not cause the switch to trigger. He wasn't sure of the power of TNT, but he was sure that there was enough present to paste him throughout the bunker, even if it didn't detonate hard enough to take the rest of the cache with it, because a surreptitious glance revealed as many crates as he'd seen under Bran. There were also radios here, Russian surplus and shortwave. That meant messages could be sent, to either start or stop bombings. But which? If they hadn't been ordered yet, all he had to do was kill this jerk, which was easy. Grabbing him and shaking him would do it.

Which would also kill Kyle.

It wasn't that Kyle was against dying for his mission. This way would be relatively painless, in fact. But he wasn't eager for the process if he could think his way out of it.

He must have telegraphed just a bit of his intent. The smirk was back as al Asfan said, "That is the difference between us. I don't fear death."

"I don't fear it, either. I just like to make mine

count for something," Kyle said. "I'm not sure killing you is worth the effort." He was going to harass this asshole until something happened. The worst that could happen was death, and that meant a qualified kill of a terrorist. "I mean, you're going to stand before God and tell him you helped blow away innocent children? Won't he be so proud?"

"I am changing the course of nations," was the response. But he wasn't quite so firm or assured.

"Right, you're scaring people into changing so you don't kill their kids. Big, brave man. Even here, you strap on explosives, because you know with any weapon or bare hands, I'd rip your fucking head off."

"And which of us is known? Whose name makes people shake in fear?"

"Mine does, to shitballs like you," Kyle said, growing more confident. "You heard about me in Pakistan. And I don't need to flaunt my name to know what I am. I'm the best fucking shooter in the world, and you know it, I know it, the people I work for know it, and I don't give a damn what anyone else thinks. I don't get a kick out of scaring kids. Matter of fact, I love kids. I'm not afraid to admit it, either. Die to save a kid? Yeah, I'll die to save a kid. That's what a *man* does. It takes a special kind of person to kill a kid and be proud of it. And do you know what we call that kind of person in the civilized world? Usually something along the lines of 'pussy.'" He was leaning forward now, and had his hand nearly in his jacket.

He was going to die, he decided. He was terrified of the event, and not afraid to admit it to himself. But as soon as he could reach that pistol, he was going to try a shot for that switch. Worst case, he died. Best case, he disabled the switch and made a followup shot. Either way, he accomplished his mission and this freak died.

"So says a man who can't die!" al Asfan challenged. "Death is not to be feared. Allah chooses his own and brings them to paradise. Infidels afraid of how they will be judged fear death."

"Yeah? Well I'll be happy to look your God in the face, tell him I splattered four baby-killing, woman-scaring, scumbag terrorist assholes personally, along with three dozen junior-grade assholes who worked for them, and let him judge me on that. I've got no problem at all, pal. Go ahead, tilt the switch!" Kyle had known reverse psychology to work sometimes. Perhaps this would be one of them. Because he had his hand inside his coat and brushing the Ed Brown. That was his confidence. Not a bomb to blow up everything and make a mess, but a surgical tool to eliminate this cancer, if he could get hold of it.

"You're bluffing." Al Asfan grinned and shook the switch, seeing if Kyle would react. Just a bare jiggle, but how much would be needed to set it off?

"TILT THE FUCKING SWITCH, YOU COWARD!" Kyle shouted, snarling to hide the sheer terror he felt. He gripped the .45 and started to draw, knowing it to be the last thing he would do.

The terrorist grinned hugely, and the mindless hatred shone through his eyes. He shifted his hand and turned it sideways, a loud popping sound disturbing the air.

That's an odd last sound to hear, Kyle thought, the pistol clearing his coat and coming up, up into sight plane. Al Asfan was staring stupidly at the switch, because it hadn't worked, and Kyle raised his aim, letting it drift up, up over that confused, wrinkled forehead. He snapped the trigger.

The first round smashed through al Asfan's forehead and the confused glint in those eyes disappeared into death. Kyle let the pistol rock back and down, snapped the trigger, and a second round went through the middle of the face, just left of the nose. Recoil, drop, and shoot, and a third round punched through the chin, making a shambles of the jaw and shattering the spine behind it.

The man was a corpse. Three 230 grain bullets at barely subsonic speed had shattered his head with nearly 1700 foot pounds of energy, like a half dozen full-strength swings of a ball bat, only much quicker. What was left was reddish-gray slop with shattered bone fragments in a rawhide bag that could only charitably be called a scalp.

Kyle was panting, sweating, shaking. He sat for nearly a minute, unable to move. Every sense was overwhelmed by the event, and by the sheer stress. He didn't know what had happened, but he knew he'd never been closer to death. His pulse had to be 240 beats a minute and was just starting to slow. His ears heard something else, but he wasn't sure what it was yet. They were still ringing from the shots.

"Yo," he heard it again, above the headache and aftereffects of shooting in an enclosed space. It was Wade.

"Yo," he said back, unable to find words of his own. He looked around to see his partner entering the doorway, AK in hand.

"Not bad," Wade said. "Three shots off under that kind of stress. You really are a sniping God."

"Thanks," Kyle said, flushed and feverish, sweating and shivering. "I don't know what happened. But it didn't go off."

Wade walked past him, carefully, and bent down next to the body. He pulled a piece of string loose and studied it.

No, not string . . . it was the wire from the mercury switch, neatly cut. Kyle stared dumbly at it for just a second. Then he knew. There was 7.62 millimeters of wire missing, that had to be embedded in that little crater in the wall he hadn't seen until he followed Wade's eyes to it. He drew a line back from the wall and figured the shot had gone over his shoulder, within a handsbreadth of his head.

That had been the popping sound he heard.

"Holy shit," was all he could say.

"Hey, no problem," Wade said.

"No problem my ass." With the situation explained, his brain came mostly back online. The inexplicable was terrifying. The rational, no matter how unlikely, was just impressive. "How far was that shot?"

"Seventy-five meters," Wade said. "From that tree." He pointed. It was a broad, spreading oak at the edge of the meadow, skeletal in the spring night. Kyle had to lean out the door to see it clearly.

Seventy-five meters, and at a target the diameter of the bullet, seeing as the bullet was larger than the wire. On the range, quite doable. From a tree, through a door, over a friendly shoulder, through a wire connected to a backpack of explosives. With wind and at night. That was one bastard of a shot.

Kyle dredged up the phrase he used at the school to students who impressed him. "Way to go, Sniper. You rock."

And had saved his life, with perhaps a half second to spare.

"I owe you one," he added. Al Asfan had been going to blow them both away. And though that was a sacrifice Kyle now knew he could make, he was just as happy he didn't have to. There were far better things to die for than that asshole.

In fact, there were far better things to *live* for.

"Hell, after Pakistan and the castle, I think we both owe each other a few," Wade said. "Let's not keep score or it'll get messy."

"Done," Kyle said.

Wade bent back down and pulled the Browning from the corpse's belt. He cleared it and handed it to Kyle. "Souvenir."

"Thanks." It was a needed distraction, and he examined it. Older, worn, but matching numbers and Belgian production. "*Fabrique National de Armes de Guerres. Herstal, Belgique.*" There were other symbols from whoever had issued it originally.

He looked back up at Wade and started to get to his feet at last.

Wade twitched at a sound in his ears and grabbed his phone. "Yes, it's safe. Come on in."

"On second thought," he continued to Kyle, "I'm calling in a favor. *You* do the paperwork on this."

"Ah, hell, just shoot me and be done with it," Kyle said.

Then they were both laughing hysterically. They were stressed as much as they'd ever been, and needed to lose it somehow. Kyle reached out a hand, and Wade grabbed it. Then they were shaking hands, hugging, and whooping.

Shouts from outside interrupted them, and

they leaned back, panting. "We're here!" Wade shouted. Kyle was still too shocky to do much.

Then Pavenic was at the door, a pistol in hand, two troops behind him with rifles. Seeing the two snipers alive, they relaxed slightly and moved inside.

"I assume that is him?" Pavenic asked, looking at the corpse. There wasn't enough face to identify. Likely dental records would be insufficient, if indeed there were any. Fingerprints might do it.

"It was," Kyle said. "It came right down to the wire."

Then he realized what he's said and roared with laughter again.

Noticing the expression on the Romanian's face, he said, "Wade, you explain. I've got to go take a whiz." He really did, very badly. He was amazed he hadn't wet himself over the incident. It wasn't every day you sat on the floor in front of a loon with half a ton of explosives in the room and his finger on the button.

He brushed past for the door as Wade said, "Ah, well, look here, because you won't believe me if I tell you."

Dobrogeanu was outside standing guard against threats, and there were two wounded who were watching each other. Kyle made it quick, draining against the side of the building, then turned back in. Pavenic was examining the wire, and his expression was priceless. But there were more important things.

"It's secure here," Kyle said. "Should we call the Army and get your casualties out?"

"We await the helicopter," Pavenic agreed. "I just called. And I have something for you," he said, turning. He took two steps forward and grabbed Kyle in a huge embrace, European style, then again for Wade.

Then he started whooping, before switching to an obscene Romanian folk song.

20

IT WAS THIRTY HOURS LATER, MIDMORNING, when they met to gather loose ends. Kyle had told his story, sketched everything he could, shared photos with their new hosts, looked at their reports and images and spent the entire day doing paperwork and loving it. No matter how bad it was, it was infinitely better than watching a madman wave a mercury switch around. He'd remember that.

Which didn't mean his current love affair with paperwork was more than a fling.

And there were no friendly deaths this time. Their wounded allies were recovering, Sam and Cafferty were unhurt, Wade was unhurt, Kyle was shaky but would be fine in a few days. The mission had been pulled off and no one had died. That alone was cause for another celebration.

He'd add that to the tally for tonight. Apparently, many toasts and drinks were planned at the DGIPI headquarters, in the section used by the counterterror platoon. For now, they were all eating catered food while they wrapped up. And it was *good* food, local, without pretension or gimmicks, just ethnic and hot and delicious. Almost dying had nothing to do with it.

They all sat back for a moment, pausing between one round of forms and another. Something that had occurred to Kyle a while back came to mind.

"Mister Pavenic, Mister Cafferty, I need to ask one favor," he said.

"Yes?" Mick prompted. Pavenic just looked at him and waited.

"The Ruger and the Browning. Could Romania officially confiscate these?"

"We can," Pavenic said. "But why? I'd thought for you to keep them as well-deserved trophies."

"That's just it," Kyle said. "The Ruger is Army property. If I try to take the Browning back, likewise. The best that can happen is they'll be stuck on display at the school. The worst is that . . . a certain person in my chain of command"—he didn't mention Wiesinger by name—"will have them disposed of. That means cut up and destroyed. No military weapons can be let into civilian hands, thanks to Bill Clinton. But if they're seized by your agency, and turned over to a dealer, I can then arrange to buy them and import them. They're perfectly legal weapons if they aren't military property." He couldn't have the suppressor for the Ruger, of course. But otherwise it was just a very nice little rifle.

"A rimfire rifle and a basic pistol are illegal for soldiers to take to a country where they can buy almost anything?" Pavenic asked. "I will never understand bureaucrats. But yes, I'll do it."

"I'll call about the import," Cafferty said. "And have the papers to you before you depart. What about you, Wade?"

"The AK has a short barrel, and automatic fire. Somehow, I don't think they'll let me have it," Wade replied. "So let the school have it for braggin' rights and I'll shoot it when I'm there. But I wouldn't mind a real tour of Bran Castle before we leave. The top parts."

"Yes, me, too," Kyle said. "Heck, it can't be nearly as scary."

"You haven't met the tour guides," Pavenic said with a chuckle. "But yes, you shall have a tour, and dinner, and we shall toast success."

"It was a good mission," Kyle said. "And I think I deserve one beer."

Author's Note

THERE REALLY ARE TUNNELS UNDER CASTLE
Bran. Publicly known are the elevator shaft
and the tunnel attached to it. Frankly, I don't believe that the only purpose of those was for
Queen Marie to reach the garden at the bottom,
and it's too close to the building to be an escape
route. The elevator does have a 1960s or later
control panel, in the photos I've seen. So there's
something down there. It might be burial cata-
combs or a "real" escape tunnel to the mountain. It might be merely a hidden study or a
cache for valuables in case of attack. Considering the recently discovered secret stairs on the
east side of the Castle, that ascend three floors to
the study, it's hard to guess. The staff of the Castle and all the sources I've seen are remarkably
reticent. There's probably something there, almost no one knows about it, and it seems as if
many people want it forgotten. If it is victims of

some old regime, or private graves, that might be best. On the other hand, even a video tour of collapsed crawlspaces taken with a remote camera would be a fascinating little addendum to the history of the castle and the area. Perhaps someday they'll arrange it.

My thanks to members of www.thehigh-road.org for support. My continued thanks to the U.S. Army Sniper School for research. As always, any errors in shooting or tools are mine, and likely intentional for dramatic effect.